Eleanor led Rachel into the bedroom with her arm around her waist and gently pushed her down onto the shiny satin bedspread. Rachel lay on her back while Eleanor busied herself undoing the girl's short skirt and drawing it down her long smooth legs.

Rachel's eyes were half closed. She adored the maths mistress's attentions. She spread her thighs apart and lay there in just her tiny white knickers. In a moment Eleanor would remove them too. Rachel shivered with delight – the new term was certainly beginning in the most delightful fashion . . .

New Term at Lechlade College

Lucy Cunningham-Brown

HEADLINE
DELTA

First published in 1997
by HEADLINE BOOK PUBLISHING

A HEADLINE DELTA paperback

10 9 8 7 6 5 4 3 2 1

ISBN 0 7472 5409 5

Typeset by CBS, Felixstowe, Suffolk

Printed and bound in Great Britain by
Cox & Wyman Ltd, Reading, Berks

HEADLINE BOOK PUBLISHING
A division of Hodder Headline PLC
338 Euston Road, London NW1 3BH

New Term at
Lechlade College

Chapter 1

It was a warm and sunny September day at Lechlade Ladies' College – the first day of the new term after the long summer vacation. A day for catching up with old friends and a day for making new ones.

Half of the students who had been in residence last term had now gone on to university – Oxford for most of them. The numbers had been made up with a new intake of sixteen-year-old girls from various schools around the country, and the newcomers had been divided between the four houses that comprised the college.

One of the girls back for her second year was Rachel Fermor, a tall black-haired charmer of seventeen. Rachel was a member of Sawby House, but that afternoon she was in the private study of Miss Eleanor Redruth, who taught mathematics and was known throughout the college as a keen and tireless chaser of young girls.

When Eleanor caught them – which never took long – she did things to them that made them squeal in delight and wriggle their young bodies in her grasp and swear to love her forever.

Supposedly, she and Rachel were discussing Rachel's programme of study for this final year before she went to university. Rachel had a gift for mathematics and the ambition to get a First at Oxford as a preliminary to a career of fame and fortune. In what, exactly, was not yet decided.

In reality, they were not talking about mathematics at all – they both had something quite different on their minds. They were sitting on the sofa in Eleanor's combined study and sitting-room, kissing each other warmly. Eleanor had one arm round Rachel's waist, and with her other hand she was stroking the girl's breasts through her shirt.

Rachel Fermor had well-rounded titties for a young woman of seventeen and this was by no means the first time Eleanor had put her hands on them. Toward the end of the previous term she'd pursued Rachel till she finally got her knickers off and diddled her to distraction. After that they became good friends and stayed that way to the end of the term. Eleanor wanted to continue the friendship throughout the new term.

There were others besides Rachel with whom she had similar close relationships. Over the next week or ten days Eleanor planned to have her hand in all their knickers for a nice long feel. And while she was renewing old friendships in this interesting way, she intended to sample as many of the new intake of girls as caught her fancy. Which would be, at the very least, a dozen of them.

The kiss on the sofa between Eleanor and Rachel was a long one, and pleasing to both of them. Rachel was trembling and running her hands up and down Eleanor's back. Eleanor began undoing the top buttons of the girl's white shirt. A moment later she slid her hand inside and held a soft round tittie in her palm and squeezed it.

Eleanor Redruth was thirty, a leggy and elegant woman with dark-brown hair. Her face was long and intelligent and her eyes had a very direct stare. Even when she was kissing, they stayed wide open. She was wearing a tan silk shirt, tucked into a darker brown skirt, and around her waist she had a leather belt with a square gold buckle.

Since arriving at college that morning, Rachel had changed into the recommended day-wear, a plain white shirt and a black skirt. In theory students were not supposed to wear mini-skirts, but 'mini' had never been clearly defined, neither in inches down from the waist nor inches up from the knee. As a result, skirts were worn very short.

Certainly skirts were short enough for smooth young thighs to be seen anywhere throughout the college. This was a permanent source of pleasure to Eleanor, who adored sleek young thighs, the more on show the better.

She also adored smooth young bodies and soft young

2

titties. To see a pair of girlish thighs spread open was a never-failing delight. And to lick her tongue up the insides of spread girlish thighs, up toward the curly-haired kitty where they joined was, in Eleanor's opinion, one of life's greatest pleasures. With so many teenage girls in the college to choose from, she took full advantage of the prettiest, term after term.

There had been one wonderful week during the previous term – a week she would never forget in her life – when she'd had five different girls on their backs in the space of six days and diddled them all. She'd had two of them on this very sofa where she was now playing with Rachel, and two others in the long grass behind the tennis pavilion, their legs wide apart for her to kneel between.

And the fifth girl Eleanor had had standing naked with her back to the wall in the showers. The showers were a very good place to cast an eye over the new talent and to make new friends. Playing with them and making them come under a heavy spray of hot water helped to fix the moment permanently in their impressionable minds.

During the course of this new term, between September and Christmas, Eleanor meant to improve on last term's record, which had been her personal best. She felt that she was off to a good start with Rachel Fermor, on the first day of term.

When the kiss finally ended and they slowly broke apart, Eleanor undid the remaining buttons on Rachel's shirt and pulled it out of her skirt. With a deceptively casual smile she reached round the girl's back to undo her bra clasp. Rachel smiled back at her and said she'd thought about her during the vacation.

'You thought about me – but did you miss me?' Eleanor asked, while her long-fingered hands were moving over Rachel's bare breasts, rolling and lifting them. The balls of her thumbs brushed over their pink bobbles to make them go firm.

Rachel smiled again and didn't bother to answer. She'd let her knees drift apart inside her mini-skirt, but Eleanor wasn't ready to feel her kitty just yet. She ducked her head and flicked the tip of her tongue over the firm pink bobbles of Rachel's titties.

'Oh, oh . . .' Rachel sighed, her eyelids drooping as she gave in to the little spasms of pleasure that ran through her body.

Eleanor straightened up and pressed kisses on Rachel's eyes and on the corners of her mouth, her knowing fingers playing slowly and very expertly over the girl's chest. Between kisses she began to ask Rachel teasing questions that meant more than they seemed to.

'Tell me who has been feeling your titties all these weeks you've been on vacation, Rachel. I'm sure there must have been someone to give you a little thrill.'

Rachel's pretty face went pink and she closed her dark eyes firmly.

'They're very sexy titties,' Eleanor said, 'and I know you like having them felt. So who had the pleasure? Do you have lots of friends at home – girls and maybe boys too? Or is there one special friend? Tell me – I'm interested in you.'

'No one special,' Rachel murmured, 'just a friend. Maybe that's why I thought about you.'

Eleanor smiled to herself and gave Rachel's smooth, soft bosom a friendly squeeze. She was very fond of handling and playing with girls' breasts – she could make some girls come just by doing that, before she even put her hand between their legs and touched their kitty. They were always surprised when they realised they were starting to come just from having their titties felt.

Eleanor was sorry that Penny Carlton had gone on to Oxford this term – Penny's melons had been the biggest and heaviest in the entire college and Eleanor had taken huge delight in handling them and licking them. So much soft and tender young flesh to play with! She'd never managed to make Penny come by sucking their bobbles, but she'd more than once come herself doing that – and then she was the one with the surprised look.

Magical moments, Eleanor thought, with a secret grin. To see that look of surprise on a girl's face when she felt the big thrill start between her untouched thighs. To stare deep into her eyes while the expression of surprise intensified, along with the sensations in the girl's belly. *Magical, mystical moments.*

For now, Rachel's titties were pleasing enough. Until Eleanor found time to inspect the new intake of girls and see if any of them was the proud owner of a really outstanding pair. If there was such a girl, then Eleanor promised herself she'd have those breasts in her mouth to suck before a week was out.

But to be honest about it, Rachel's weren't bad – in fact, when you got right down to it, they were very nice to handle. Some time passed before Eleanor had enough of them and put her hand up the girl's skirt.

'How often did you think about me?' she asked as she slipped her hand inside Rachel's tights and her thin little briefs. 'Twice altogether? Three times in ten weeks?'

'More than that,' Rachel sighed. Her thighs were open to let Eleanor reach her warm kitty and stroke it with a fingertip.

'Your not-very-special friend,' Eleanor said, 'the one you said you let play with you through the vacation – are we talking about another girl, or is there a boyfriend?'

'Oh,' murmured Rachel, her face flushed. She pretended to be too overcome by pleasurable sensations to answer the question.

'I see,' said Eleanor, pressing a fingertip between the soft lips of Rachel's chuffie. 'There's no need for you to spell it out – you've got a boyfriend. You've been letting him fondle you. Do you think that's sensible?'

'He's not really a boyfriend,' Rachel protested, 'not the way you mean it. He's someone I've known a long time. He lives not far from my home and we go out together now and then.'

'How old is he?'

'Eighteen – he's training to be a journalist. We go to discos and the cinema, but there's nothing serious about it.'

'You let him feel your titties, you said. He's had his hand inside your bra every time you've met him, if I know anything about young men.'

5

'He only wanted a quick grope,' Rachel said, not very convincingly.

Eleanor knew better than that. She snorted in derision. 'Only a grope, indeed! What else have you let him do?'

'What do you mean?' Rachel gasped, knowing very well what she meant.

Eleanor's fingertip was gliding over Rachel's nubby and sending long thrills through her body.

'Don't be silly,' Eleanor said softly, 'you know as well as I do what male creatures want to do to pretty girls. They're all desperate to get that long stiff *thing* of theirs inside you and give themselves a cheap thrill. It starts off with a hand up your skirt – they finger you until you give in and open your legs for them.'

'I'd never let Timmy do that to me,' Rachel breathed.

She was very close at that moment to the big thrill. Her smooth long thighs were straining apart as far as her mini-skirt would let them and she was trembling all over.

'What didn't you let him do to you?' Eleanor asked, pretending not to understand her. 'Are you saying that you didn't let him finger your kitty or that you didn't let him push his ugly male *thing* into you?'

'I'm a virgin,' Rachel gasped out, 'really I am, I'd never let a boy stick his *thing* into me.'

There was more she would have added to strengthen her denial, but she could say no more just then because of the tremendous sensations that surged through her quivering belly.

'Yes, that's it,' Eleanor exclaimed, two fingers deep inside the girl's slippery wet chuffie to keep her coming, 'let me feel your thrill, you little *virgin*, you!'

Rachel's white bra hung undone around her neck while Eleanor ducked her head and licked the pink bobbles of her titties. Rachel moaned and clung to her with both hands, while breathtaking thrills shook her.

'Yes, very nice,' Eleanor said when the girl was calm again. She put her hand against Rachel's cheek and stroked it gently, 'I adore seeing you go over the edge – you look impossibly sexy when you're coming.'

'Do I?' Rachel asked, sounding very self-satisfied.

'But you really haven't answered my question,' Eleanor said. 'You'd better come into the bedroom with me, so I can ask you again.'

Rachel didn't exactly understand what questions Eleanor wanted to ask her, or what she was getting at. But it wasn't important, as she had no objection to going into the bedroom with her.

This was next to the study; it was not a large room, but well-furnished and bright. The bed, with its head to the wall, was a single – there were no double beds at Lechlade Ladies' College. That had been considered too suggestive by whoever was responsible for furniture buying. But single beds in all the rooms had never yet stopped either girls or teaching staff from 'doing a double' with a friend.

Eleanor led Rachel into the bedroom with an arm around her waist, closed the door behind them and gently pushed the girl down on the shiny satin bedspread. Rachel lay on her back with her feet apart and waited while Eleanor bent over her and busied herself undoing the fastener of the girl's short skirt and dragging it down her long legs. Next the teacher pulled the girl's shoes off and rolled down her tights.

Rachel's eyes were half closed. She spread her thighs apart and lay there for Eleanor's inspection in just her small white knickers. She was waiting for Eleanor to take them down, too, and tongue her – that was an act of true friendship which Eleanor performed very ably, as most of the second-year girls at the college knew from personal experience.

Eleanor was in no hurry to oblige Rachel. She sat on the side of the bed and let her eyes wander hotly up and down the girl's body. She was very desirable, this nearly-naked seventeen-year-old, with a pair of good sized round breasts and a smooth broad belly. A dark shadow showed through the thin, almost see-through material of her knickers – Rachel's pubic hair, like the hair on her head, was virtually raven-black.

To bring the delay to an end, Rachel slipped her hand under Eleanor's skirt and up between her thighs, until her fingers touched the warmth and softness where they joined.

She felt Eleanor's chuffie through sheer tights – she couldn't discern any knickers underneath.

That didn't surprise Rachel in the least. It was widely known among the young ladies of the college that Eleanor very often went without knickers. If asked why, she would say she liked to be ready for a quick feel, wherever she was at the time.

Rachel squeezed Eleanor's warm chuffie through her tights and Eleanor responded – though not exactly as expected. There was a look of intense concentration on her face as she eased down the front of Rachel's white briefs and revealed the broad patch of thick dark hair underneath.

Rachel was famous in the college for the luxuriant bush of black hair between her legs. She'd been nicknamed 'Monkey' by her friends because of it. Not in a disparaging way – it was an expression of genuine admiration. When Rachel was naked in the showers every girl around stared at her glossy black thatch and sighed, wanting to run her fingers through it.

Rachel wriggled her bare bum on the satin bed-cover. 'Are you going to make me come again?' she asked.

'In a while,' Eleanor said, 'but first I need to be certain about an important matter.'

She was rubbing the palm of her hand slowly over Rachel's impressive bush. Rachel's mouth was open and she was sighing.

'Lick me,' Rachel begged.

'There are questions to be asked before I consider doing that,' Eleanor answered, 'I invited you into my bedroom to settle a matter between us that I regard as absolutely vital. I'm afraid you'll have to wait for anything else.'

'Why am I lying on my back on your bed with no clothes on, if all you want to do is ask me questions?' Rachel murmured. 'I know and you know that you brought me in here to do me – so please do me!'

Eleanor smiled to see that the thin material of the girl's knickers was wet from her excitement. She used both hands to pull them down a little way, over her hips, down her thighs an inch or two – then with a fingertip she made a parting in the thick bush of black curls to reveal soft lips.

'You said that you're still a virgin, Rachel, but anyone can say that. I want you to tell me the truth about this boyfriend of yours.'

'I've told you already,' Rachel insisted, waggling her thighs to draw Eleanor's attention. 'There's nothing else to say.'

Eleanor's fingers were stroking slowly up and down the moist lips of Rachel's chuffie, giving her little spasms of pleasure and arousing an urgent desire for more.

'You've told me nothing at all,' she said. 'I asked you if you'd let this Timmy person feel your kitty and you didn't answer me. So tell me now – have you let him touch you here between your legs, where my fingers are now? Has he felt you a lot? More times than you can remember?'

Rachel's face went red and she closed her eyes.

'He touched me there once or twice,' she said in a whisper. 'I only let him because he was so persistent.'

'Men or boys, they're all the same,' Eleanor commented acidly. 'They can never keep their hands off girls' bodies. When we get right down to it, the simple truth is that this so-called "virginal" kitty of yours has been tampered with lots of times by male fingers.'

'Not all that often,' Rachel murmured, red-faced.

'Did your friend Timmy know enough to get his middle finger inside you and find your lovely little nubby?' Eleanor demanded. 'Did he give you a thrill?'

'He tried,' Rachel confessed, 'but he never found it. And he never managed to give me even a mild thrill. Why are boys so hopelessly ignorant?'

'The answer is wretchedly simple,' Eleanor explained. 'Pathetic, almost – it's because their own miserable *thing* is exposed and on show all the time. It dangles down between their thighs most of the time and then stands up straight when they see a girl. And when you consider further, a male organ is remarkably uncomplicated in its operation – a quick rub and it's all over. In their male arrogance they assume that we women are as basic in our bodily functions as they are themselves.'

'Oh, I see now,' Rachel said.

'Whereas we women are demonstrably their superiors and we are divinely complex in all our responses,' Eleanor went on. 'This is something that the male sex totally fails to appreciate. But lack of response never yet stopped a male when his *thing* was standing up stiff – you must remember that their brains, such as they are, switch off completely when they get their hands on a pair of breasts, or inside a young girl's knickers. I'm quite certain that Timmy had a hard-on while he was fingering you.'

Her middle finger slipped between the lips of Rachel's kitty to touch the little nubby inside with the finesse of years of experience with teenage girls and their tender bodies.

'Well?' she prompted Rachel when there was no reply to what she had said. 'Was his *thing* standing up stiff?'

'Yes, it was,' Rachel said in a small voice. 'I couldn't help noticing because he'd unzipped his flies and it was sticking out like an iron bar. He kept rubbing it against my leg while he was feeling me.'

'You must tell me the occasion of this abuse of your body,' Eleanor said in a curious voice. 'Bearing in mind what you've just said about his flies being open and his *thing* exposed, I find it impossible to believe that there was only one time when he diddled you.'

'It was one night when I went back to his place to listen to his CDs after we'd been for a hamburger. His parents were out and we had the house all to ourselves.'

'I see,' Eleanor said thoughtfully. 'That was a dangerous situation to put yourself in. This was the occasion when you let him go further than I ever imagined you would, if he had his *thing* sticking out of his trousers. Did you handle it?'

'He begged me to,' Rachel muttered, 'but I didn't stroke it, I only held it in my hand.'

'An exceptionally dangerous thing for a young girl to do, hold a man's hard-on in her hand – surely you know that much. Did he actually come while you were holding it?'

'Yes,' Rachel admitted. Her voice was so faint that Eleanor had to bend down to hear the words.

'In your hand?' she asked.

Rachel said it was a terrific surprise at the time.

'Horrid males, shooting their sticky stuff all over the place,' said Eleanor in a highly disapproving tone. 'Although you say it was a shock to you, it's obvious that you must have been rubbing it to make him come like that.'

'No, I just held it,' Rachel said quickly.

'Was that the first time it happened?' Eleanor demanded.

'First time what—? I don't understand,' Rachel countered.

'Was that the first time he came in your hand?'

'Yes, of course it was. And before you ask, it was the first time that I'd held his *thing*.'

This was a barefaced lie Rachel told to soothe Eleanor's sensibilities. In reality, she'd been giving her boyfriend a regular 'finger-wave' all through the summer vacation. It was either that or open her legs and let him do her – and that was something she didn't want to happen.

To keep Timmy happy, she had pulled his *thing* out as often as they were alone together and given him a brisk fingering. He'd lain back with his legs spread apart and his flies open, his eyes closed and a foolish smile on his face, telling her how sexy and beautiful she was, while she thrilled him with light strokes and took him all the way to a fast sticky splurge in her hand.

He was a strong and well-fed young man, this Timmy, with an insatiable appetite for the sensations Rachel gave him. Sometimes she finger-waved him three times in a day, and the next time they met he always wanted more. She wasn't going to tell Eleanor Redruth any of that, however. Eleanor's help and support were essential to Rachel's end-of-year exams.

'Well,' said Eleanor, greatly relieved to be told that the incident in question was the first and only occasion when Rachel's girlish hand had touched a vile male *thing*, 'after he'd done it in your hand, at least that was an end to it – they lose all interest in you after that.'

'No,' Rachel said, pleased to be able to score a point at last and feeling very daring, 'he didn't go limp. In fact he'd no sooner helped me wipe his *stuff* off me than he begged me to let him put his *thing* in me and do it again.'

'Good heavens – the boy's a sex maniac!' Eleanor

exclaimed, 'I hope you had the sense to say no to him.'

'I didn't let him,' Rachel confirmed.

All this time Eleanor's long thin fingers were playing inside Rachel's chuffie, making her more and more excited, but not allowing her to go too far. Eleanor herself had been more aroused than she'd ever admit by the tale of Timmy's male insensitivity.

She bent down over Rachel's titties, set her mouth to the nearest one, sucking the firm little pink bobble into her mouth. Her tongue lapped over it in quick little strokes, while she held the other one between her thumb and forefinger and tugged it gently. Rachel's back arched off the bed and she came with a long gasping moan.

Her little white briefs were halfway down her thighs and she was still in the throes of the big thrill when Eleanor sat up and pulled the knickers all the way off. Her hands slithered up the sighing girl's long bare thighs and she used her thumbs to prise her wet chuffie open, revealing the pink interior and the slippery little nubby.

'Oh, Eleanor,' Rachel sighed, 'I do adore you for the marvellous things you do to me. Are you going to tongue me now?'

She wanted Eleanor to do that to her more than anything in the world. But Eleanor was in a strange mood and the tone of her answer was not at all cosy.

'I am seriously concerned about you, Rachel, dear,' she said. 'You've not told me the whole truth, I think. You are trying to mislead me with this account of how you refused to give in to the sexual manipulation of your young man. I'm sure there were other occasions, apart from the one you've described. So be frank with me now. When was the last time you saw him before you came back to college?'

'Last night,' Rachel said, turning her head to the side to avoid Eleanor's eyes. 'We went to the cinema together.'

'And afterwards?'

'We went to the late-night pizza-house for something to eat. Timmy put his hand on my thigh underneath the table, but I was wearing jeans, so he didn't get anywhere with that.'

'Go on,' Eleanor said, 'tell me everything he did to you.'

Her tone was friendlier now, because she had realised that disapproval might lose her the pleasures of Rachel's soft young body if they should fall out over a boyfriend. 'You can tell me anything – you know I have your interests at heart.'

'And you like to diddle me,' Rachel said with a giggle, quite aware of the reason for the teacher's change of approach. 'It must have been about midnight when we got back to Timmy's. Everyone was in bed and the house was dark. We went into the sitting-room and he dragged me down on the sofa and started kissing me – we hadn't turned the light on in case we woke anyone up.'

'He felt your titties, didn't he?' Eleanor said. 'What were you wearing with the jeans – a shirt he could unbutton?'

'A college tee-shirt with the crest,' Rachel said, giggling, 'and no bra. Timmy pulled my tee-shirt out of my jeans and put his hand up it for a good long feel.'

'And you liked that?'

'In the dark I couldn't really tell who was feeling me,' Rachel said. 'It was a hand on my titties – it could have been your hand.' She felt she could be cheeky now she knew that Eleanor wanted to stay close friends with her.

'No,' Eleanor said, 'if it had been my hand on you it would have made you come in next to no time. I'm willing to bet he didn't make you come.'

'That's true,' Rachel agreed. 'After a while he unzipped my jeans and put his hand down my knickers.'

'Were you wet, Rachel?'

'Only a little bit. He fumbled about till he managed to get two fingers in, but he couldn't seem to find where my nubby was and I didn't get turned on. He was sliding his fingers in and out, as if he was trying to do me with them.'

'Arrogance and ignorance,' Eleanor said with a thin smile. 'Males are all alike in that way – they know nothing and don't even know that they know nothing. What about his *thing* – had he got it out by then?'

'Yes, his flies were open and it was sticking out against my leg, stiff as a rolling pin. He asked me to hold it, but I said no – I didn't want him shooting off over my designer jeans.'

13

'Did he undress you any further?'

'He said it was our last time before I left for college and he wouldn't see me again till Christmas – he begged me to let him see me naked. He'd only seen my breasts – I never let him take my knickers off.'

'But didn't you say you were in the dark?' Eleanor's eyebrows arched up her forehead.

'We were, but he switched a table-lamp on – he was very serious about seeing me naked and he kept telling me how beautiful I was. Do you think I'm beautiful?'

'You are beautiful and sexy and irritating,' Eleanor said. Her hand was between Rachel's thighs and her palm was clasped over her black-haired chuffie, as if to protect it from a rampant male *thing* piercing it and penetrating it and doing dreadful things to it. 'Go on with what you did last night.'

'I couldn't help feeling just a bit sorry for Timmy,' Rachel said. 'He sounded so desperate. I sat up on the sofa and took everything off for him – everything. But first I made him promise seriously that he wouldn't try to do me.'

'The promises men make when they've got a hard-on are worthless,' said Eleanor vehemently. 'They'll say anything to persuade you to lie on your back and open your legs. They are shameless. From what you've told me so far, Monkey dear, I fear the worst.'

Her hand covering Rachel's warm kitty clasped it tighter, trying to save it from heaven knew what ravaging.

'I know you can't trust boys when they've got their *things* out,' said Rachel. 'I'm not stupid, you know.'

'I'm pleased to hear it – but you seem to take dangerous chances.'

'What I don't understand,' Rachel said with a sly grin, 'is how you know so much about what men get up to when their *things* stand up stiff – unless you had some real experiences with them when you were my age. Am I right?'

'That's beside the point,' Eleanor said instantly. 'We are discussing your conduct, not mine. But I don't mind telling you that I have never allowed any male person to put his big hard ugly *thing* inside me.'

'From the way you speak, some have tried,' Rachel said

knowingly, 'and that's why you know all about it. You're an attractive woman and they'd still try now, if you ever let them.'

'There's no chance of that,' Eleanor said with determination. 'I can say with pride that I fully intend to preserve my integrity from all the depredations of lustful men.'

'So do I,' Rachel said with an impudent grin. 'Will you tell me about the men who tried to put their hands up your skirt?'

'Certainly not!' Eleanor exclaimed – and then, seeing that Rachel was grinning, she steered her away from the subject. 'As I understand the situation so far,' she said, 'you were naked and lying on a sofa in someone's dark sitting-room late at night, letting an eighteen-year-old sex maniac see your pretty body and run his hands all over you. Did he take his clothes off too?'

'Oh, yes,' Rachel said. 'He stripped naked and showed me his hard-on. He held it in his fist and jerked it up and down and it looked enormous – it was jumping in his hand like some kind of live creature he'd caught.'

The balance of advantage had somehow changed. Eleanor could disapprove all she liked, but now it was Rachel who was making the running. She drew her knees up and spread them, her black bush bigger than the palm of Eleanor's hand over it.

'Why don't you tongue me?' Rachel asked. 'You used to like doing it to me last term.'

With a muffled gasp Eleanor lay down beside her on the bed and kissed the soft pink lips between the girl's thighs.

'This boy,' she said, 'what did he do to you?' She slid her tongue between the lips and flicked it gently over Rachel's pink nubby, making her tremble.

'He lay on top of me,' Rachel whispered, 'he wanted to feel his belly on mine, he said – it was very exciting, lying there with my legs open and feeling his weight on me.'

'Did you let him put his *thing* in you?' Eleanor gasped, raising her head for a moment to stare up along Rachel's smooth young body. 'Did he get it in? Tell me!'

'He was desperate,' Rachel sighed. 'He'd promised not

to, but he was begging me to let him. It was trapped between his belly and mine and I could feel how stiff and big it was – and it was throbbing . . .'

'No, no!' Eleanor moaned between the girl's parted thighs. 'Tell me you didn't let him . . . tell me you're still a virgin . . .' Her tongue lashed at Rachel's nubby, as if to punish it.

'You're going to make me come,' Rachel said shakily, 'I'm going to . . .'

'Tell me!' Eleanor gasped out between her rapid licks, 'I must know, Rachel . . .'

'He pulled back and tried to push it in . . . as if he was stabbing me.' Rachel was almost sobbing as she reached the last seconds before her big thrill. 'I could feel it touching me and I thought I was going to be *done* – and given a bellyful when he shot his load . . .'

'Oh, no,' Eleanor groaned, her voice muffled between Rachel's thighs. 'Oh no . . . no . . .'

'I was trying to wriggle away from under him before he could get his *thing* into me – I was suddenly afraid his *stuff* would give me a big belly and I'd have to leave college. But it was all right – he was too far gone to get it in before he came and I felt his cream shooting over my bush and between my thighs . . .'

She squealed suddenly and bucked energetically under Eleanor's probing tongue as her climax hit her. Eleanor tongued her furiously until she finished and lay trembling, with a happy smile on her pretty face.

'What a dreadful risk to take,' Eleanor said in a voice that shook with powerful emotion.

'All's well that ends well,' Rachel said with a cheeky grin, 'and I'm still a pure young virgin.'

Eleanor was breathing hard, her face scarlet and her eyes bulging as she stared down at Rachel's wet chuffie from a distance of a few inches.

'Did he make you come?' she demanded hoarsely.

'No – I told you, I was trying to avoid being done.'

'That's good,' said Eleanor. 'My tongue's much better than a boy's ugly *thing*. He's only using you for his pleasure – I can make you come every time, Monkey darling . . .'

The teacher's emotions were too strong for her and they had taken control – she fumbled in desperation at the square gold buckle of her belt and dragged her skirt down her legs and off. She had no knickers on; Rachel could see the neatly trimmed triangle of dark brown curls through her sheer tights.

Rachel reached out, smiling again, but before she could touch the curls exposed to her, Eleanor let out a long wail and rolled over on top of the girl.

Her legs locked round Rachel's hips and her slim body began jerking in sudden involuntary orgasm on Rachel's hot belly. Through her tights Eleanor was grinding her palpitating kitty against the thick black thatch between Rachel's spread thighs.

'Well, well,' Rachel said to herself as much as Eleanor, 'you're just as bad as Timmy – you want to do me all the time.'

'I think you did me that time,' Eleanor said shakily, 'even if I was on top of you. Did you see my face?'

'You had a very surprised look when you came,' Rachel said.

Chapter 2

The printed prospectus for Lechlade Ladies' College mailed to parents of potential students claimed that it was an entirely female establishment. The Principal and teaching staff were all women, as were lesser employees such as the kitchen staff and college servants and cleaners.

The prospectus overlooked the fact that the position of caretaker was held by a man and always had been. There were boilers to be attended to, showers and changing-room floors to be mopped, large items of furniture and equipment to be moved about, electric fuses to be replaced, ladders to be climbed – a whole range of repair and maintenance tasks not much to the taste of women.

The post of caretaker was residential, but the caretaker was not actually allowed to live within the college grounds. That would locate a male much too close to the young ladies' bedrooms, which was out of the question. Men were notoriously unreliable, not to say untrustworthy, when in close proximity to young women dressed only in underwear or nighties.

The caretaker was required to live in the gatehouse, a good five or six hundred yards away from the main building, at the entrance to the grounds from the main road. Needless to say, the caretaker had to be a married man. The theory was that if he had a wife to take to bed nightly his natural urges would be satisfied and he would be much less of a risk to innocent young college ladies.

The current man had been there for nearly five years. His name was Keith Mason, he was in his late thirties and he was married to a thin blonde woman named Sally. He was good at his job, cheerful and willing and handy. But unbeknown to the college authorities, Keith Mason was a Peeping Tom. His blonde whippet of a wife suspected him, but she had no proof of his prowling activities.

For a man of his enthusiasms there could hardly be a more congenial place of employment than a girls' boarding school. It had a gymnasium, with changing-rooms, showers and a locker-room, and there were pavilions by the tennis courts and the hockey field. There was also an Olympic-size swimming pool – to say nothing of almost two hundred bedrooms, some of them sited on the ground floor with windows that could be approached unseen.

Leaving aside the teaching staff, there were a hundred and sixty young women at Lechlade, from sixteen to eighteen years old. Even to think of them in the abstract gave Keith a raging hard-on inside his clean white overalls. There were dark-haired girls and fair-haired girls and redheads – some with big melons and some with little peaches. As Keith went about his daily tasks he devoted great ingenuity to observing as many skimpily dressed or nearly nude girls as possible.

Tennis was actively encouraged at Lechlade and the courts were a fine place to watch young girls in the summer. They wore short white skirts or shorts that showed their bare thighs, and thin sleeveless tops that gave a glimpse of smooth girlish armpits when they reached up to hit the ball. There were round young titties bouncing under the tops, hardly restrained by little sports bras. And when the girls leaped and stretched for a save, there were glimpses of neat little white knickers.

There was nowhere to hide near the tennis courts, so Keith had to see the sights while he was passing by. He always dawdled for as long as he dared, but it wasn't possible for him to use his binoculars on the move to get a close-up view of bouncing breasts or sweet young bums in close-fitting knickers.

The binoculars were more use to him at the swimming pool. There was a useful stand of trees about a hundred yards from the pool that gave him cover. He could lie upon the ground behind a tree trunk and keep watch on the girls in their sleek little swimsuits. He watched them run and dive – they practised diving a lot, their long legs straight up in the air as they plummeted from the top board and their slender bodies cut into the water with hardly a splash.

He watched them sitting on the tiled edge of the pool, talking while they swung their feet in the water. He gazed open-mouthed when they adjusted shoulder-straps and he caught glimpses of soft young bosoms.

Sometimes he lay there in the wood for an hour to enjoy the exciting views of pretty teenagers. He loved it when they stood on the diving boards and put their arms back, pushing their titties out provocatively against the thin wet material of their suits. And when they bent over ready to dive off the edge of the pool and showed their bare bums, with a narrow strip of coloured swimsuit pulling up tight between the cheeks.

That was a sight that drove Keith half-crazy with lust as he lay there visualising the curly-haired little chuffies under their tight wet swimsuits. At times like these he usually stuffed a wadded hanky down inside his underwear in case he shot off accidentally while staring at the girls.

A simple pleasure he never missed, morning and evening, was the sight of a party of twenty to thirty girls jogging through the grounds, out the gate and down the road. Girls in little shorts that hugged their bums and thin tee-shirts that clung to their chests. They were volunteers, following the Sports Coach, a straggling line of pink-faced high-spirited girls – all long legs and pretty faces.

It was when they came jogging back through the gate that Keith most enjoyed himself. After a brisk outing the tee-shirts were soaked with sweat and clung to bouncing breasts as if painted on. Keith lurked out of sight to watch – the sight always brought a smile to his lips and a hardness to his twanger. He followed the girls' steady progress toward him through his binoculars, shifting the focus from swaying titties to pumping thighs and back again.

Gymnastics were not a compulsory exercise, so only the girls who had a talent for it took part – and in Keith's experience they were well worth watching. They were lean

21

athletic girls, the ones who used the gym; they had small high-set titties, narrow hips and long legs – and they all had a grace of body and movement that thrilled him.

By good luck, the gymnasium was an easy site for peeping activities. It was a modern single-storey oblong building and it stood alone, away from the main complex. Apart from its roof, it seemed to be made almost entirely of glass. It had plate-glass windows from the ground up to the roof, the whole length of both sides.

The architect's purpose had been to let in as much natural light and sun as possible. This was ideal for Keith. He could lie up in a clump of ornamental laburnum bushes less than thirty yards back from the glass side of the building and through his binoculars enjoy charming and intimate views of young girls concentrating and sweating as they exercised their bodies.

On the first day of the new term everyone was too busy settling in to use the sports facilities, although Keith thought it worthwhile going to see if anyone was having a swim or a game of tennis. By the second day of term everything was in full swing, both classes and sports. In the late afternoon Keith was hidden in the shrubbery, fascinated by what he saw in the gym.

Half a dozen girls were in there, in colourful close-fitting leotards that clung to their bodies and left their arms and long legs bare. Some of them he knew from the previous term, but it was a newcomer who caught his attention. She would be sixteen and some months – he knew that for sure because they had to be past their sixteenth birthday to be accepted for the two years at Lechlade that got them into a decent university, usually Oxford.

Keith didn't know her name, which was Vikki Herbert. She had long light-brown hair, hanging down her back in a pony-tail. Her white-and-scarlet leotard nicely showed off her long thighs and tight round bum. When Keith set eyes on her she was bending forward with her feet wide apart and her arms hanging down in front of her to touch the springy wooden floor with her fingertips.

She was doing her loosening-up routine before she started

the serious stuff. From where he lay Keith had a rear view of her, showing him the round cheeks of her bum with the stretchy leotard pulled tight between them. He stared, sweating slightly with the emotions that gripped him. He focused on the narrow strip of white material between her wide-splayed thighs, his eyes following it up the split between the cheeks of her bum.

Her sweet young kitty was hidden under that strip of cloth, Keith told himself. He was sure it would have light-brown curls and soft pink lips. He wanted to kiss that thin and narrow strip of leotard, to draw his wet tongue along it from front to back. He'd wet it through by licking it, so the outline of her little sixteen-year-old kitty would show through.

Keith had a consuming passion for young girls. In his view a girl of sixteen was the most wonderful creature on earth. At that age they were at their luscious prime – if he had his way he'd spend his life playing with a vast harem of them. He'd have them on their backs on silk-covered divans while he fondled their titties and pushed the end of his tongue up their deliciously *do-able* little chuffies.

At Lechlade there were crowds of these fascinating creatures for Keith to drool over. Sometimes he believed he was in Paradise when he thought about his life. Especially his fantastic job – he might just as easily have wound up caretaking at a down-market comprehensive, yet by the greatest of good luck he had been taken on at Lechlade.

Sixteen-year-old girls soon become seventeen-year-olds. In fact, there were as many of these at the college as there were sixteens. In Keith's view girls of seventeen were all right – he liked to watch them undress through the windows of their rooms. But by seventeen they'd already lost some of that youthful freshness that drew him like a moth to an electric light. The sad truth was that by the time they were seventeen their chuffies had been handled a lot.

At eighteen they were grown up. Far too often they'd had boyfriends' shafts up them by then. A chuffie that had been done by boyfriends was a chuffie that had been done to death, in Keith's belief. He didn't want to imagine poking his tongue into them when they'd been broken in and ridden

23

to a stand-still – he fancied them untouched and innocent.

This girl in the scarlet-and-white leotard bending over to display her pretty bum – he was sure her kitty was untouched and virginal. Untouched by *boys*, he meant, not completely untouched. He had no illusions about what the young ladies did to each other at night, when they climbed into each other's beds. They diddled each other – he'd heard their little moans and sighs from outside their windows many a time.

The girl in scarlet and white bent over further to put her hands flat on the floor. The suppleness of her young body was a joy to watch, and so was the stretch of her leotard up the crease of her bum. She was bending over so far that Keith could see between her open thighs to where her small round titties dangled underneath her.

Her titties moved inside the leotard to the swing of her arms, a sort of sliding motion. The material was pulled so tight that he could see the firm little bobbles of her titties pushing against it. He sweated and sighed, longing to feel her bum-cheeks filling his hands. He'd strip her leotard right off and go down on his knees behind her, and he'd lick those tight cheeks while she did her exercises.

Under the concealing bushes he held the binoculars to his eyes with one hand while he pressed the other flat over his stiff twanger to control its twitching inside his close-fitting overalls.

Vikki stood upright, hands on her hips. She began twisting her body from side to side in a steady rhythm. *Oh my god yes*, Keith moaned inwardly as he watched the ripple of muscles along her thighs, *oh god yes* . . .

She had long beautiful thighs – and firm flat muscles from exercising. The thought was in Keith's overheated mind that the grip of those thighs would be very powerful. He constructed a complicated fantasy in his mind about persuading her to lie on her back on a tabletop while he stood close between her legs. She'd wrap her legs around his waist and tighten her muscles and squeeze him with all her strength.

He'd be like a Brazil nut in a nutcracker, her lovely long

24

thighs crushing him between them, her feet crossed behind his back. She'd be naked while she was doing this to him, not hiding her young body in a leotard. Her round little titties would be within his reach, so that he only had to stretch forward to touch their little pink bobbles with a fingertip. And all the time the steely grip of her thighs would be pulling him fiercely against her, holding him tight into her groins, so close that the light-brown curls of her chuffie were touching him.

He'd be naked himself and his twanger would be standing up like a flag-pole – pointing out over her smooth bare belly. As the squeeze of her thighs grew relentlessly harder, it would become so tight that she was flattening his naked body – squashing him so cruelly that he knew he was going to faint and fall down on the floor.

Before that happened he was going to come – there was no way to stop it now. Her savage grip was forcing his cream out of him, just like a hand squeezing toothpaste from a tube – it was so desperately exciting that in another few seconds he'd shoot his load over her belly and her titties in a long wet swoosh . . . *Oh god yes* he was moaning to himself.

Keith dropped his binoculars on the ground beside him. His legs were twitching out of control and his twanger had grown so big and hard it was painful in his tight white overalls. He undid the front, from his neck all the way down to his groins, to give himself air and freedom – but his hard-on still kept jerking about inside his jockey-shorts.

If only he could follow this fantastic sixteen-year-old into the showers when she'd finished her exercise routine. He imagined how she'd look standing naked under the spray and washing her slender sweaty body with soapy hands. She was sure to play with herself – he was certain all the girls diddled themselves in the shower. And he wouldn't need to use his binoculars if by some miracle he could stand naked himself in the stall beside her and watch her hand gliding between her thighs.

Keith was sure young girls played with their kitties in the shower because there had been an occasion the previous term when he actually saw one of them at it. He'd managed to hide inside a locker in order to watch a big-tittied young charmer named Penny Carlton under the hot spray. She'd gone on to university this term, so there was no chance of seeing her naked body again, which was a great pity. But perhaps just as well, because she'd caught him in the locker with his hard-on in his hand and scared him half to death.

Under the shrubs outside the gym Keith's hard-on was straining upward so strongly now that he couldn't bear the confinement of his underwear. He slid his shorts down inside his open overalls to let his twanger jut out free in the air – it was throbbing like a battery-powered vibrator.

Vikki was moving again. He snatched up the binoculars and trained them on her through the distant window. She bent over forward and placed her hands flat on the floor, then she flipped her legs up behind and stood on her hands, her long body straight up in the air.

She must have unexpected strength in her slender arms, Keith thought, nearly as much as in her thighs. He fantasised for a moment or two about being pinned down helpless on the floor by her in a cruel and vicious wrestling grip. Her long strong thighs would be gripping his head so tight between them that she might crush it like an eggshell.

He'd be flat on his back and begging her for mercy. But she would ignore his pleading. She'd have one arm over his waist, the other arm between his legs, her hands clenched together behind his back and almost ripping his body in half. *Yes, yes*, he moaned, *crush me to death*. In that position, his body twisted painfully in her grip, he'd shoot into her pretty face when he came.

He brushed the thought away and tried to concentrate on what she was doing. He watched awestruck as, from her handstand position, she let her elbows bend outwards slowly so that her head sank down toward the floor in a controlled movement. She balanced on her forearms, her legs starting to move apart sideways.

It all happened slowly to Keith, but there was nothing he could do to help himself. Vikki gracefully parted her legs all the way, until they were horizontal – she was doing the splits upside-down. Where her legs joined he could see a domed mound under the stretched leotard. He moaned when he spotted wisps of light-brown curls peeping out at the sides.

He wanted to jump up from under the laburnum and rush into the gym as fast as his shaking legs would carry him. With his white overalls undone from top to bottom, to expose his broad hairy chest and his belly – and his twanger sticking out in front of him like a horizontal flagpole on a public building.

He told himself that it wouldn't matter if anyone was watching him or not. In fact, he'd like a whole crowd of girls to see him like that in his male pride. He'd dash straight across the gym to where she stood on her head with her legs wide apart. He'd drop to his knees and kiss that pretty little mound where the leotard covered her . . .

While this vision was whirling through his fevered mind, his twanger was bounding in his hand and he knew he was going to shoot his cream. But at that very moment he heard voices behind him, some way off but getting closer. He guessed that there were more girls heading for the gym – and their path would take them within twelve feet of where he was concealed. He lay twitching on his side on the ground, doubled up and moaning. He gripped the base of his shaft between fore-finger and thumb and squeezed hard to stop himself shooting off.

He did his overalls up in a hurry and crept further backward under the bushes until the girls – four of them – went past him, chatting and laughing. They were in shirts and shorts – Keith eyed their pert titties and their long smooth thighs. Then they were past the bushes and their backs were to him. One of them had a neat round bum that made his eyes bulge.

The cheeks moved up and down in time with her steps. They rolled against each other, these cheeks, like a pair of puppy dogs playing in a basket. Keith pressed both hands tight over the bulge in his overalls to stop the twitching of his shaft. *Oh my god, it's all too beautiful for words* he was thinking, *this is the most fantastic place in the whole world* . . .

As soon as the girls were safely inside the gym he backed out of the bushes and slipped away, his heart thumping inside his chest at how close he'd come to being caught. And that made it all the more exciting for him, at the time and also in retrospect.

But pleasures have to be paid for, and the rest of that afternoon was a nightmare for Keith. His hard-on refused to subside. It stood up rigid and defiant inside his white overalls and demanded his attention.

The head rubbed on the inside of his underwear when he walked and that made him more desperate. He considered going behind the tennis courts to give himself a quick 'finger-wave' as the girls called it – if he shot his wad it would relieve the tension right away and let his shaft go slack. But after watching Vikki's gymnastics he wasn't in the right mood for a simple hand-job. What he wanted was to finger a chuffie and part the lips and play with it for a while before he shot his load into it.

He looked at his wristwatch and saw that it was nearly four-thirty. No one would know if he knocked off half an hour early. He turned and made for the gatehouse and his wife – she wasn't a sixteen-year-old, but between her legs she had what he urgently needed, and she'd never yet said no to him, whatever the time of day.

It was a longish walk back to the gatehouse for Keith in his condition – and it was an uncomfortable walk, with his hard-on grazing the inside of his jockey-shorts at each step. Two or three times he was forced to stop and bend over, his hands on his knees, while he waited for his urges to calm down a little. Otherwise he'd have squirted his sticky lot into his tight underwear and collapsed. By the time he reached the gatehouse and opened the front door with a trembling hand he was breathing hard.

He called out hoarsely from the entrance hall, his hand rubbing over the bulge in his boiler-suit in happy anticipation of setting it free to do what it wanted to do.

'I'm in here,' he heard Sally say.

The door to the sitting-room stood open and inside a welcome sight greeted him. Sally had stripped down to her knickers – pale pink and see-through – and the blondish curls round her chuffie showed through. She was lying back

28

in an armchair, with her knees wide apart. She was waiting to be done.

With a long moan of delight Keith hurled himself across the sitting-room, ripping his overalls open as he went. He dropped down between her feet and kissed her a score of times through her knickers. His hands slid underneath the cheeks of her bum to grip them hard and raise her belly higher up toward him.

When he'd seen her sprawled on the chair he was so blinded by emotion that he didn't notice the surprised expression on her face.

Nor was he in any state to wonder how she'd guessed that he would arrive home early in urgent need of a soft warm chuffie to ravage. Which was just as well, because it wasn't him that Sally had been waiting for in her knickers and nothing else.

The fact was that she was expecting the Sports Coach to come in and do her. Keith wasn't the only male employed at the school. One term ago the Governors had appointed a man to take the place of Miss Maureen Plessy, the former Games Mistress. She had damaged a knee on the tennis courts and was advised to resign and give up sports.

The Board of Governors was responsible for all teaching appointments – and the Board was made up entirely of women, every one a former student of the College. Nowadays they all held important positions – some were in the higher ranks of the Civil Service and some held senior posts at universities. Some were in law or merchant banking. Maybe they had felt that the college should move with the times when they appointed a man to the vacant position.

The Principal of Lechlade Ladies' College, Miss Enid Uppingham, had been amazed when she heard the Governors' decision. She was shocked – the idea of a man at the college, in any post other than caretaker, was utterly outrageous. But she had no say in the matter, and an athletic twenty-seven-year-old by the name of Toby Dundale came to the college as its first male teacher.

The Principal refused outright to let him be called the

Sports Master. The word *master* suggested a superiority over women, which was completely absurd – everyone of importance understood that women were very superior to men. She got her way over the job-title and the new member of staff was known officially as the Sports Coach.

She also made certain that he wasn't allowed to live inside the actual college, even though he was a member of the teaching staff. He was put in the gatehouse with the caretaker and his wife. It was a good-sized Victorian house, built in the days when married caretakers typically had families of five or six children, and there was space enough for Toby to have a sitting-room and a bedroom, well separated from Keith and his wife.

In the one term Toby Dundale had been at Lechlade so far, Keith hadn't noticed his wife's interest in the younger man. Keith was too busy spying on skimpily dressed girls swimming, jogging and playing tennis. There were a hundred and sixty girls for him to watch, and young teachers as well, but there was only one target for his blonde whippet of a wife – Toby Dundale.

As Toby lived in the same house, Sally had opportunities to see him in his little tennis shorts. She was impressed by his well-developed athletic body, and found ways of seeing more of it – particularly by taking him a cup of tea in bed in the early mornings.

She began a daily routine of tapping at his door at seven-thirty a.m. and going in with his tea. In bed he wore only pyjama bottoms – she could look closely at his broad bare chest with the golden hairs on it. And even more closely at the outline of his body below the waist, under the bed-clothes. Men often woke up with a hard-on, she knew. She scrutinised the bed-clothes for a long bulge in the right place.

When he propped himself up in bed with his back against the pillows and took the tea-cup from her, Toby was naked down to the waist. He would sit most mornings with his legs spread apart under the sheets, and then Sally would be able to make out the long hard bulge along his belly. She thought it was a marvellous sight – he'd only to say the word and she'd flip the bedclothes right off him, kneel down on the

30

floor and take his twanger in her mouth.

When she was alone in the afternoons Sally amused herself by imagining the look of disbelief on Toby's face if without a word of warning she were to do just that – uncover him and suck his hard-on into her mouth. While she played this scene in her mind, she squeezed her own titties through her blouse and plucked at their bobbles to make them hard as berries.

She imagined Toby gasping in amazement at the unexpected sensations her sucking sent surging through him. And by now, alone in an armchair in her living-room, Sally had her hand down inside her knickers and two fingers inside her blonde-haired slit. She imagined the sudden spurt of warm cream in her mouth as Toby moaned and shot his lot. *I'm going to have to come*, she sighed as she brought on her big thrill with short fast rubs.

Desire as strong as Sally's couldn't be denied for long. One evening Toby came back from taking a dozen or more girls jogging. Keith was out doing a repair job, or so he'd said. In reality he was hiding near the showers with the urgent hope of seeing the girls strip naked and wash their beautiful sweaty young bodies.

Sally was waiting for Toby behind the front door of the gatehouse. She was determined to pounce on him and get him to do her. She'd already stripped to her bra and knickers, so he'd understand what she expected – and the instant he came in she threw herself at him, wrapped her arms round his neck and clamped her legs around his waist. In the next fifteen minutes she'd been done twice and was crazy for more of him.

Keith had no suspicion that Sally had been done almost every day last term by the new Sports Coach. Or that she intended to be done again by him daily this term. The only thought in his mind when he came home early to find her sprawling nearly naked on an armchair was delight that she was ready for him. And he meant to take full advantage of her willingness.

Sally was a thin woman with fluffy blonde hair. She was long-legged and slim-thighed with small pert titties. Her age was thirty-one, but her skinny body was packed with so much sexual energy that her appetite was as ravenous as when she was twenty.

It was a shock to her when Keith rushed into the sitting-room instead of Toby, but she was just as pleased to be done by him – she could lie on her back for Toby later on, when Keith went out to do his final check that the college was all locked and secure for the night. Toby would be in bed by then; she would go into his bedroom in a see-through nightie and straddle him as he lay on his back – she liked doing men as much as being done by them.

Meanwhile, Keith had pulled her little pink knickers down her legs to get at her chuffie – he had his tongue inside it and was making moaning noises. She rubbed the wet, open lips against his mouth and grinned.

'Keith – what have you been getting up to this afternoon?' she asked as she put a bare foot in his open overalls to press his bounding hard-on flat against his belly. 'You've had your hand down some girl's knickers for a feel, haven't you?'

It was a joke of hers – she often accused him of interfering with the girls. Privately she didn't believe he had the nerve to even try it, but it amused her to make out that he was a would-be lover of sixteen-year-olds.

If she'd ever discovered the truth about his Peeping Tom interests she'd have been very surprised. And she'd have been annoyed that she wasn't his only interest in life – she was a demanding woman.

'I've been thinking about you all afternoon,' Keith said, raising his head from her belly. 'It gave me such a hard-on that I had to come home and do something about it.'

'I felt exactly the same myself,' she said in case he began to wonder why he'd found her already undressed. 'I've been here waiting for you this past hour.'

Keith pushed his briefs down his legs inside the overalls so she could hold his bare and jumping hard-on between the smooth soles of her feet. She rubbed it up and down slowly, as if she had it between the palms of her hands.

Keith was moaning softly while he played with her soft little titties. He was quite sure he'd shoot his cream between

32

her bare feet in another three seconds if she kept on doing that to him.

'I'm going to do you like never you've never been done before,' he gasped, 'I'll do you stupid . . .'

'Come on then,' Sally was moaning. 'What are you waiting for?'

He dragged her see-through pink knickers all the way down her legs and stuffed them in his overall pocket, then wriggled in closer on his knees and steered his hard-on into her wet and open chuffie. A long hard push took him into her slippery depths and he pressed his hot belly against hers while he slid in and out powerfully.

'Oh my god, I'm coming already,' she sobbed – she was overwhelmed by the force of his assault.

Keith's hands were clenched on her cheeky titties and he was already on the short strokes, seconds from shooting off, his mind filled with images of a pretty teenage girl in a leotard standing on her head and doing the splits with her legs. Sally's belly was shaking under him. She'd slipped her hands into his open white overalls and was clawing at the cheeks of his bum.

He felt the rake of her fingernails and came instantly, shooting his cream into her soft belly. Sally had already passed her big thrill and was disappointed that he'd come so quickly – she'd wanted him to last out and take her there again before he lost interest.

Even so, once was better than nothing, however fast. And about eleven o'clock that evening, while Keith was making his rounds of the college buildings and grounds, she did as she'd promised herself – she went into Toby Dundale's bedroom. Being a professional athlete, he was very much an early-to-bed, early-to-rise fanatic.

He was propped on the pillows reading a book, his golden-haired chest bare. Sally didn't bother to knock, she went straight into his room and flicked the bedclothes off him. She stared down at his soft dangler, which had slipped out through the long slit of his pyjama trousers. Even limp it was a good size – and with the proper encouragement, she knew, it would grow to a very satisfying length and thickness.

She smiled down at him. There was no need for words, he knew why she was there in her short see-through nightie. She sat on the side of the bed and ran her fingers along his dangler. It stirred instantly at her touch. She kept on playing with it this way while it grew to full stretch, then changed to a full-handed up-and-down pumping.

'Anything I can do for you?' she asked jokingly.

'You witch,' Toby sighed, 'you only want me for my body.'

'And I'm going to have it,' she said.

She slipped off the bed and knelt on the floor beside it to take his long stiff twanger into her mouth. Toby spread his legs wide, lay back against the pillows and let her do what she wanted to him. After a minute or two of hard sucking, when his hard-on was as solid as it would ever get, she jumped up on the bed and threw a long lean leg over him.

'You think you're going to have your way with me, don't you, you sexy bitch?' he said with a grin.

'I'm going to do you stupid,' she said, grinning back at him as she repeated Keith's words. Keith had disappointed her when he came too soon, but she wasn't going to let Toby disappoint her. She had about forty minutes before Keith got back from his round of inspection – and in that time she intended to get full satisfaction from Toby.

She was sitting over his thighs with her fist clenched round his hard-on. Toby felt between her legs to stroke her kitty, and she spread her knees to let him get his fingers inside her.

'Who have you done today, Toby?' she asked. She was pretty certain he did things he shouldn't do to some of the college girls. 'That's why you go to bed at half past ten every night, because you're exhausted from doing girls all day long. You'll get into real trouble one day, mark my words.'

Toby grinned lazily at her. She was half-joking, but she was closer to the truth than she knew.

'I don't care how many schoolgirls you do,' she said, 'you won't put me off by saying you've worn yourself out. I'm going to have you, Toby.'

She pushed his hand away from her chuffie and guided his twanger up into herself. She sat down hard to drive it all the way in, then she was riding him, bouncing up and down to make him slide in and out smoothly. Her titties jiggled up and down – he reached out and held them.

'I'm going to make you come with me,' she moaned.

Chapter 3

During the first week of the new term Toby Dundale, the Sports Coach, tried several times to get Sharon Pomeroy on her own. He failed to do so and from that he knew she was deliberately avoiding him.

Sharon, who taught geography and geophysics, was a slim, long-haired woman of twenty-eight. Toby had enjoyed a hot little affair with her in the final weeks of the previous term and was anxious to get it going again. Obviously she was not.

When he tried to get her alone, she was always with other people. He wrote a note and slid it under her door. She didn't answer. Even then he didn't give up – he was good-looking in a blond, athletic way and he had a fine opinion of himself. He felt sure he could talk her round, if given a chance.

Ten minutes alone with her, that's all it'll take, and I'll have my hand in her knickers, he promised himself. *Five minutes after that she'll be flat on her back with her legs wide open and I'll have my shaft up her. She loves it – once she's had it up her again she won't be able to get enough of it.*

During the long summer vacation he and Sharon had gone away together. Being exercise-minded, it was totally out of the question for him to stay at a comfortable hotel and loll on a beach all day long. He needed to be active all the time, so he borrowed a boat from a friend and took Sharon yachting around the Channel Isles.

The weather was kind to them. While the boat drove on under full sail with the automatic steering in charge, they lay naked on the deck in the sunshine and played with each other. Toby was in top condition; the open-air life suited him very well and Sharon had never before been done so thoroughly and frequently.

It was a new thrill for her to spread her legs on a hard deck rolling and pitching with the waves. She was nervous at first about being seen from other boats passing within binocular range, but that feeling wore off after Toby convinced her that the people on other boats in the distance were bound to be too busy having each other or too drunk to notice anything.

On Sharon's insistence, Toby tied up in a harbour every night and they went ashore for dinner in a restaurant. Late evening would find them back on board having a final drink, then climbing into a bunk together for a long good-night rattle before they fell asleep.

For Toby it was the ideal holiday. He could happily have sailed the boat right round the world, eating, sleeping and having Sharon. But after a while Sharon found the holiday not so perfect – she was spending twenty-four hours a day with a man who had nothing to talk about except sex and sport. As far as she could tell, he'd never read a book in his life after leaving school. He never went to the theatre or the cinema or concerts. He watched nothing on TV except tennis, swimming and athletes in vests running, jumping and throwing things.

They parted friends when the holiday ended. But when Toby suggested they should go to Stuttgart to watch the European Amateur Tennis Finals, Sharon told him she'd promised to stay with her parents in Cumberland. His eyes lit up at that – he said that if he went with her they could go rock-climbing and fell-walking. Sharon hurriedly persuaded him to go to Stuttgart on his own.

Toby returned to college for the new term with the fondest memories of his sailing holiday and couldn't understand why Sharon was avoiding him. But he was certain he could talk her round, whatever the problem. He lurked near her rooms one evening until he was sure she was alone.

The teaching staff at Lechlade were all given the same accommodation, a suite of rooms each, most of them on the ground floor. Except Toby, who had been farmed out to the gatehouse with the caretaker and his wife in an effort to keep him a safe distance from the young ladies' bedrooms.

The students shared, two to a bedsitting room, but each teacher had a sitting-room, a bedroom, a bathroom and a kitchenette for making tea and toast.

Toby knocked at Sharon's door in Wexby House. She opened it and as soon as she saw who it was she began to make excuses. She had work to do, papers to mark, and so on.

'I'll only stay a minute,' Toby said, giving her the smile that charmed the knickers off girl students and teachers.

She finally let him in and he took a seat on the sofa, hoping she'd sit beside him. If she did, then before she could say no he'd have an arm round her waist and give her a long kiss while he felt her titties.

She didn't sit beside him. She went to the desk under the window and sat on the upright chair, to make the point that he was interrupting her work.

There were papers on the desk, for she really had been busy. She made a small concession to politeness by half-turning the chair toward him. He tried to talk about their holiday afloat, to remind her of non-stop sex on deck under the blue sky.

She resisted his attempts to draw her into conversation and after a while he got up and went across the room to the desk. He perched on her side of it, facing her and close enough to put his hand on her shoulder. What was the matter, he asked, weren't they friends any more?

Sharon hadn't really gone to stay with her parents up in Cumberland after the boating holiday. Her parents didn't live in Cumberland, they lived in Surrey. She simply didn't want to go to the Tennis Finals with Toby, so she'd said Cumberland on the spur of the moment because it sounded a long way off. Though that hadn't deterred a health fanatic like Toby.

While he was abroad watching the tennis, Sharon had actually gone to Torquay to lie on the beach and be waited on in a comfortable hotel. She would rather have gone to

Rhodes or Corfu, but not on her own. After yachting with Toby she wanted a rest from lying on her back with a hard-on inside her – and on any of the Greek islands she'd be pestered night and day to do just that.

Torquay seemed a safe place. The men there would be married and with their families. That wouldn't stop them trying to get a feel if they found her alone in a lift or sunbathing in a concealed corner, but she could cope with that easily enough.

On her second day at Torquay, to her great surprise she heard her name called on the beach. She put down the book she'd been reading and raised her sun-glasses to look – and there was another of the Lechlade Ladies' College teachers in a bathing-suit, Claudine Stanhope.

They sat together in the sun and gossiped. Claudine was wearing a one-piece swimsuit in white that showed off her figure very well. She had a body worth looking at – all the males within fifty yards were staring at her thighs and bosom and pretending not to. Sharon herself was in a scarlet bikini – she was proud to expose her flat belly and the all-over tan she'd acquired lying naked on a sailing-boat deck.

She too had been an attraction for all the males on the beach between the ages of fourteen and sixty-five. She found that fairly flattering, so many eyes on her – all those hot lustful glances like hands pawing at her body. All those males who wanted to rip her bikini off and do her right there on the hot yellow sand.

Only in your dreams, boys, she said to herself with a secret smile, hoping that they'd all get hard-ons in their bathing-trunks. Then they'd have to try to hide the awkward state they were in from their wives sitting in the deck-chairs next to them. They'd have to lie face-down on the sand to hide their bulge and hope it would go slack.

The eyes didn't turn away when Claudine joined her. Now there were two slender and pretty women in swimwear to stare at. And something else, Sharon noticed – she could feel Claudine's eyes on her now, sizing up her near-naked body while Sharon asked why she had chosen Torquay.

'The hotels are full of young girls who are bored by having

to go away on holiday with their parents,' Claudine answered at once. 'They're easy to pick up. Some of them turn out to be hot little devils when you get their knickers off. Why are you here, Sharon?'

Sharon was in a relaxed and confiding mood. She told Claudine all about the sailing holiday with Toby. Claudine laughed and said, 'Men!'

They were staying in different hotels, but around twelve-thirty they dressed and had lunch together in a small restaurant. After that they went to Sharon's hotel – Claudine had said she'd like to see her room, to judge how the two hotels compared. It was a hot day, and after hours in the sun before lunch, Sharon felt ready for a nap. She suggested to Claudine that they should meet in the evening.

'Why not?' Claudine said with a knowing smile. 'You want to come out on the prowl with me for young girls. After all that abuse from a male *thing* you feel the need to play with a kitty – I understand perfectly.'

No such thought had been in Sharon's mind, but she decided not to say so in case Claudine took offence. She said she needed a siesta.

'I'm sure you do, after all you've been through,' Claudine said. 'I'll stay here while you take your nap – it's friendlier that way.'

Sharon shrugged, kicked her sandals off and lay down on her bed. It was a single bed and Claudine was sitting by the open window near it, skimming through a magazine. Sharon closed her eyes and had just begun to doze off when she felt a hand on her belly. It slid under her untucked shirt and moved slowly up over her breasts.

A cool and soothing palm rotated over her little pink bobbles till they stood firmly upright. *Oh*, Sharon murmured, keeping her eyes closed. The hand slid underneath her, forcing its way between her back and the soft bed, and undid her bra. There were two hands on her titties now, tugging the bra away – then they gripped hard and squeezed.

Sharon sighed and kept her eyes shut. A mouth came down from above her and pressed itself against her mouth, a tongue slid between her lips. Sharon lay still and calm with

41

her arms at her sides, feeling too languid to respond to what Claudine was doing to her.

The mouth moved away. Sharon felt the hands slide down her body to her waist. Fingers fumbled at her belt and the zip of her cut-off jeans. Her flies were opened wide, and the fingers moved to the elastic waistband of her knickers. A cool hand insinuated itself inside, moving down towards her kitty.

At Lechlade Claudine was not known to be one of the voracious teachers who pursued girls day and night – as Eleanor Redruth did, for instance. Claudine had a reputation for discretion, though it was widely thought that she dabbled with a chosen few. A very few.

On holiday she was a different person altogether. She talked openly about prowling for girls and getting their knickers off. Now she was well into seducing Sharon Pomeroy, without being given any active encouragement.

Her searching fingers touched the thin curls and the soft lips between Sharon's thighs. A fingertip pressed a little way between them and was withdrawn almost at once. Sharon waited – her calm was disappearing and she was trembling, her eyes closed in expectation now.

She could sense Claudine bending over her, and a moment later felt her knickers being pulled below her hips inside her open jeans. Then Claudine was on the bed and her head was between Sharon's legs.

Her chin was inside the open jeans, her tongue licking the lips of Sharon's kitty. Her fingers parted them as the wet tip of her tongue probed inside and flicked lightly over Sharon's nubby.

By this time Sharon's calmness had been totally shattered. She moaned and opened her legs wider, pushing her kitty at the tongue that was devastating her.

'Claudine . . . you've never given any sign you wanted me,' she gasped. 'We've known each other for years – why now?'

Claudine raised her head and smiled down the length of Sharon's body. 'Why not?' she answered. 'You've had enough of a man's big thick *thing* in you this vacation to last you a lifetime – it's time for a little proper loving.'

She dropped her head again and Sharon gave a tiny shriek as she felt her nubby being sucked into Claudine's mouth and held between her lips. Such powerful sensations surged through her belly that she felt herself start to come. Quick throbs of delight made her moan softly.

All considered, it turned out to be a most enjoyable holiday. Claudine diddled her day after day on a bed just as often as Toby had done her on a yacht's deck. An agile tongue inside her instead of a thick hard-on, that was the most obvious difference. Either way the end-result was the same – thrill after thrill, climax after climax.

There was another distinct difference, too. Claudine loved to play 'heads-and-tails'. Sharon knew all there was to know about tonguing and being tongued, but it was odd at first to lie with her face between Claudine's thighs and her tongue in her friend's kitty – while Claudine's tongue was probing her own kitty at the same time. But she came to prefer 'heads-and-tails' to the more usual 'diddle-me-first-and-then-I'll-diddle-you'.

When the new term started and they went back to college, their close girl-to-girl friendship continued. That was the reason Sharon was wearing fancy knickers under her casual clothes – for Claudine's benefit if she happened to drop by and put her hand up Sharon's skirt. Nothing had been arranged, but she was half-expecting Claudine to drop in this evening – not Toby Dundale, who had arrived without warning.

'Aren't we friends any more?' Toby asked, sitting on the side of her desk, his hand on her shoulder.

'Of course we are,' she said, feeling awkward, 'it's just that I've so much to do.'

She stood up to let him know that his minute was over and it was time for him to leave. Still sitting on the desk, he put his hand under her skirt, between her knees, and slowly slid it upwards. The smooth feel of her flesh was very exciting. It was a warm September evening and she had changed her formal day clothes for a loose cotton skirt and a pink shirt worn outside it.

43

'That's all right then,' he said with a smile, 'as long as we're still friends, that's all I came round to ask.'

His hand slid all the way up her bare leg and touched the warm secret place where her thighs joined. All that lay between his fingers and the silky lips of her chuffie was the delicate thin material of her knickers.

'I don't think you should do that, Toby,' she said, her face suddenly pink. She was still fond of him, but she didn't want him as a bed-friend this term.

'You're right – I'm leaving,' he said, smiling as he turned his hand between her legs to cup her kitty in his palm. 'Just a friendly pat.'

Their affair last term had started unintentionally on both sides. Toby was a qualified physiotherapist as well as a coach. But he wasn't allowed to massage the young ladies of the college – the Principal had emphatically ruled that out. She was horrified by the thought of a man's hands on innocent young female bodies – there was no telling what might happen!

Sharon had ricked her back badly on the tennis courts one afternoon last term and begged Toby to treat her, even though it was also against the rules for him to give therapy to the teachers. He put her spine back in place and then massaged her to relax her jangled nerves. One thing led to another, and Sharon was soon lying naked on her back on the massage table with her legs apart.

At this point he stopped massaging her, unzipped his flies and flipped his twanger out. Two seconds later he was poised above her belly, steering his hard-on into her. 'Oh no, no!' she moaned when she felt it pushing up into her. 'I don't let men . . .'

She had to leave the protest unfinished as Toby's rapid thrusts took her over the edge and she came. She didn't scream or thrash her legs; she didn't arch her back or drum her heels. Faint little tremors ran through her and she gave half a dozen sighs. Toby felt his sap rising and in the nick of time pulled his throbbing shaft out and shot his cream onto her bare belly.

For the rest of the term he'd had her on her back every

day. He kept up a mild pretence of treating her back for a few days – he made her lie face down while he massaged her neck and down her spine to her bare bum, but that was to excite her, not to treat her. By the time she felt his fingers probing between her thighs she was ready to turn over and invite him to lie on her belly.

On the boat with him out in the Channel, she remembered how pleasant his massaging was and asked him to do it again – this time as she lay face up and naked under the broad sky. Toby was very good at it – his trained hands started at her neck and worked their way down her body, over and round her titties, over her belly. By then she was trembling and sighing and on the verge of the big thrill. And he, naked while he massaged her, had a hard-on sticking out like the bow-sprit at the front end of the boat.

All that pleasure they'd had together, Toby said to himself, for him it had been a dream holiday. But now they were back at Lechlade, Sharon didn't want to know – something had changed while she was staying with her family in Cumberland.

'What's wrong, Sharon, don't I make you happy?' he asked.

Though she was casually dressed, she seemed to be wearing very fancy knickers – his fingertips told him they were lacy and small, and the strip between her thighs was so narrow and thin that he was able to stroke the bare lips of her chuffie.

'You said you were going,' she murmured, red-faced.

'And so I am,' he agreed, thinking that he would like to come before he went.

He pressed his middle finger between the lips of her kitty and touched her nubby. It never took much to excite her.

'I don't want you to do that,' she murmured.

'You're very tense,' he said. 'Too much work too soon in the term – too much responsibility, that's what it is. It can exhaust you and pull you down and destroy your appetite for living. Let me give you a massage, it will relax you.'

'This is neither the time nor the place,' she said.

'Has your back been giving you trouble?' he asked, with

45

sympathy in his voice. 'Have you been having little twinges when you move quickly? Sometimes the type of injury you sustained on the tennis court returns after a time and needs further treatment.'

'My back is perfectly all right,' she said, 'and it really is time you left.'

'Better to be safe than sorry,' he insisted. 'Stand up while I check. It'll only take a second. These things have to be caught in time and treated before they get really painful.'

Reluctantly she stood up. Toby stood behind her with his hands on her hips and turned her gently to face the desk.

'Bend forward and put your hands flat on the desk,' he said.

When she did so he asked if she felt any strain in her back from the position. She shook her head and he undid the side of her white cotton skirt and let it slide down her legs. Then he turned her shirt up her back to expose her bum. He'd been right, she was wearing very fancy knickers, so small and lacy that the cheeks were hardly covered.

He put his hands under her loose pink shirt, flat on the small of her back, and rubbed lightly. His fingers worked along her spine, feeling for signs of tension. Sharon was breathing heavily – she was tense, all right, but that was because Toby was touching her. Very soon, though, under his expert fingers, all her tension dissolved.

Her new mood was transmitted to him through his stroking hands – he knew he was more than halfway to winning his campaign and it wasn't long before he was massaging lower down, on the round cheeks of her bum.

He pulled her little lacy knickers down her thighs to bare the cheeks, then rolled them under his hands and squeezed them. His fingers dug into the soft flesh, Sharon began to sigh – she knew his technique. She told herself she ought to make him stop now and send him away before anything happened.

By 'anything' she meant, in particular, that she wouldn't want Claudine to come in and see what was being done to her – such as Toby's hands stroking her bare bum. Or worse than that, his fingers between her thighs stroking her kitty.

But surely if Claudine was coming to see her this evening, she'd have been there before now. In the circumstances Sharon decided that letting Toby have one last time with her couldn't do any harm.

His twanger was standing up and jerking in his tight little jockstrap. He slipped a hand underneath Sharon, his palm flat against her belly. His other palm lay on her back and he bounced her body gently up and down between his hands.

'You've never done that before,' Sharon said.

'I'm testing the springiness in your spine,' he said, starting to breath hard. 'It's a well-known diagnostic test.'

It was nothing of the sort, but it gave her such pleasant sensations that Sharon didn't care what it was. His hands slid along her back and belly until one was over her tailbone and the other between her thighs and over her kitty. He bounced her gently between the two, sending tiny tremors of pleasure through her.

Where he'd learned this particular technique he couldn't remember, but he knew he could make Sharon come if he kept it going long enough. His middle finger lay along the lips of her kitty, not pressing inside but rubbing gently with each little bounce. With his other hand he was doing the same on her backside – his finger lay along the crease between the cheeks of her bum.

'I can feel the benefit already,' she gasped.

'Backs need very careful handling,' he told her.

He dropped to his knees on the carpet behind her, his face so close to her round bare bum he could have nibbled at it with his teeth. But that was for later. He massaged firmly down the backs of her thighs and she was sighing loudly now. He stood up behind her, flicked his zipper down to free his hard-on and held it in his hand.

He was handsomely equipped, as befitted a Sports Coach. His twanger was as strong and well-exercised as all the rest of his body. He steered the purple knob toward Sharon's kitty – one push between the half-parted lips would take him into her.

Sharon's sighs of pleasure turned into a hard gasp of fear.

'What's the matter?' Toby asked. He'd slid his hard-on up

47

her so many times in the past that she couldn't possibly be nervous about it.

'Enid's coming across the lawn!' she exclaimed. 'You'll have to stop before she sees us.'

Toby had been too occupied stroking Sharon's body to look out of the window above the desk. But now he did look out and he too saw the still-distant but unmistakable figure of Enid Uppingham, the Principal of Lechlade Ladies' College.

Enid was a commanding figure – a well-fleshed woman of about forty. She had glossy black hair which she wore in a bun, a pair of big heavy breasts, a plump belly and sturdy legs.

It wasn't likely that she'd noticed two faces looking out through a ground-floor window of Wexby House. She was still too far away to see anything, Toby decided. Of course, if she *had* noticed the two faces at the window, she might wonder why they were not side by side as anyone would expect, but one above the other.

Common sense would suggest to her that one person was standing behind the other person. But even so, that was not a completely satisfactory explanation. The two faces were lower down in the window than if the two persons concerned were standing up. It would require a lot of thought and imagination for a spectator outside to decide exactly how the two persons were placed in regard to each other.

Enid Uppingham was no fool. She knew what went on in the college. She was aware that some of her teaching staff diddled girls of their choice, and some of them diddled other teachers. That was their business, as long as they were discreet and caused no gossip. Healthy young women needed an outlet for their sexual energy, and it was far, far better that they do each other instead of chasing after men.

Enid was strolling around the college grounds, enjoying the calm warm evening air, when she saw the two faces at a far-off window. She wasn't sure whose window it was, but she recognised Toby Dundale's firm features and golden shock of hair even at that distance. He was in someone's room, and he was pressing himself close to the back of whoever it was. This was the immediate conclusion that sprang to Enid's mind.

His male *thing* was sure to be hard, she said to herself, because men were always in that condition in the presence of pretty women. He must be pressing it against the female standing in front of him . . . against her clothing . . . or, hideous thought, could it be out of his trousers? Could it even be pressing against naked flesh?

Was he exposing himself in a state of arousal, was he abusing the body of whoever it was standing in front of him?

Enid had never got over her sense of outrage at the appointment of a man as Sports Coach. She had had it in for him from the day he arrived. The last term – which was his first term – she'd attempted to make Toby's last by getting him sacked for moral depravity. So far she'd had no luck – but if she could catch him interfering with a girl he'd be dismissed instantly.

From where Enid was, it looked as if she'd got him this time. But proof would be needed – she changed direction to take her close by the window. She didn't walk any faster, though, because that might have warned him.

Inside the room, with Sharon bent over her desk and her chuffie only an inch from his throbbing twanger, Toby had no qualms. Enid was surely too far away to see anything, he had convinced himself. He shuffled closer to Sharon, his trousers down round his ankles, and eased his hard-on between the cheeks of her bum.

'Feel that,' he said, sliding the head slowly up and down the crease.

'Big and hard,' she said.

She was excited by how wet her chuffie was – ready to be penetrated and stretched by his length of hard flesh. Toby put his arms round her, his hands on her belly under her shirt, and slid them up to clasp her titties. Sharon had small but nicely shaped titties, set high on her chest, with pink bobbles that stood up as firm as little acorns the moment they were touched.

He was panting to do her over her own desk, to push his shaft up her and slide in and out until he came in a long wet splurge. But he could see Enid moving closer across the broad lawns and it was sensible to move away from the window before she got near enough to guess what he was doing with Sharon.

'I think we should go into the bedroom to finish the treatment,' he said, his voice shaky.

'Yes, be quick, be quick,' Sharon urged him. He hadn't specified which treatment he meant and if she was in any doubt, she didn't bother to ask – she knew what he wanted to do to her.

Two minutes later she was sitting on the side of her bed while his hands glided over her titties inside her loose shirt. 'Oh yes, Toby,' she sighed when his fingertips touched her little pink bobbles.

Her legs were apart and her patch of blondish curls was fully in view. Toby was kneeling between her feet, trailing his tongue down her belly and flicking it over the curls and the soft lips.

'Toby . . . yes . . . yes,' she said in a hoarse, excited voice.

If it had been Claudine kissing her nubby, Sharon thought, they'd wriggle round on the bed to get their faces between each other's legs. She'd tongue Claudine at the same time as Claudine tongued her. Which of them hit the big thrill first was a fascinating question each time they did it together.

It wasn't like that with Toby, though. In the long days on the boat she had kissed his hard-on lots of times. She'd flicked the tip of her tongue over the head and heard him moan with pleasure. But she never took it fully into her mouth and risked having him shoot his cream. She wanted to feel his hardness inside her chuffie – and now, to her surprise, the idea of being penetrated was exciting again after Claudine's twice-daily tonguing.

She pulled her shirt above her titties, then right off over her head, and threw it across the room. She used both hands to pull her knees up to her chest, pressing her heels down hard on the edge of the bed while opening her thighs wide apart until the slippery pink interior of her chuffie was exposed to view.

Toby was sighing continually as he kissed the smooth flesh

50

along the insides of her thighs, up into her groins and around her neat little patch of blondish curls. He pulled the lips of her chuffie even wider apart and pushed his tongue between them. He flicked the tip of her nubby, making her moan and shudder – he saw that she was going to come very soon.

'I want it inside me,' she gasped. 'Put it in, Toby . . .'

'Then we're still friends,' he panted. 'I thought you'd never let me do you again, Sharon.'

He wasn't telling her the truth. He'd been cocksure he'd get his shaft into her if he could only get her on her own for fifteen minutes.

'I want you to do me, Toby,' she said breathlessly.

Enid had reached the sitting-room window where she'd seen faces. She looked in, but no one was there, only papers untidily strewn about on the desk below the window. But her worst suspicion about Toby was confirmed when she spotted a pair of fancy lace knickers lying on the floor.

Enid had recognised whose room it was. Sharon Pomeroy's. There was one inescapable conclusion to be drawn from all this – that Toby Dundale was doing disgraceful things to the geography teacher. *What a pity it's not a student that depraved wretch is sexually abusing,* Enid thought, *that would be grounds for instant dismissal and possible prosecution.*

But she consoled herself that perhaps something could be made of this shameful physical liaison between two members of the staff who were of different genders.

The bedroom window was next to the sitting-room window, further along the building. Enid sidled along the wall until she could peep round the window-frame and get a good view of the bed. The two of them were there, as she knew they would be, obscenely engaged. Sharon sitting naked on the side of the bed, Toby kneeling on the floor in front of her.

Sharon's knees were pulled up so high they touched her titties – Enid could see right into her pink open chuffie. Toby was naked, his clothes lay scattered on the rug. Enid was captivated by his broad chest with the golden fuzz on it, his lean belly – but most of all she was fascinated by the length of flesh that stood up stiffly from between his muscular thighs.

While she watched with a knuckle between her teeth to prevent herself whimpering, she saw Toby straighten his legs slowly and push himself upward. His mouth moved up from Sharon's kitty, over her belly, up to her titties. Then higher still, and he was rearing over Sharon, his body between her spread thighs. As he positioned himself, Sharon reached for his throbbing *thing* and guided it straight into her.

Enid felt moist between her sturdy thighs while she watched Toby doing Sharon with quick little jabs. He was on the short strokes before there were any long strokes. Enid forced her eyes to stay open, but her vision was blurred – sensations were surging through her belly that demanded her attention.

'Oh my god, he's going to come inside her,' she gasped.

Sharon's hands were on Toby's shoulders, gripping hard. She was ready to come, and he was so far gone now that he doubted if he'd last another five strokes. He hoped she'd come first – and at that moment she did. She didn't cry out or arch her back; instead genteel tremors ran through her and she gave a few little sighs. That was her way. Toby convulsed as he felt himself start shooting off – he flicked his leaping hard-on out of her chuffie and squibbed his cream up her bare belly as high as her titties.

Outside the window Enid groaned to see him fountaining his load onto Sharon's perfectly shaped titties. She'd never in her life expected to see such a sight – it confused and excited her. She turned away from the window and walked slowly back to her own quarters, her mind filled with whirling images of Toby's bounding shaft spurting its juices while Sharon's proud-standing and pink-tipped bosom received the flood.

Safe in her own sitting-room with the door locked, Enid flung off her jacket and reached under her pleated skirt to slip her knickers off. She was a full-bodied woman and she took the larger sizes of underwear. But in spite of her severe manner and appearance, she wore the frilliest and most feminine knickers she could buy.

52

The ones she took off now were of white satin, embroidered and edged with lace. And they were damp from her excitement where they had touched her chuffie on the walk back. Above her dark stocking-tops – she rarely wore tights – her thighs were sturdy and smooth all the way up to her groins and her thicket of black curls. She sat on her brown leather chesterfield, spreading her legs wide.

'He did Sharon,' she murmured aloud to herself.

Her fingers plucked at the plump lips between her thighs.

'Sharon was naked and he was on his knees and he pushed his long hard *thing* into her. It looked enormous but it went right in and she didn't flinch.'

Enid's skirt was pulled up round her hips. She leaned back on the chesterfield with her fingers inside her chuffie, teasing her wet little nubby.

'He pulled his huge *thing* out of her and sprayed all over her titties,' she sighed, 'I saw it all – from his first penetration to the moment when he shot off. Sharon loved what he was doing to her, she was sighing and shaking . . . *oh my god I'm coming already . . .*'

Chapter 4

The girls of Lechlade Ladies' College were by nature ambitious young women or they wouldn't have been there. They had their sights set on the old universities, first-class degrees and important careers.

They were interested in boyfriends to some extent, as all teenage girls are, but not during term, only at home during vacations. Because of their ambitions, they didn't want permanent boyfriends and they had no intention of ruining their future prospects by taking the risk of being put in the club for the sake of a teenage boy's quick thrill.

In their late-night discussions at college the girls always reached the same conclusion – that letting a boy stick his *thing* into them was idiotic. Boys couldn't be trusted, whatever they said beforehand, as soon as they had it in they'd shoot their sticky little load into any girl who was fool enough to let them. They'd never give a thought to what could happen to the unlucky girl as a result.

Boys would promise absolutely anything in order to get their *thing* between a girl's legs. But there was nothing in it for the girl because boys were useless. All they thought about was their own satisfaction – as soon as they'd got their twanger in they didn't care whether the girl enjoyed it or not.

Some of them didn't seem to realise that girls came at all – to them a girl was just a creature with breasts to grope and a slit to get their hard-on into. They didn't understand girls. Girls understood each other, they knew how to play nicely with a chuffie, how to give it an expert finger-wave and diddle it till the big thrill came.

When the girls came back to college for the start of a new

term they always told each other about the fingering techniques of the boys they'd been out with and let put a hand down their knickers. They had a good giggle about male stupidity and inadequacy. They told each other funny stories about boyfriends they managed to get so worked up that they shot off in their trousers. It was rated a victory for any girl to claim she'd sent a boyfriend home with sticky underwear.

It wasn't all that difficult to achieve. Practically every teenage boy was so desperate that half an hour of French kissing and tittie-fumbling would put him in such a fraught condition that a quick rub on the front of his jeans would make him come in his jockey-shorts.

Orline Ashby had a rattling good tale to tell about a boyfriend she'd been out with a few times. He was eighteen, she said, and his name was Matt. He'd left home after finding a job and lived in a bed-sitter, and one evening she'd gone with him to the launderette.

He had been after Orline for a long time, all this vacation and last vacation, trying to persuade her to let him do her properly. She let him feel her titties when he took her out and two or three times she'd let him slip his hand inside her knickers and finger her kitty. He always asked her to get his twanger out and stroke it, but Orline was very wary of going this far.

If she pulled it out and gave him a rapid finger-wave, that would cool him down. On the other hand, while she was diddling him he might get overexcited – she didn't trust him not to fling her on her back and ram it into her. She played safe and refused to diddle him when they were alone, which made him even more rampant.

She'd had his shaft out a couple of times in the back row of the local cinema, where he couldn't do anything. Even then she was cautious about holding it in her bare hand. She wrapped a hanky round it and diddled him through that until he shot his lot with a groan that could be heard ten rows away. When he'd finished twitching and squirting she wadded up the wet, sticky hanky and put it into his pocket.

He tried it on again after they came out of the cinema, but Orline insisted that once a night was enough for anyone. What she meant was that once was enough for *him*. When she and her girlfriends played together at college, once was never enough, nor was twice. Three or four times was more like it, but that was different because they were girls.

At the launderette Matt stuffed his washing into a machine and put his money in the slot. It was after nine in the evening and the launderette was almost empty; just two other people doing their laundry. Orline wanted something to tell when she got back to college, and so she started to tease Matt.

When she told the story in the common room after dinner one day early in the new term, three of her friends were there, all second-year girls like herself – Hilary Landor, Marjorie Newmill and Pru Renwick. Orline giggled as she told them about what had happened in the Superclene Launderette. She'd set the ball rolling that night by accusing Matt of playing with his own *thing*.

'You've got your hand in your pocket nearly all the time,' she'd said to Matt, staring pointedly at the front of his jeans. 'You've got a permanent hard-on from fingering yourself.'

Matt's face turned bright pink. He pulled his hand out of his pocket and insisted he wasn't doing anything of the sort.

'Playing with his twanger in public,' Marjorie Newmill commented, 'and while you were with him – what a beast.'

'Let Orline tell us about it,' Hilary said, 'we know boys are beasts. What did you do then, Orline?'

'Matt was leaning on the washing-machine and I was standing in front of him,' she said. 'Nobody was watching us, so I put my hand on his flies and gave him a good hard squeeze to make him yelp. I insisted that he *was* feeling himself and it was no use saying he wasn't because he'd got a big hard stand. "It's only natural," he told me, "I'm in love with you."'

Then Orline grasped his *thing* through his jeans again and he was staring at her with round bulging eyes and very red cheeks.

'You're not in love with me, you just want to *do* me,' she said, giving his shaft a rub through the jeans.

Matt had a good-sized one – it stood up like a stick and twitched in her hand. She rubbed her palm up and down half a dozen times to take him nearer to boiling-point.

'It's your fault I've got this hard-on,' he said, trying to stroke her titties without anyone seeing. 'You're so sexy that just looking at you makes it stand up hard. It's only fair if you come back to my place so I can do something with it.'

'But you didn't go, did you?' Pru Renwick interrupted Orline's story.

'I told him not to blame me for the state he was in,' Orline said, 'he did it to himself.'

There were only two other customers in the launderette. A woman at the far end finished her drying and packed her stuff into a big bag and went out. That left only one man, apart from Matt and Orline. He was sitting on a plastic chair some distance away, looking at a girlie magazine featuring women with huge bosoms while his washing went round and round in the machine.

'That man's just like you,' Orline said to Matt, 'he's got a giant hard-on.'

She stood closer to the red-faced Matt and slipped her hand into his jeans pocket, where his own hand had been before. He grinned at her and said boastfully, 'Feel how big and hard it is.' He was sure she'd go back to his bed-sitter with him now she'd had a feel of what he was offering.

'I've handled bigger,' she said, just to keep him in order.

'Oh, yes? Whose?' he demanded jealously.

'Lots of boys have bigger ones than yours,' Orline said, neatly sidestepping his question. She asked him one of her own.

'Have you ever done a girl, Matt – really *done* her?'

'They always say yes if you ask that,' Marjorie broke in, 'especially the ones who've never even had their hand in a girl's knickers.'

'Shut up, Marjorie,' Hilary said, 'otherwise we'll keep interrupting you when it's your turn.'

'Of course he said he had,' Orline confirmed with a grin, 'and he sounded outraged, as if the question was a slur on him. He said he'd done lots of girls and they loved it.'

At that moment her fingertips were touching Matt's shaft through the pocket of his jeans and she was rubbing slowly up and down. He was as easily deceived as teenagers usually are, imagining that she was feeling him to find out what she'd be getting when he stuck it up her.

'Do you like what you feel?' he asked with a sly grin.

'You're so conceited you think you only have to flash a hard-on at a girl and she'll rip her knickers off and lie on her back for you.'

It was a statement to which there was no riposte Matt could think of.

'So *who* have you done, Matt?' Orline asked him while he was trying to devise something to say. 'Tell me.'

It bothered him, this request for specifics, and he said that he'd done lots of girls – but nobody she knew.

'Is that so?' she said, her fingertips still sliding up and down. 'Tell me the names of a few of them.'

The man with the magazine halfway down the line of washing-machines was looking at them now. He suspected they were up to something because they were standing so close together. But he couldn't see what was going on, because he was on the side away from Orline's hand in Matt's pocket.

'I suppose you've had this *thing* of yours up Ruthie Browning,' Orline said, naming a girl they both knew. 'From what I've heard, she's been done by everybody in trousers over the age of thirteen. I'm sure you wouldn't have missed your chance to stick it up her big sloppy kitty.'

'I'm choosy who I put it in,' he said.

He sounded so offended that Orline guessed that Easy Ruthie was probably the only girl whose kitty he'd had it in.

'You say you're choosy about it,' she said, 'but you haven't mentioned any names yet.'

She stared into his face with a smile. He was racking his brains for names. It had to be girls she didn't know, in case she checked later.

'When was the last time you had this great thick *thing* of yours in a girl's kitty?' she asked, just to prod him along.

'Last Saturday night, after the disco,' he said, after a longish pause.

She could tell that he was making it up – there was a shifty look in his eyes. She asked him who the lucky girl was.

'Beverley Tate,' he said, and instantly turned a bright red.

'I know Beverley,' Orline said, although she didn't believe there was any such person. 'She's a tall, thin blonde girl with long hair in a pony-tail.'

She'd reduced Matt to such a state by playing with his hard-on that he could hardly speak for puffing and sighing. He nodded weakly, accepting her bogus description of the alleged girlfriend.

'Bev's very pretty,' Orline said. 'She's got a reputation as a goer. Some say she's a nympho – not as bad as Ruthie, maybe, but very keen to have a boy's shaft inside her. Did you shoot off in her?'

She could feel his twanger straining in his jeans under her moving fingers.

'Yes,' he gasped, 'right up her kitty – oh! . . . I'm coming . . .'

'Did he come?' Marjorie asked, her own face pink.

'He went off like a sky-rocket,' Orline said with a grin. 'His *thing* was leaping and jerking in my hand while he shot off in his underwear – it felt warm and wet when it soaked through the pocket lining. I had to laugh at the silly look on his face – he was flopping back against the washing-machine with his mouth wide open.'

'Does he still think you'll open your legs for him when he's got a stand?' Hilary asked.

'That's not the end of it,' Orline said. 'The man with the magazine jumped up and came towards us, looking furious. "I know what you're up to," he was shouting, "I'm going to call a policeman and have you both arrested." The funniest part was that you could see he'd got a great big hard-on under his trousers.'

'What did you do?' Marjorie asked breathlessly.

'I was going to tell him to sit down and diddle himself and mind his own business,' Orline said, 'but Matt was embarrassed because he'd come and so he grabbed my arm and dragged me out of the launderette. We ran off down the street, with the fool of a man shouting after us. And Matt was complaining all the while that his underwear was wet and sticky.'

The four girls laughed as they discussed Matt and his ineptitude for a while, and Orline's three friends all rated her highly for her achievement. They looked to Hilary next, knowing that she was certain to have something tantalising to report.

'We went on holiday to the Algarve,' Hilary began. 'Daddy picked a hotel near a golf-course. One afternoon he took both my brothers there with him and Mummy went to get her hair done. I was on the balcony of my room, soaking up the sun and reading a paperback, when I noticed this man on the next balcony.'

'Young or old, handsome or ugly?' Marjorie asked at once.

'He looked about forty,' said Hilary, 'he was wearing green shorts and flip-flop sandals, that's all. I could see he was plump-bellied. He was stretched out on a lounging-chair, reading a newspaper. When he folded it over to get to the inside pages I saw *Paris-Matin* printed at the top and I deduced that he was French.'

'Oh, a sexy Frenchman,' Orline sighed. 'But you said he was forty – that's much too old to be sexy. And they drink too much, you know. I bet his dangler wouldn't even stand up.'

'I didn't say he was sexy,' Hilary told her, 'and as to his dangler, I've something to tell you about that in a minute. There we sat on our separate balconies reading, but after a while I saw he wasn't really reading his paper. I was wearing my blue bikini and he was using the newspaper as a screen while he stared at my body.'

'I should think he was, too,' Marjorie sighed – everyone knew she had a passion for Hilary. 'When you're in your blue bikini I can't keep my hands off you.'

'Yes, well, I pretended not to notice him,' Hilary said, 'but I got up from my lounger and stood with my arms on the balcony rail, and I leaned forward to look down at the

61

beach so as to give him a good view of my bum. I was wearing my sunglasses so I could watch the Frog out of the corner of my eye without him knowing I was looking at him.'

'That's turning the tables,' Orline commented with a grin. 'He didn't know he was being watched while he was watching your bare bum – but did it make his dangler stand up?'

'It certainly did,' Hilary said, 'I saw him drop his hand into his lap and hold it over the front of his shorts. I was giggling to myself and I thought, *Monsieur whatever-your-name-is, you're a dirty old businessman on holiday with your family, your wife's taken the kids somewhere and you're all alone on your balcony with a stand, staring at my body. Well, I'll give you something to stare at, you filthy beast.*

Hilary was going to give him a run for his money. She raised her arms over her head and stretched them wide and arched her back, as if she was loosening up cramped limbs – she was really making her titties stand out enticingly. She had a very kissable pair of titties, so her friends at college told her. They looked very feelable too, Hilary's titties, and indeed they were felt and kissed very regularly in term time.

She was thinking about taking her bikini top off and letting the Frog have a good look. *That'll send his blood-pressure up,* she thought with a grin. *No, let him sweat a while before showing him anything.* She gazed out at the sea and the little sailing boats, or pretended to, while she turned her head a fraction and checked what he was doing from behind the cover of her dark glasses.

He'd stopped pretending to read the newspaper. He was making believe he was asleep, with his head back and his eyes closed, the open paper spread over his lap. His face was flushed and there were beads of sweat on his forehead, under his short dark hair. It was a very hot day, but there was a nice sea breeze and he was sitting in the shade – the heat he was feeling came from inside him.

His hand was under the newspaper. Her guess was that he was giving his twanger a good feel. She also guessed that his eyes were not completely closed. He was looking at her from under his eyelids – staring at her titties and playing with himself. She turned and leaned back on the rail, her hands on it, one bare foot resting against the knee of her other leg, a casual schoolgirl pose, she told herself. It opened her thighs and gave her admirer a good view of the spot where her bikini briefs covered her kitty. She kept a sharp eye on his newspaper and could see furtive movement beneath it.

He's undone his shorts and pulled his hard-on out, she said to herself with a silent chuckle. *He's holding it in his hand and diddling himself.*

Hilary was pleased that she'd been able to make him go that far. The situation promised to be a good tale to tell back at college next term. It wasn't the usual sort of thing the girls bragged about – ordinary tales of how they got a boyfriend all hot and bothered and teased him so much he shot his sticky little load into his underwear.

This was a grown man she was teasing, not a teenager with a permanent stand. She was teasing a foreigner, in an expensive hotel, left on his own for an afternoon and stroking his twanger because Hilary had got him into a comical state of arousal.

The newspaper over the Frenchman's lap was definitely moving. She saw it stirring over the fist she guessed was sliding up and down his shaft. There was no need to take her bikini top off and let him look at her kissable titties – he was going to shoot his lot under the newspaper soon enough. A dark stain would soak through the page to give him away.

'His face was scarlet,' she told her listening circle in the common room. 'I could see he was on the short strokes. I'd done nothing at all except wear a bikini, and I started to wonder just how far I could get him to go if I put my mind to it.'

'That sounds dangerous,' Marjorie said, 'especially with a foreigner – they're all sex maniacs, everybody knows that. What if he tried to jump on you and ram his shaft up you?'

'It was safe,' Hilary said. 'The gap between the balconies was too wide for him to jump across, unless he was an acrobat. I called out to him and went to the railing on his side.'

The man on the other balcony went redder and redder in

the face and ignored her at first, pretending to be fast asleep on his lounger. His hand stopped moving under the newspaper. Hilary called across again and he opened his eyes.

He stared at her – mostly at her pointed titties in their bikini cups, but he didn't miss her smooth bare belly and thighs. Then he was staring at the mound between them.

'Do you speak English?' she asked – she wasn't going to let him know she was doing A-level French at college.

When he shook his head she smiled sweetly at him and pointed to his lap. He blushed to realise she knew what he was concealing under the newspaper, the secret of his unzipped shorts and his exposed stand.

She smiled at him again and made a gesture of flicking the newspaper away. He pretended not to understand. She nodded her head vigorously and held up her right forefinger and slid the fingers of her other hand up and down it in a lewd gesture nobody could mistake.

He looked at her doubtfully. She nodded again two or three times, then put her forefinger into her mouth and sucked it noisily. The man stared open-mouthed at her, especially when she pointed to his lap again while still sucking her finger – a little pantomime which conveyed to him the blood-racing possibility of having his twanger inside the mouth of this pretty and almost naked young girl.

That decided him. He flipped the newspaper aside to the balcony floor and spread his legs. As Hilary had thought, his belt and zip were undone, his shorts gaping wide open, and his twanger standing up bold and thick. She nodded in approval of his action and he ran his fingers up and down the shaft. There was a smile on his face, a dreamy expression.

'That's a beauty,' she said, uncertain whether he understood any English or not. 'Give it a rub – I know you want to.'

She jiggled her fist up and down at waist height and he understood her meaning well enough, if not her words. His eyes glowed with pride at her approval of her shaft and her request to see it perform. He wrapped his hand round it and jerked up and down strongly.

64

Hilary leaned over the balcony side-rail, her titties thrusting toward him. She made little kissing movements with puckered lips at the purple head of his twanger. He moaned and she stuck her long pink tongue out at him and then flicked it rapidly from side to side, as if she was doing it to his bounding hard-on.

He began to babble away in his own language – and with his free hand he was making *come-here* signs at her. He wanted her to climb the rail and jump across the gap to his balcony. Whereupon he would do all sorts of exciting and disgraceful things to her beautiful young body.

'Don't get too ambitious,' she said, grinning across at him, 'I'm not letting you put it in my mouth. And you're certainly not going to put it in my precious kitty.'

When she said *kitty* she put her hand between her legs, down inside her blue bikini bottom. The excited Frenchman took this to mean that she wanted to feel his shaft between her legs. Perhaps she was promising to climb the rail and leap across into his arms, so he could rip her bikini off and have her flat on her back on the sun-lounger. He was holding his shaft just below the swollen dark head and jiggling it up and down fast.

'If you ask me, you're a dirty middle-aged old beast,' Hilary told him sweetly. 'They say all foreigners are sex maniacs, and I believe them now I've seen you sitting there in broad daylight in the open air with your shaft in your hand diddling yourself. You ought to be locked up for thinking the things you're thinking about young girls.'

Obviously he didn't understand a word and thought from her tone that she was saying encouraging things to him. There was a wild look in his eyes – with his free hand he made gestures of snatching her bikini top off. He begged her in garbled French she couldn't understand to let him see her titties.

'Show you my gorgeous titties?' she said. 'Are you mad? If I let you look at them, you'll hurl yourself across here to feel them. And after that you'll want to see my kitty. You'll be down on your knees, ripping my bikini briefs off and kissing me between the legs. I know your sort – you'll try to push your tongue into my kitty, you beast.'

He was babbling nonsensically and his clenched hand was jerking up and down very fast.

'I'm not an idiot,' Hilary said to him with a most promising smile. 'You're sitting there giving yourself a hand-job and all the time you're imagining it's my hand round your shaft. You'd like that, wouldn't you? Well, you're out of luck.'

To tease him past the limit she put her hands behind her back to undo the straps of her bikini top. He moaned when he saw the straps dangling loose from her hands – in another half-second she'd pull the top away from her body and her sweet young titties would be completely bare for him to look at . . .

His moan of appreciation turned into a long wail of surprise and dismay as he came explosively. Hilary stared across at his leaping twanger shooting its bounty high into the air. She grinned. There was no need to take her bikini top off now – and she'd never intended to, anyway; undoing the strap was the final step in her teasing.

The Frenchman lay back trembling on his lounger, wet and sticky all up his bare chest. His shaft was losing its firmness and dwindling now it had performed its little act so heartily. When he had his breath back he turned to look at the young girl who'd persuaded him to do this to himself. She wasn't on her balcony, she'd gone inside her room, but he suspected she was still watching him from behind the shutter. Maybe with her hand down the front of her bikini briefs.

'That's fantastic,' Pru said. 'I'd never dare tease a man that far – I'd be afraid he might be waiting for me the next time I went out.'

Marjorie was staring at Hilary with an expression of affection on her face, her dark brown eyes gazing into Hilary's pale blue ones.

'I want to diddle you,' Marjorie said breathlessly, 'let's leave here and go to my room.'

'I'm sure you want to,' Hilary said, 'there's nothing new about that.'

'I'll diddle you senseless,' Marjorie promised.

'Not till you've told us what you got up to in the vacation,' Orline cut in. 'Fair's fair – you've got all night to do Hilary.'

'All right then, I'll tell you about my trip to the doctor. I got the better of him, though I had to show him everything first. And I let him grope me.'

'It doesn't count if a doctor feels your kitty, does it?' Pru said at once. 'I mean, they're supposed to. They don't even get a stand because they've been trained not to get excited.'

'Doctors are not supposed to feel you the way this one did,' Marjorie retorted. 'When I got there the receptionist said Dr Dilton, our regular doctor, was away on holiday and Dr Tremlake was standing in for him. So I sat down to wait. When it was my turn I went into the consulting room and he was standing there by the desk with a cup of tea in his hand.'

'Was he young or old, handsome or ugly?' Orline asked the question this time that Marjorie herself had asked before.

'Good-looking,' said Marjorie, 'still in his twenties, tall and slim and dark-haired. He was a massive improvement on old Dr Dilton with his cold hands and pot belly and bald patch.'

'This young doctor looked at you and he saw a pretty young brunette,' said Hilary, 'who later tonight is going to be done till she screams. He saw a girl with luscious plump titties and whether he'd been trained or not, he wanted a feel. You were a change from the bored middle-aged women and pregnant young wives he'd been seeing all day – am I right?'

'You're always right,' Marjorie said admiringly. 'When he looked at me he put his teacup on the desk and sat down fast with his legs pressed together. So I knew he fancied me. I decided I'd have a little fun with him. I'd really gone there to ask what I could do for my freckles – but I thought I'd ask the new doctor to give me his advice on contraceptive pills.'

'Contraception – at your age? Do your parents know about this?' Dr Tremlake had asked Marjorie.

'They don't have to, I'm old enough to decide for myself,' she told him.

'That's true,' he admitted, 'you're sixteen and so you're over the age of consent.'

'I'm seventeen,' Marjorie said, 'and I'll consent any time I feel like it.'

Dr Tremlake thought he should try a question or two, so he asked, 'Are you a virgin or have you already started having sex, without the pill?'

Even while he was asking the question, he was visualising Marjorie in the back seat of an old car with a boyfriend, her knickers off and her legs spread open. As a matter of fact, when he was a medical student he had done it in the back of a car many, many times, mainly with trainee nurses.

It needed a certain amount of agility and ingenuity to get your twanger in all the way on the back seat of a car, but it was well worth the effort, the doctor thought.

'Since you ask,' Marjorie said, grinning, 'I haven't had a boy's *thing* in me yet, so I must be a virgin. But I'm not exactly untouched, if you know what I mean.'

He grinned and said he knew exactly what she meant and there was no harm in that.

'Have you got a regular boyfriend?' he asked.

Marjorie shook her head. She had several regular girlfriends at college, but she wasn't going to tell him about them. He took her head-shake to mean that she'd let herself be felt and fingered to a climax by various boys she knew. And that if she was telling the truth about not letting them put their hard-ons inside her, she must have given the boys concerned a seeing-to with her hand.

Looking at the plump round titties inside her open denim jacket, the doctor decided he wouldn't mind being one of her boyfriends and having a feel.

'Before I give you a prescription, I think I'd better examine you to make sure all is well and in good order, before you make a start on your active adult sex life,' he said.

Marjorie smiled at that. She was willing to bet she'd come more times in her life than he had, though he was about ten years older. She stood up and took off her jacket and denim skirt. Dr Brian Tremlake remained seated – his legs crossed to keep his hard-on trapped and out of sight.

'Slip your knickers down and lie on the examination couch,' he said in a husky voice.

He could hardly believe his luck. Naturally, doctors were forbidden to take advantage of their female patients, but it was his duty to examine this pretty seventeen-year-old with the bouncy titties. It was a duty he was looking forward to with a twitching stand.

Marjorie didn't turn away from him while she took off her skirt and slipped her knickers down her legs. She was wearing white cotton briefs and she dropped them with apparent casualness on Brian Tremlake's desk. He stifled a gasp at that and hoped his face wasn't crimson.

The couch stood along the wall opposite him. Marjorie sat on it and swung her legs up.

She stretched out on her back and the doctor stared almost open-mouthed at her bare round belly and smooth thighs. He liked the look of her plump kitty, which had dark-brown curls of fine, soft-looking hair. He could imagine a teenage boy putting his hand inside her knickers and feeling her. But he didn't have to just imagine it, he was going to have a feel of her kitty himself, only he called it *examining* her.

Marjorie was watching him closely without seeming to. When he stood up from his chair she nearly giggled to see the long bulge in the front of his grey trousers – he had a massive hard-on. He didn't bother to put on a pair of the thin plastic gloves doctors usually wear when they carry out internal examinations. Marjorie knew he meant to give her chuffie a very thorough feel.

He took his time over it – in medical school he'd been warned over and over again that he must stay calm, detached and in control when examining women's bodies. He was enjoying the moment too much to rush things – and anyway, he had no intention of actually *doing* this sexy seventeen-year-old. Anything as unprofessional as poking his shaft into her was out of the question. He was only going to feel her kitty. For good medical reasons.

He asked Marjorie to spread her legs wide and he stroked in her groins with his fingertips before he parted the plump brown-haired lips. If the truth were told, he'd very much

69

like to get on top of her and do her – he had to admit that much to himself when he opened the pink inner lips of her chuffie. He touched her nubby and couldn't help sighing.

Marjorie lay with a little smile on her face while he was feeling her and when he slipped his fingers into her. At least he knew where and how to touch a girl to make her excited, she thought. Maybe it was a part of doctors' training. She saw he was very red in the face – feeling her was certainly making *him* excited.

She turned her head to one side so she could stare at his flies while he fingered her. He was mumbling on to her about checking this and that and testing her reflexes and similar excuses for giving her a good feel. His bulge was impressive, long and upright and twitching.

She could guess what was going through his mind. He wanted to slip his twanger into her and shoot off – in fact he was desperate, the twitching in his trousers gave him away. He was telling himself he mustn't take advantage of a patient, especially not a young girl who said she was a virgin.

While he was playing with her for his good medical reasons it became apparent to him that her chuffie had been handled a lot. It wasn't tight and virginal at all. Delicious sexy things had been done to it, and done often. The thought made his hard-on jerk more strongly.

Marjorie decided it was time to torment him even more and she asked if it would be painful the first time she let a boy put his *thing* in her.

'I shouldn't think so,' he gasped, sliding two fingers as far up her as they would go. 'You're very well developed for your age.'

'I've heard that some men have absolutely enormous *things*,' she said. 'Surely if one of them rammed it in hard, that could hurt, couldn't it?'

'You mustn't listen to old wives' tales,' he said in a reassuring tone of voice. 'The average male part is about six inches long when erect, and that is well within the capacity of the average woman to accommodate without any discomfort. I fear you're more likely to encounter smaller ones than oversize ones.'

70

'Six inches long?' Marjorie said, sounding dismayed. 'But that's massive – I could never cope with that much inside me – it would split me wide open. Six inches sounds gigantic – how big is yours, doctor?'

He was panting as he subjected her open and slippery chuffie to a thorough digital examination. He ignored her question – so she reached out and pressed the back of her hand to the lurching length in his trousers.

'My god, it's huge!' she exclaimed, rubbing the back of her hand up and down fast. 'You've got a giant of a twanger.'

Doctor Tremlake moaned and convulsed and shot his sticky juice inside his underwear. *Oh oh oh* he was moaning as he slid very slowly down to his knees, his face coming to rest on Marjorie's bare belly.

She could feel his body jerking rhythmically to the surges as he came and came. She grinned and pushed his head away.

'Oh, doctor!' she said. 'Whatever have you done?'

Chapter 5

This year as in previous years, girls coming back to Lechlade for their second year were given a different roommate. The arrangement had been in force so many years that the reason for it was long forgotten.

Its origins actually lay in events that took place about eighty years earlier. The college had been honoured to have the youngest daughter of a very rich peer as a student – the Hon. Emily Rackover, a pretty sixteen-year-old with long fair hair done in ringlets. But at the end of her first year, Emily informed the then Principal that she would request her noble Papa not to send her back to Lechlade after the summer vacation.

The appalled Principal, Miss Dinah Cranford, asked why. Emily said it was impossible to share a room over a long period with someone whose views differed greatly from one's own on certain matters that could not be spoken of openly. For a brief time such a problem could be disregarded, but to encounter the situation nightly was intolerable.

The Principal deduced that the Hon. Emily's roommate had been trying to take advantage of her at bedtime. Girls often formed attachments to each other, which led to hand-holding and hugging. Even kissing, if both were warm-natured.

Girlish crushes had been known to lead to sharing a bed and touching each other's bodies under the long nightgowns that were then worn. The Hon. Emily seemed to Miss Cranford to be a good prospect for girlish advances – her ringlets of long fair hair were delightful, as were the big round titties under her chin-high blouse and the graceful long legs under her ankle-length skirt.

Apparently, Emily had found the idea of being 'finger-waved' by her roommate unacceptable. The Principal persuaded her to return to Lechlade after the summer vacation by promising to give her another roommate – one the Principal would herself pick.

Later on, when Miss Cranford was looking through the list of names to choose a suitable girl for Emily, she realised that to part two roommates after only a year together would cause gossip. Idle and wicked tongues would suggest that unmentionable lusts had been detected.

The solution was to change *everybody*'s roommate at the end of their first year and claim it was an academic tradition. So it was done – and the Principal chose Miss Maria Palgrave to share with Emily. Maria was the only daughter of a Church of England bishop, a plain girl, devoted to her studies.

The Principal never found out that she had misunderstood Emily's objection. She'd got it the wrong way round – Emily was fed up with her roommate, Jane Quibley, not because Jane tried to lure her into bed, but because Jane refused, night after night, to get into bed with Emily for a diddle.

It turned out that Maria Palgrave was keen on nightgown-lifting and Emily's second year at Lechlade was a success. She and Maria diddled each other diligently at bed-time, they went to their room after lunch every day for a quickie, and they often enjoyed another before dinner. Marie had a lean, lithe body that she loved to slide over Emily's fuller form – it was a body massage in the truest sense of the phrase.

By the end of their first term together, Emily had shed a half-stone in weight, as a result of her exertions on her back with her legs apart. Marie was even more lithe and muscular from her frequently repeated exercises. The two girls formed a lifelong attachment and continued to meet several times a week even after Emily was married to the younger son of a duke and Maria to a curate.

That was all a long time ago, but the new room-sharing rules quickly became an unquestioned tradition at Lechlade – and unquestioned traditional things rarely change much.

Marjorie Newmill and Hilary Landor shared a room in their

first year, and they formed a hot passion for each other. After the summer vacation Hilary found herself sharing with Linda Knight, a ginger-haired girl she didn't like much. Marjorie, to her amazement, was paired with a first-year girl. This was unusual, but that was how the numbers worked out.

Or so said Miss Joy Locksley, the Head of Wexby House, when Marjorie went to complain about being landed with a newcomer. Marjorie suspected there was a plot to separate Hilary and herself, though she couldn't see why. She and Hilary liked their Head of House, a slender dark-haired woman. They'd told each other many a time they'd like to be diddled by her, but she had never showed that sort of interest in either of them.

'She has very elegant titties,' said Marjorie to Hilary. 'I'd love to feel them and lick her bobbles while she had her hand up my skirt. I bet she puts a dab of French perfume in her cleavage.'

'She has lovely legs,' Hilary said dreamily. 'Just imagine seeing her naked with her legs open while you feel her kitty.'

'She's very dark-haired,' said Marjorie. 'I wonder if she's got the same shade round her kitty – what do you think?'

'Bound to be,' Hilary said, 'darker than yours even, though yours is a sexy colour.'

'I'd love to open my legs for her to tongue me,' Marjorie sighed. 'I'd come three times on the trot.'

Despite Marjorie's protests, Miss Locksley would not change the room-sharing plan now it was up on the Wexby House notice-board and Marjorie had no choice but to make the best of sharing with the new girl. Her name was Caroline Wilton and she was a tall sixteen-year-old with medium-brown hair.

A few days after the start of term, Marjorie went to their shared room at about nine o'clock in the evening. To her surprise, Caroline was huddled up in bed, early as it was.

'Are you all right?' Marjorie asked.

'No, I'm not.' Caroline peeped over the edge of the bedclothes that had been pulled over her head. 'There was a man at the window – I think he was trying to break in.'

'What did he look like?'

'I didn't see him very well,' Caroline said as she hitched herself up in bed, still clutching the sheets around her, 'I was changing into jeans and a sweater. I looked up and saw a shadow on the window. I didn't know what to do, so I jumped into bed naked and pulled the sheet up over my head.'

'It was Keith Mason, for sure,' Marjorie said. 'There's no need to be afraid of him. What you should do is run to the window and open it and stick your finger in his eye.'

Caroline stared at her as if she'd gone mad.

'Attack a man?' she said. 'Are you crazy?'

'He's timid really,' Marjorie explained. 'If you pretended to go for him he'd turn and be halfway across the grounds before you got to the window. You're in no danger from Keith.'

'Who is he?' Caroline asked, sounding puzzled. The sheets were still wound tightly round her body, but she was less anxious now that Marjorie was with her.

'Keith is the caretaker,' Marjorie explained. 'He's harmless. He lives in the gatehouse and he's always hanging round the showers and the swimming-pool hoping to see a pair of titties.'

'Oh,' Caroline said, sounding shocked. 'Is he a flasher?'

'He's not brave enough for that. All he does is lurk about trying to get a look at a kitty. Everybody knows about him and they pull their curtains across when they're changing or getting ready for bed.'

'If everybody knows about him, why hasn't he been sacked?'

'I mean *we* all know about him, not the staff.'

'Why doesn't somebody report him?' Caroline asked.

Marjorie sat down on the side of her new roommate's bed and grinned at her. Caroline sat up with her back against the headboard and the sheet slipped a little to expose her bare shoulders.

'It would spoil the fun to get him sacked,' Marjorie said. 'The thing is, we're cleverer than Keith and some girls like to play tricks on him. There were two in this house last term who caught him hiding in a locker in the shower changing-room to spy on them.'

76

'Actually hiding inside a locker?'

'He'd crammed himself into the broom and bucket locker. They whipped the door open and found him with his jeans down round his ankles and his *thing* in his hand – just as he shot off.'

'No! That's incredible,' Caroline said. 'They saw him actually *coming*?'

'The story went right round the college and gave us all a laugh. Keith crept about with his eyes on the ground for a week afterwards. He simply daren't look anybody in the face.'

'Do you think he had his *thing* out while he was looking at me through the window?' Caroline asked in dismay.

'Of course,' Marjorie said with a grin. 'He'd have had his zipper down and his hard-on in his hand. My friend Hilary and I spotted him up a ladder behind the gymnasium once – he was pretending to repair the guttering, but he was spying through a window to see girls undressing.'

'Well, I suppose he's seen all he wants of me,' Caroline said, cheered up by Marjorie's off-hand attitude to Keith's hobby. 'He'll go after the other new girls now.'

Marjorie shrugged. 'How long was he watching you?' she asked.

'Don't know. I sat on the bed while I took my shoes and tights off and then I stood up and took my skirt and top off. And my bra. Then I sat down to check my tights because I thought I saw the start of a run . . . I stood up again to take my knickers off . . .'

'Never mind about all this standing up and sitting down,' Marjorie interrupted. 'The truth is that you treated Keith to a proper strip-tease show. Must have made his day.'

'I didn't know anybody was watching me,' Caroline said, her cheeks turning pink. 'I was standing with my knickers in my hand when I saw this face at the window. He could have been there all the time.'

'I'm sure he was,' Marjorie said with a smile. 'That's why we always draw the curtains. I'm sure that now he's seen you naked, in his hot little mind Keith believes he's felt your titties and fingered your kitty.'

'No . . . surely not!' Caroline exclaimed.

She sat up higher in consternation and the sheet slipped down to her waist. And as she'd said, she'd jumped into bed naked to escape Keith's lustful stare. Marjorie looked at her new roommate's titties – they were tiny, no larger than a pair of apples.

'Let's face it, Caroline,' she said teasingly, 'he didn't get all that *much* of an eyeful, did he? When he got a look at mine, before I'd been told about him, he had a lot more to pretend he'd got his gummy little hands on.'

Caroline stared at the chubby pair of titties under Marjorie's blouse. She reached for the sheet, to cover herself again, but Marjorie took her wrist and stopped her.

'I'm not laughing at you,' Marjorie assured her. 'Your titties may be small but they're a nice shape. If you hadn't spotted Keith in time and scared him away, he'd have made his underwear sticky looking at them.'

'You think he diddled himself?' Caroline asked, her face still pink.

'I'm sure of it, that's why he lurks about spying. And you'd be a treat for him, with your tiny titties. He especially likes girls who look very young. And you're very pretty, too – if it had been me watching you play with yourself through the window, I'd have had my hand in my pants.'

'I wasn't doing that!' Caroline said. 'I was only undressing.'

Marjorie smiled slyly and put her hand on Caroline's bare shoulder. A sigh from the younger girl encouraged her and her fingers moved slowly to the pink bobbles of Caroline's tiny but perfect titties. Caroline closed her eyes and leaned back against the headboard of the bed.

'They're nice, your titties,' said Marjorie with a friendly smile. 'I love them – I bet all the boys you know try to get their hand down your dress for a feel.'

'They usually prefer girls with bigger ones – like yours,' Caroline said with a pout.

'That's only because boys are so stupid. Even when you let them feel your titties they don't know what to do next after they've given them a bit of a squeeze,' Marjorie said in a tone of contempt for the entire male gender. 'All they think about is getting their *thing* inside you.'

She bent forward to kiss Caroline's titties and breathe hotly on them. When she heard Caroline sigh, she flicked the tip of her tongue over the little pink bobbles.

Caroline slid down the bed, pushing the sheet to her waist. She lay with her head on the pillow and her hands under her head, enjoying what Marjorie was doing to her.

'Would you let a boy stick his *thing* in you?' she asked.

'No chance,' Marjorie said, raising her head from Caroline's titties for a moment to look her in the eyes. 'Boys are a dead loss at it – it's much nicer to play with other girls.'

'I like the feel of a hard-on inside me,' Caroline surprised her by saying. 'Being diddled by another girl is all right – I'd never say no, but it's not as exciting as a long stiff *thing* sliding in and out.'

Marjorie sat up and looked at her, astounded.

'Are you serious?'

'Why shouldn't I be?' Caroline said, looking her in the eyes without the least sign of embarrassment.

'It's not worth it,' Marjorie insisted. 'If a boy shoots his sticky little load in your kitty, he thinks he owns you and can tell you what to do. He tells all his friends that you're *his* girl. And besides, think of the risk if you fall unlucky.'

'You do have to be careful,' Caroline said with a knowing grin.

'Yes, that helps, but what about the other thing – a boyfriend thinking that he owns you because he's had it up you – doesn't that bother you?'

'I haven't got a regular boyfriend. I know lots of boys and go out with each of them in turn. My choice, not theirs.'

Marjorie was struggling in her mind to grasp the implications of what Caroline was telling her. 'You mean there's not just one boyfriend you let stick his *thing* up you, there's a lot of them – is that it?'

'That's right,' Caroline agreed, 'I've had a lot of them. Don't you understand yet? They're so desperate to get it inside me that they'll go down on their knees and beg. I can tell *them* what to do.'

Marjorie could hardly take it in. There was a puzzled look on her face as she turned the bed-clothes aside to uncover

Caroline completely. She looked down at the girl's slender body – her belly was long and flat and the button was so small as to be hardly noticeable. It wasn't round, it was more of a shallow oval dent.

Her thighs were slender and girlish – but her chuffie was full-lipped and prominent. There was not much hair on it, just a light-brown fluff.

Marjorie ran her hand down her new friend's narrow belly. 'Open your legs,' she said, 'I want to see you.'

'You mean you want to finger me,' Caroline whispered.

'We'll see about that – open your legs.'

Caroline stared up at the ceiling and swung her legs apart. Marjorie's fingers went to the lips between them; she stroked lightly up and down.

'How many boys have fingered you?' she asked.

'Don't know – dozens,' Caroline said lazily.

Marjorie opened the soft lips and tickled the nubby inside.

'Oh,' Caroline murmured, 'that's nice. Is that how you do it to your friend Hilary? I suppose you've been doing it to her tonight.'

'Tell me the truth now,' Marjorie said with a slight frown. 'You may have let your kitty be fingered by dozens of boys, but you haven't had dozens of hard-ons in it, have you?'

'Yes, I have,' Caroline murmured. 'Long ones and short ones and thick ones, some that came before they were hardly inside me and some that rattled away for fifteen minutes before they shot off.'

Marjorie hardly knew what to say. She held Caroline's kitty open with one hand while she tickled the exposed nubby and looked for indications that this ordinary-looking slit had accommodated so many twangers.

'You're wet inside,' she said.

'Did your friend Hilary diddle you tonight?' Caroline asked, gazing up at the ceiling. 'Is your kitty still wet? I suppose when you shared a room with her you used to do each other every night at bedtime.'

'You suppose correctly,' Marjorie admitted. 'We always got into one bed together. We're very close friends still.'

Caroline yawned as if bored. 'All girls together,' she said.

'You were playing with yourself when Keith spied on you,' Marjorie countered. 'Did he see you come?'

'I didn't come,' Caroline murmured. 'I nearly did, but when I saw him watching me I was so startled that it put me off.'

Marjorie stood up and stripped her clothes off. Caroline didn't bother to watch her, she just lay on her back with her long legs parted and waited. Marjorie dropped her clothes on the floor, skirt and shirt, tights, bra and knickers. She slid on to the bed naked, her chubby titties swinging.

'You feel like diddling me now,' Caroline stated. 'I knew you would, the minute you came in and found me so terrified. You thought you could take advantage of my state of shock.'

'You mean the minute I came in and found you waiting for me naked in bed,' Marjorie said.

She placed herself with her head above Caroline's thighs, so she could use her tongue on her.

'You're every bit as bad as the man at the window,' said Caroline. 'You think you can do what you like to me because I'm new here. You want to ravish my helpless body.'

'You deliberately stripped and waited naked for me in bed to tempt me to play with you,' Marjorie countered. 'You're the one who's as bad as Keith – you're a sex maniac like him.'

'Yes, I am,' Caroline said, grinning, her fingers stroking her own tiny titties to make their bobbles stand firm.

'If you're not as sexy as you think you are,' Marjorie said in mock-threat, 'I'll hold you down while I pour cold water over your belly.'

'You don't know what sexy means till you've been with me,' Caroline replied.

Marjorie plunged her hot tongue between the parted lips of Caroline's chuffie and flicked very rapidly at her nubby.

'That's not bad – for an amateur,' Caroline said, her narrow belly quivering. 'Being tongued is the next best thing to being done. I expect you'll want to do it to me every night, as you did to your friend Hilary.'

Marjorie's tongue was much too occupied for her to reply, but she was surprised by the forwardness of this first-year

81

girl. By rights Caroline should be on her knees tonguing the senior girl and feeling grateful for the privilege. But if she really did have as much experience of being done as she claimed, that seemed to give her the upper hand.

'Oh,' Caroline breathed, 'I'm coming, Marjorie . . .'

She wriggled her bare little bum on the bed and gasped a few times and then lay still again, tremors shaking her slender body.

'That was lovely in its way,' she said, 'but I shall expect you to do better now that we're friends.'

Marjorie rolled over on her back and parted her legs. Her fleece was dark-brown and very curly.

'I'm dying for it,' she moaned. 'Help me.'

Caroline lay beside her and sucked at the bobbles of her chubby titties while she pushed two joined fingers into her wet chuffie.

'You've a lot to learn, Marjorie. I'll start your education by giving you some idea of how it feels when a boy has his hard-on up you and is sliding it in and out. I'm using only two of my fingers because you've never had one in you.'

'Don't want any boy's *thing* in me,' Marjorie sighed as she spread her legs wider, her hand between Caroline's closed thighs.

It was in Marjorie's mind that things had turned out better than she'd expected with her new roommate. She could have been put in with someone boring – if she couldn't have Hilary, she'd been lucky to get Caroline.

'Secretly you really do want a hard-on in you, but you're afraid to admit it,' said Caroline.

'I'm not afraid of anything of the sort,' Marjorie sighed, her plump belly shaking.

'Your trouble is that you've no idea at all what it's like to feel a hard-on throb inside you when it gives you a quick gush of warm cream,' Caroline said.

She was moving her fingers in a steady rhythm in and out of Marjorie's open wet chuffie, while the ball of her long thumb slid against the slippery little nubby.

'Oh no, no!' Marjorie gasped, trying to imagine how the spurt of warm male *stuff* inside her chuffie would feel.

'How many times can you come before you're tired?'

'Wouldn't you like to know,' Marjorie sighed, her head rolling from side to side on the pillow as powerful sensations surged through her.

'I'll soon find out,' Caroline said. 'Did your friend do you more than once tonight?'

'That's my secret,' Marjorie gasped, and then her shaking body arched off the bed as she came convulsively.

Arms around each other, they chatted and giggled while they rested for a while.

'All that talk about me not knowing what it feels like to have a boy's *thing* in me and then using your fingers to demonstrate,' said Marjorie, 'as a matter of fact that wasn't the first time I've been done with straight fingers up me.'

'I'm sure you've had girls experiment on you,' Caroline said indifferently, 'but it's not the same.'

'It was a man who did it to me like that – a grown up,' Marjorie said.

'When was that?' Caroline sounded more interested.

Marjorie told her about her little adventure on the examination couch in Dr Brian Tremlake's consulting room.

'As soon as he'd got me on my back on the couch with my knickers off, he put two fingers up me,' she said. 'I knew he was panting to get on top and do me and I was laughing to myself at him.'

'How can you be certain he wanted to do you?' Caroline was sceptical. 'He might have been examining you in the usual way – doctors are trained to handle girls as if they're no more than sides of beef.'

'He had this massive bulge in his trousers,' Marjorie insisted. 'It was long and thick, and I could see it throbbing under the cloth – I knew I'd got him where I wanted him.'

'That does sound as if he was keen on having you,' Caroline conceded. 'So he was playing with you, not examining you – did he make you come?'

'No, the object was for me to make *him* come in his trousers – he didn't know we were playing a game against each other, he thought he was having a free feel.'

'And you won the game?'

'Easily. After he'd been sliding his fingers in and out of me for a while he started shaking and moaning and then he sort of collapsed on his knees beside the couch. I knew he was shooting his little lot in his underwear. His face was down on my belly and I thought he'd tongue me. But it was only his legs going rubbery while he was coming.'

'What did he say afterwards?' Caroline asked with a grin.

'He was red in the face and didn't know what to say. When he got back on his feet, there was a dark stain starting to show through the front of his trousers – he'd really shot his bolt. I played the innocent and pretended I didn't know what he'd done. I asked him if he was all right. He said he'd felt faint for a moment and he was better again.'

'You were playing the power game with him,' Caroline said, 'the same way I play it with the boys I go out with. But you don't let your victim get his *thing* in your kitty, which means you can't make him do anything much for you after he's shot his bolt – he thinks he's got the better of you by having a free come.'

Marjorie wasn't sure she understood that and she asked when was the last time Caroline had been done by a boyfriend.

'On my last night at home before I came here,' Caroline said without hesitation. 'I was with a boy called Hugo Walters. He borrowed his dad's car to take us to a party. On the way home afterwards he parked and we got in the back seat.'

'I've been fingered by boys in the backs of cars,' said Marjorie, 'but is there room to lie down and be done properly?'

'In a big car, there is,' Caroline said. 'This one was a Volvo. There isn't much room to lie down flat, but you can squeeze yourself along the back seat – you have one foot on the floor and the other knee up. It's very uncomfortable for the boy to get on top, but once they see a chance to get their hard-on into you, they'd hang on barbed wire to do it.'

'You certainly need to know acrobatic boys.'

'There are easier ways,' Caroline told her, 'I usually sit on the back seat with my knickers off and my skirt pulled up and open my legs wide. Hugo or whoever it is gets down on his knees on the floor and pushes his *thing* in.'

'That's how he did you?'

'When he'd got it in me it felt so hard and thick that it seemed to reach right up inside my body to my titties – it was wonderful. He came like a firework going off. He was so grateful I'd let him that he'd have kissed my feet if I'd told him to. The next time we meet he'll beg me to let him do me again.'

Ten-thirty was the official time for Lights Out, but that wasn't the end of all social activity for the young ladies of the college. After that time they mustn't leave their rooms, according to the rules, and some of them did stay in and share a bed with their roommate. But there were some who wanted variety and went visiting other rooms after Lights Out.

These were the girls who slipped silently along empty corridors in their nighties and dressing-gowns. The Heads of Houses knew this went on by night and had a good idea of who went prowling and which rooms they went to. But as long as there was no noise or disturbance, no action was taken to stop nighttime socialising.

Marjorie and Caroline were still lying on the bed talking and giggling when there was a brief tap at the door and it opened. In came Hilary Landor and her new roommate, Linda.

'I see you two have made friends,' Hilary said, staring at the two naked girls holding each other. 'I hope we haven't come too late and missed the fun.'

'No such thing as coming too late,' Marjorie said with a grin. 'We can come any time you like, can't we, Caroline?'

Hilary and Linda took off their dressing-gowns and sat on the sides of the bed, facing the occupants. Both wore shorty nighties that hardly covered their titties and ended halfway down their thighs.

'Keith's been creeping about tonight,' Marjorie told them. 'He was at the window spying on Caroline while she undressed. He ran off when she spotted him.'

'That means he's outside somebody else's window, if he

was interrupted before he'd done it to himself,' Hilary said. 'There should be a notice on the board to tell new girls to draw their curtains.'

'He startled me – but I'll get even with him before the end of term,' Caroline said firmly.

Hilary looked at her with a thoughtful expression on her face. 'We've got a confident one here,' she said to Marjorie.

'You don't know the half of it,' Marjorie said. 'According to her she's been done by dozens of boys – really done, with their *things* up her.'

'Have you really?' Hilary asked Caroline.

'Is that what you've come here for?' Caroline countered. 'To question me about my private life?'

'Oh, no,' said Linda seriously – the first time she'd spoken since she came into the room. 'What we came for is to diddle you because you're a new girl. We want to have a feel of your kitty and see what it's like.'

'Don't mind Linda,' Hilary said to Caroline, 'for an intelligent girl she sometimes sounds a bit dim. We're here to make friends with you.'

'By diddling you,' Linda added, still in a serious tone.

Both girls pulled their nighties over their heads and dropped them on the bed. Hilary was fair-haired and had pretty titties and a blondish little patch of curls between her thighs. Linda had bright ginger hair – and not only on her head. Down between her legs was a thatch of bright carroty-coloured curls. Caroline stared as if enchanted.

She reached out to touch the curls and then clasp Linda's remarkable kitty in her hand. She stroked and combed through the curls with her fingers.

'That's truly gorgeous,' she said. 'I've never seen one that colour before – will you let me play with you, Linda?'

'If I decide to let you have her,' Hilary said. 'I'm in charge here.'

Without another word said, she and Marjorie and Linda crowded in on Caroline to put their arms around her and hold her tight. She giggled and pretended to resist for a moment, as if unwilling. They took hold of her slim thighs and pulled them open to expose her wispy-haired kitty.

'Take a good look at her,' Marjorie advised her friends. 'Dozens of boys' hard-ons have been up that innocent-looking kitty.'

'Hardly any hair on it,' ginger Linda said, 'not like mine.'

'If she's telling the truth, she's not a virgin like us,' Marjorie added. 'What do you think about that?'

'What do you mean, she's not a virgin?' Linda asked, as if she found the idea difficult to grasp.

'Never mind that now,' Hilary said. 'We'll soon find out if she's up to much.'

Caroline struggled up to her knees laughing. Marjorie was holding her from behind, her arms about her and her hands over her tiny titties. Hilary was kneeling on the bed in front of Caroline, with a hand between her open thighs. She cupped Caroline's wispy-haired kitty and sank her nails into the soft flesh of her groins.

'Let's have her on her back,' Hilary commanded her helpers.

Marjorie tipped Caroline over sideways, Hilary and Linda grabbed her by the arms and turned her on her back. Linda then got hold of her ankles – Caroline struggled to keep her legs together but Linda was stronger than she looked and she slowly forced them far apart. All three girls stared down at Caroline's exposed chuffie.

'When you said that she's no virgin,' Linda said, 'did you mean that she lets boys do her?'

'You've got it,' Marjorie said encouragingly.

'She has to learn she's only a new girl,' Linda said.

Hilary smiled coldly and threw herself face-down on the bed between Caroline's splayed legs. Her fingers prised apart the lips of the younger girl's chuffie and her tongue pressed in. Caroline jerked as the tongue found her nubby and lashed over it wetly. She was excited by the presence of the group of naked girls and she came quickly, her body jerking wildly in the grip of the hands holding her down.

Hilary moved away, a grin on her face, and Linda took her turn. This time it took longer for Caroline to reach her thrill, but Linda kept at it until she did. Then came Marjorie's turn – she bent over Caroline and rolled her tiny titties in her hands and stroked the pink bobbles with the balls of her thumbs. She slid her chubby body over Caroline till her face was between her thighs and her tongue could find her nubby.

'I don't think I can come again,' Caroline sighed.

They laughed and ignored her. Marjorie opened her wide with her thumbs and tongued her, first fast and then slow and then fast again, on and on until Caroline moaned and came.

'She has promise,' Hilary said. 'More than you'd expect from a girl with tiny titties and hardly any hair on her kitty. You'll be all right with her at bed-time, Marjorie.'

They left Caroline alone to recover while the three of them slithered and writhed over each other's naked bodies. Caroline had never seen a threesome of girls before and she watched in fascination, curled up on her side, close to the headboard to give them room to thrash about and pleasure each other.

They came differently – Hilary moaned and shook for the longest time, Marjorie went *Ah ah ah ah ah* and jerked her belly up in the air. And Linda, with Marjorie's finger inside her ginger-haired chuffie, gave a little screech and kicked her legs up high.

'You're all beautiful,' Caroline said, 'I love you all.'

After that it was a game of kissing and feeling and licking, Caroline included. She was on her back again and the others used their hot mouths all over her body. She felt wet lips and tongues on the insides of her thighs, on the firm pink bobbles of her titties, on her mouth, on her belly-button, between her legs and inside her wet, slippery chuffie.

Linda rose up and sat on Caroline's face, legs splayed sideways on the bed. She rubbed her ginger-haired chuffie against Caroline's mouth; the warm little lips were half-open.

'There you are,' she said gleefully. 'You said you wanted to play with my kitty – now you can kiss it.'

Caroline's mouth was open and she was gasping with excitement. Linda felt hot breath on her kitty.

'Please lick me,' she begged. 'Do me, Caroline.'

Hilary and Marjorie, one on each side of Caroline, grinned at each other and together stroked Caroline's belly and then parted the lips of her chuffie and tickled her nubby, each with a forefinger.

'Caroline's giving Linda a good tonguing,' Hilary said, 'I wonder if we can make her come before Linda does.'

But it was Linda, squatting over Caroline's face, who got the big thrill first – Caroline came half a minute later, her wet tongue still pressed inside ginger Linda. When she recovered she rolled sideways to tip Linda off her face and threw herself at Hilary.

The games continued with hardly a pause for breath, till Caroline lost count of how many times she'd come. Her body throbbed and shook with racking pleasure, her back arched off the bed again and again in time with her little shrieks. Her chuffie was so wet that she knew the insides of her thighs would be shiny halfway down to her knees.

When she woke up from a refreshing nap she found herself lying between Linda's parted legs, with her cheek resting on her ginger-haired kitty. Hilary's head was pillowed on Caroline's belly, and her hand rested idly between the new girl's thighs. Caroline heard little sighs of pleasure and turned her head to look – further down the bed lay Marjorie on her side, with her head between Hilary's thighs.

It was a final, one-sided tryst – the sighs were all coming from Hilary in her throes, and her breath was light and warm on Caroline's bare belly.

Chapter 6

Although Enid Uppingham would have liked to get her hands on the titties of many of the girls at the college, and down between their firm young thighs, she felt that as Principal it was her duty to behave properly toward her students.

She often dreamed at night about fondling girls and feeling their kitties. She would wake in the dark, hot and bothered, with her nightie up to her waist and a moist feeling between her legs. She had seen most of the girls naked in the showers and knew which ones she fancied. Tall, fair-haired Hilary Landor was the star of many of Enid's dreams and nightly fantasies.

Not only at night but at times during the day when Enid's mind was not occupied by college business, she found herself day-dreaming about Hilary, letting her thoughts play over the topic of diddling the lovely girl. Enid imagined herself inviting the girl into her bedroom, where they would both strip naked and she would kiss Hilary's high-set, pointed titties, tasting the tang of the perspiration trickling down between them.

She could easily imagine putting her hand between Hilary's long thighs to feel her kitty. The hair on it was blondish and fine – Enid knew that from her observations in the showers. She thought about pressing the tip of a finger into Hilary's kitty and touching her nubby.

After she'd seen Sharon Pomeroy being done by the Sports Coach, Enid's nocturnal imaginings took a different direction and became even more vivid. Observing that little scene through the window had made a much deeper impression on her than she would have believed possible. When she went to bed and turned out the light and tried to compose herself for sleep, the disturbing image of Sharon naked would edge into her mind and keep her awake.

The unusual position of the participants was one reason why the scene refused to be forgotten or dismissed. Like most of those who have little personal experience of sex-games between men and women, Enid imagined that the woman usually lay on her back and let the lucky man jump on top of her and rattle away.

But Sharon hadn't been lying on her back with her legs apart and Toby Dundale on top of her. Even that would have agitated Enid – simply seeing the real thing taking place before her eyes – but it wouldn't have moved her as much as what she actually did see through the bedroom window. Sharon was sitting naked on the edge of her bed, while Toby was kneeling on the floor in front of her with his throbbing twanger poised to thrust into her kitty.

The sheer athleticism of the scene was striking. To Enid's limited way of thinking, a woman lies at ease on her back and lets herself be done by the panting man on top. He is required by nature and custom to do the necessary work, by jabbing in and out until he comes. And, it is to be hoped, makes his partner come too – though in Enid's view that hardly ever happened, and it was an accident if it did.

Certainly she had never managed to achieve a climax on the few occasions during her student days when she had allowed a man to take her knickers down and put his stiff *thing* inside her. She regarded it as a sort of weakness in women if they let men persuade them to lie down and spread their legs.

Girl-to-girl – that was where the pleasure was to be had, that was how the big thrill could be guaranteed every time. If all the girls in the college learned how to satisfy themselves that way and forget men, so much the better, in Enid's opinion.

But hard as it was to explain in terms of her own experience, in the incident Enid witnessed through the window Sharon seemed as enthusiastic and active as Toby was. She wasn't just lying back and allowing him to vent his male lust on her pretty body. She'd positioned herself with

92

her knees pulled up to her titties and her chuffie wide open. And when Toby pushed his body steadily upward between Sharon's spread thighs to slide his long thick *thing* into her, Enid was surprised to see that Sharon was actually holding it and guiding it into herself. Then as soon as Toby was all the way inside and began stabbing into her, Sharon flung her arms around his neck and jerked her belly against him hard and fast, meeting each of his thrusts with one of her own. It seemed to the onlooker outside the window that Sharon was *doing* Toby as much as he was doing her.

Enid found this hard to comprehend. Well-brought-up young women might permit men to do certain impolite things to them, for reasons of their own, but in Enid's scheme of things they did not do sexual things for men.

She couldn't deny what she'd seen with her own eyes, however, and as she stared fascinated through the bedroom window she could have no doubt what would happen next as a result of the combined exertions of Sharon and Toby. He was going to come inside her. To judge by her jerking and moaning, Sharon might very well come at the same time – which was another circumstance Enid found extraordinary.

Toby didn't actually shoot his lot into Sharon – at the very last moment he pulled his twanger out of her chuffie with a loud moan and sprayed her titties with his cream.

That final moment, when Sharon was moaning and shaking and Toby was splattering her, affected Enid strongly. Lying in bed at night she couldn't get the picture out of her mind – there wasn't the remotest chance she'd be able to sleep before she'd relieved her tensions by giving herself a finger-wave.

She lay on her back in the dark, her sturdy thighs well apart and her long nightie pulled up round her waist. Her fingers were moving slowly to bring on the tremendous thrill she was panting for. The thrill she was convinced came only from girl-to-girl loving, not from letting men handle your body and subject it to indignities.

Oh yes, any minute now she sighed as she slid a fingertip over her slippery nubby – *oh yes, yes, I can feel it starting.*

She raised her knees and parted them, held the soft lips

93

of her chuffie open and diddled herself with a practiced touch. Her mind was filled by the image of Toby pulling out and splashing his *stuff* over Sharon's bare belly and titties – and it didn't take long before Enid's mouth gaped wide open and she gave a long loud moan as the big thrill hit her and made her plump body shake like pink blancmange.

Night after night Enid had to finger-wave herself before she could fall asleep. And once was never enough – some nights it took three times, and sometimes more. Enid decided that she must take positive steps to free herself from this obsession.

She was a direct and resourceful woman. She sent for Toby Dundale the afternoon after her decision was made. He arrived straight from the tennis courts wearing a striped red-and-white blazer over a cream sports shirt – and abbreviated white shorts. Between his white ankle-socks and his shorts there seemed to be yards of muscular leg – and much of that display of male flesh was thigh. He was very fair-haired and there were golden hairs on those thighs, which Enid tried not to notice.

In his first term at Lechlade there had been words between her and Toby on the suitability of his tennis shorts. In Enid's view they were highly improper. When he demanded to know why she thought that, she tried to explain, but without actually stating it plainly, that his show of bare thigh might inflame the passions of young girls.

He knew perfectly well what she was getting at, and was pleased to think that girls' passions might be inflamed – he liked the feel of young titties and wanted to get his twanger into as many girls as he could. To calm Enid he promised to buy longer and baggier shorts during the vacation, or at least she thought that was what he had promised.

The summer vacation was past, the new term had started and Toby was indeed wearing new shorts – but they were more revealing than his former ones, if that was possible.

Enid sat at her polished mahogany desk and stared at his very short and very close-fitting white shorts. She knew she'd lost that battle and there was no point in restarting it. There were other and better ways to get rid of the muscular-thighed Sports Coach – this man with a fleshy *thing* dangling inside his too-short tennis shorts, this male despoiler of young girls' bodies, this depraved and lustful creature who had no place in a college for young ladies.

'Sit down, please,' she said, indicating a chair in front of her desk. He took it as a bad sign that she didn't address him by name – he guessed it meant that he was on the carpet, though he couldn't think why. So far that term he'd seen the Principal only at staff meetings and there'd been no obvious sign that she was any more annoyed with him than usual. He was very well aware that she had been against him since his arrival at the college and fully intended to get him sacked, if she got the chance.

Toby sat down and smiled across the desk at the Principal. She was wearing a dark blue skirt and jacket that day, over a pale grey roll-top sweater. She was a generously fleshed woman, wide of hips and broad of bum, with solid thighs and heavy titties. She might be getting on for forty but, Toby thought speculatively, if she were undressed and on her back she'd be a sight to gladden a man's heart.

'We must consider your position at the college,' she said in a neutral tone. 'You know that discretion and integrity are essential at an educational establishment for young women.'

Toby didn't like the sound of that. He kept quiet and studied the way her jumper outlined her full bosom. He was always surprised to see a woman over thirty with big breasts wearing close-fitting cashmere knitwear – they usually tried to minimise the bulk of their titties, not accentuate them.

Except film stars, of course – they always dressed to make out that they were blessed with oversize chests. Enid's had a comfortable look about them. He decided he'd like to put his face between them. And his twanger.

'It has been brought to my attention that you have formed a relationship with another member of the staff,' Enid said.

'I don't understand,' Toby said, trying to sound baffled, though he understood her very well.

'You are on terms of physical intimacy with Sharon Pomeroy – I can't put it plainer than that.'

'Gossip,' Toby said. 'Rumours, speculation.'

'I think not,' Enid said, her face red. 'There is an eye-witness to an act better left undescribed. You were both naked at the time. And on her bed.'

She wasn't going to admit that she was her own eye-witness. It would put her at a disadvantage to be known to have spied on her academic staff through a bedroom window.

Toby shrugged. 'If we're going to discuss who's having who on the teaching staff,' he said, 'I'm sure you know about Claudine Stanhope and Sharon. And about Eleanor Redruth and Joy Locksley. And about Monica Howlett and . . .'

'Enough,' Enid interrupted him quickly. 'You cannot excuse yourself by accusing others.'

Toby had only found out about Sharon and Claudine because Sharon had told him. The three of them had reached a sort of unspoken agreement – Sharon was to be shared between Toby and Claudine on different days. Being an eternal optimist, he was hoping that this unusual arrangement might in time lead to him getting his twanger up Claudine as well as Sharon.

So far Claudine showed no sign of interest in him. And to his dismay, she seemed to be having Sharon more often than he was.

'Accusing others?' he said. 'Lord, no – I'm all in favour of the staff being on terms of the closest friendship – it's good for morale.'

Enid stared silently over her desk at him. She was wondering if he was having her on.

'If you're concerned about the friendship between Sharon and me,' he continued, 'then you must be concerned about Claudine and Sharon – have you spoken to Claudine?'

'That's entirely different,' Enid said, on the defensive.

'I don't know why you say that,' Toby said. 'You claimed that someone had seen Sharon and me naked together – though I can't imagine how that's possible. Has anyone seen Sharon and Claudine naked together, giving each other a thrill?'

Enid felt she was losing control of the interview – and she

didn't want to get into a discussion with a *man* of what naked women did together.

'You are missing the point,' she said. 'I have been seriously worried since hearing of your association with Sharon. So much so that it has begun to affect my health.'

'How?' Toby enquired, raising his eyebrows.

He thought he could hear something different in her tone. She had started by accusing him of doing what came very naturally to him and harmed nobody, but now she seemed almost to be asking for his understanding, and even for support.

'How can your health possibly be affected by anything I may or may not do with Sharon in our leisure time?' he asked, trying to sound reasonably sympathetic about her problems.

Enid told him of her difficulty in getting to sleep, though not the real reason for it, which was her recollection of seeing him doing Sharon. She mentioned a recurring dream she had, though not the actual content of her dream, which was him looming over Sharon and spraying her bare titties with his *stuff*. She said that several times a day when she was working she found herself drifting into bouts of absent-mindedness.

She didn't tell him the subject of her fantasies during these spells of reverie, which was herself taking Sharon's place on the edge of the bed and feeling his hard-on push into her chuffie. She spoke so vaguely that Toby was baffled about what was truly ailing her.

'You live a sedentary life,' he said earnestly, 'so you need to take more exercise – that would put you right in no time.'

'Do you really think so?' Enid asked in surprise – that sort of advice wasn't what she wanted to hear.

'A brisk game of tennis two or three times a week,' he said, 'five or six lengths of the pool every other day. That's what you need, believe me. And a gentle jog round the college grounds, morning and evening, with the crowd of girls I take out for half an hour or so.'

Enid tried to imagine herself in track-suit and trainers, accompanying Toby and the girls jogging. She didn't care for the idea at all. Toby was imagining the same scene – and he liked it. He could easily visualise Enid's heavy titties bouncing up and down in a track-suit, the cheeks of her big bum rolling to her trot.

Sports and games were an important part of the curriculum at Lechlade, so Enid had to show an interest she didn't feel. A daily walk round the grounds was her limit, not leaping about on a tennis court in clothes that would reveal her broad bum and her plump thighs.

'Yes, you're right,' she said without enthusiasm, 'but I've been inactive for so long now that there would be a serious risk of strain.'

'I'll work out a programme for you that will eliminate any such risk,' Toby offered, smiling at her in the friendliest manner.

'Thank you.' What else could she say? 'I'd better have a check by my doctor to be sure.'

'No need for that,' Toby said, feeling that he had the upper hand now. 'I've had physiotherapy training, as you know, so I'm fully capable of giving you the necessary check. Let's do it now, then we can make a good start this evening with half an hour in the pool when the girls have gone.'

'I'm not much of a swimmer,' Enid objected.

She still had a swimsuit, but it was ages since she'd had it on. It was a black one-piece that clung very closely to her ample body when it was wet. The last time she'd worn it was five years earlier at a conference of female head teachers at Bognor Regis.

It was an expensive and well-designed garment – it supported her heavy titties very well and prevented droop. Her bobbles were very visible through the material, though. A waiter bringing a tray of cold drinks to a group of the female teachers relaxing by the hotel pool had stared at Enid's prominent bobbles until he developed a bulge in his trousers and she blushed pink.

Apart from that, the swimsuit held her broad, plump belly in very well, so that she looked somewhat slimmer than she was, which was all to the good. But it fitted so closely round her thighs and between her legs that it made her chuffie seem rather prominent. She was sitting on a deck-chair when the lecherous waiter appeared, and kept her legs closed so he couldn't ogle *that* part of her, at least.

He was a foreigner, a Mediterranean type, so God knows what would have happened if he had seen the mound between Enid's thighs, so closely and clearly outlined by her expensive swimsuit. The lustful fellow might even have shot his lot in his trousers right there by the pool, in front of the whole group of female head teachers.

If that was the regrettable effect her swimsuit had on lewd men, Enid wasn't at all sure she wanted Toby Dundale to see her wearing it.

'It doesn't matter if you haven't swum for a long time,' he said. 'I shall be right beside you, every stroke of the way, helping and guiding, encouraging and supporting you.'

To Enid's way of thinking, Toby's swimming trunks were even more scandalous than his tennis shorts. Not that they could rightly be called *trunks* – that word suggested a garment that fully contained the lower part of the wearer's body, from waist to halfway down the thighs. Toby's did not.

She'd observed him many a time in the pool and his body was virtually naked. All he wore to coach swimming was a shamefully tiny posing pouch that only just contained his male parts. It did nothing to hide their shape or size.

Listening to his offer to be beside her in the pool and to support her, she could easily imagine him swimming alongside her, in close contact. His hands would be on her shoulders or on her back to encourage her – perhaps they'd slide over her bum or under her plump belly . . . and his body might glide against hers in the water, letting his oversized *thing* in its pouch momentarily press against her . . .

'You're very kind,' Enid said a little breathlessly. 'In spite of the differences between us I know I can rely on your professionalism and sympathy. If you'll check me over, I'll go swimming this evening.'

'Oh, good,' he said cheerfully. 'I'll have to ask you to take some of your clothes off, so I can check you properly.'

'What do you want me to take off?' she asked carefully.

'Strip down to your knickers, please.'

He stood up to shed his blazer and hung it on the chair-back. He put his hands together and interlaced his fingers, bending them backward and forward to make them supple.

Enid's face had turned noticeably pink at his request. And as to his matter-of-fact reference to her knickers – she was not accustomed to men speaking of her underwear in such a familiar way. Men were *beasts*, she was convinced of it; their minds were occupied all the time with lustful thoughts about women's bodies.

When a man mentioned knickers he was not thinking about the actual garment, but what was inside, that is, the wearer's thighs, bum and sex organs. Male minds knew no delicacy – a man speaking about knickers would visualise the wearer's chuffie. He would fantasise about feeling it and getting his lascivious fingers inside it . . . Enid's blush grew deeper as the full extent of male depravity forced itself on her attention.

She knew that men's natural baseness didn't stop at getting *fingers* into a chuffie – that thought would always lead them on to every male's most indecent ambition, to get his *thing* into it and satisfy his lust on a hapless woman's body. Men were gross and vile.

'Wait here,' she said, 'I'll call you when I'm ready.'

She went into her bedroom and closed the door behind her. Toby didn't understand why he was shut out for three minutes while she took her clothes off – he'd see her without them soon enough. He went to the window and stared out while he tried to organise his thoughts about Enid. She was neurotic, he was convinced of that much.

It didn't take a genius to understand why. Enid was a big, full-bodied, warm-blooded woman. In Toby's expert opinion she needed frequent male attention to keep her healthy and happy: she needed a regular seeing-to. This she continued to deny herself, out of her concept of duty or modesty or plain old-fashioned inhibition.

As a result she was neurotic and twitchy. She wanted to and she didn't want to, both at the same time. She wanted a man to stick his hard-on up her and ride her to glory – but she also despised men for wanting to do that.

100

Toby was in an awkward situation as the only male teacher at the college – the only member of staff with a twanger. The girls were attracted to him because of it and almost begged him to feel their titties and kitties. In just one term at Lechlade he's handled more girlish kitties than in the previous two years.

Enid didn't want him there on the staff. She had made that clear enough. She hoped to catch him interfering with a girl and get him sacked. She also wanted him to push her down on her back and do her, but she didn't think she should allow any man to take such liberties. She was confused, and in these circumstances Toby was confused himself.

'You can come in now,' she called from the bedroom.

He found her sitting on the edge of her bed. Presumably she had taken her clothes off, but as she had put on a long green satin dressing-gown, he couldn't be sure. She was holding the top tightly closed so that he wouldn't get a look down the deep valley between her big titties.

'Ready?' he asked, raising one eyebrow.

She nodded, pink-faced, not trusting herself to speak.

'You strike me as pretty healthy,' he said briskly. 'We'll soon check the obvious things – get on the bed, please.'

Enid wanted to keep some control over the situation and not surrender her body unconditionally into a man's hands. Hands that would touch her, she thought, hands that would slide over the parts of her body normally kept decently concealed.

He was sure to touch her belly, she thought fearfully. And her thighs – his hands might feel up the insides of them. But he wouldn't dare touch her chuffie, she was sure of that.

'Am I to lie face-down?' she asked him.

Toby had no intention of letting her decide how he was going to check her body.

'I'd like to have you on your hands and knees,' he told her, straight-faced. 'On the bed, please, your back straight and horizontal, your shoulders relaxed, your neck loose and your head hanging down.'

'Why is that?' she asked, astounded. 'I've never before been asked to take that position.'

101

'I believe you,' Toby said, trying not to grin, 'but I need to make an exploratory diagnosis and for that I need your backbone straight.'

'I see,' she said doubtfully, not moving.

'This is meant as a compliment and I hope you will not take offence,' he said. 'You are a full-bosomed woman, with a well-rounded belly. When you lie on your front, your backbone will not be straight and level, if you see what I mean.'

'Oh,' said Enid.

She knew that when he said *full-bosomed* he meant she had big titties. Which was perfectly true, but it troubled her that he was thinking about her titties. Men being as they were, even to mention them meant that he was thinking about getting his hot hands on them.

She stood up and turned to face the bed before untying the cord round her waist and slipping the dressing-gown off her fleshy shoulders. Toby watched it descend down her body to the carpet, revealing her broad back and the full round cheeks of her bum – which were very stylishly encased in ivory satin knickers that looked expensive.

Well, well, he thought, *she gives the impression of being prudish but she buys fancy knickers to put her chuffie in – which means she gives it a lot more loving thought and care than anyone would believe of her.*

'On the bed,' he said kindly, stepping forward beside her, one hand on the small of her back to urge her gently on.

Her flesh was soft and warm and touching her gave Toby an instant hard-on inside his skimpy tennis shorts. She put one chubby knee on the bed, then the other, the thin ivory satin of her knickers stretching tight over her bum as she bent forward. He positioned her in the middle of the bed on her hands and knees, facing the polished wooden headboard.

In the general way of things Toby played with seventeen-year-old girls with figures kept slim and pliant by daily stints in the pool and on the tennis courts. Or he played with teachers in their twenties, fit and athletic young women like Sharon Pomeroy. And he played with Sally Mason – a thin nympho with little titties. Enid Uppingham's full-fleshed body

102

was an exciting change for him.

She knelt on the bed, her heavy titties swinging underneath her, her big round bum like a full moon. Toby swallowed and vowed to have those satin knickers off her before long and sink his finger-nails into her plump cheeks. And his teeth too, if things worked out right.

He stood at the bed-side and ran his hands slowly down the length of her broad back. *Creamy* was the word that came into his mind to describe the feel of her skin. If her back was like that, what would her titties be like when he got his hands on them? Offhand he couldn't think of any suitable word except *deluxe*, which didn't seem adequate.

Inside the close-fitting little jockstrap he wore under his shorts, Toby's twanger was standing upright and throbbing. He slipped his hand under Enid's plump belly and gave it a good feel. But only her belly – he didn't touch her dangling titties yet, nor try to slip his hand inside her fancy knickers.

'I'm checking your internal organs,' he said by way of explanation. 'Your liver and spleen and womb. Everything seems to be in very good order.'

One of his palms lay flat against her belly, the other flat on her back – it was the little trick he'd used on Sharon to get her going. He was confident it would work on Enid, too, if he bounced all that soft warm flesh between his hands. He flopped her belly gently up and down in a light and pleasing rhythm, to arouse her desires.

'Very good,' he said. 'There's no creakiness in your back at all, and nothing out of place in your tummy.' He knew his manipulation was having the right effect because he could hear Enid starting to breathe hard.

'That's reassuring to hear,' she said, her voice breathy.

'Swimming and jogging and tennis – they all have one thing in common,' he told her. 'They strengthen the leg muscles – but you need adequate leg muscles before you start any of them.'

He took a step sideways toward her bum and felt underneath her, so he could put his hands between her strapping thighs. He felt up and down slowly and deliberately, stroking and gripping alternately.

'Great potential there,' he said ambiguously.

Enid wasn't sure how to take it. Did he mean her thighs had potential for developing muscle for athletic purposes? Or did he mean something else – something gross and immoral?

If she could have read his mind, as his palms slid up and down the insides of her thighs, from chubby knees up to hot groins, she would have been in no doubt. He was thinking that her fleshy thighs could clasp a man between them as snugly as a girl's hand could grip a hard-on.

Only that morning Toby had been working in the gym with a new girl who had great promise – a sixteen-year-old named Vikki Herbert. She'd shown him what she could do on the rings and bars, and afterward he took her into his little office to plan a programme of exercise with her – and to urge her not to let intensive study get in the way of her athletic ability.

Vikki was a very pretty girl, with long light-brown hair in a pony-tail. She had demonstrated her skill to him wearing a white-and-scarlet leotard which showed off her long thighs and her taut round bum. Toby was interested, and she was impressed by her new coach.

Inevitably, one thing soon led to another as they sat in his little office, their heads close together. They started by talking about gymnastics – but eventually Vikki was behind his desk with him, sitting on his lap.

Toby took advantage of the situation to stroke her nicely-shaped titties through her thin leotard. He put his hand between her long legs and stroked along her thigh to her little mound. He slipped his fingers under the edge of the stretched leotard and felt her soft curls.

She surprised him by saying she wanted to hold his hard-on.

'Why do you think it's hard?' he asked with a grin.

'I can feel it pressing against my thigh,' she said, grinning back at him. 'It's like a cucumber. Let me hold it.'

Toby had never passed up an offer like that in his life. He put both hands on her waist and lifted her as she turned and sat down on his lap again, facing him. Her thighs were open so wide that he could see wispy light-brown curls at her groins, peeping out from the sides of her leotard.

She unzipped his shorts, pulled down the silky transparent pouch he wore for underwear and took his thick twanger out. It was hard, as she'd said, but in her palm it grew harder and longer still.

'Oh,' she said, clearly impressed, and held it tightly while she pumped her hand up and down.

'When we get to know each other better,' Toby said with a happy sigh, 'I'll have it up you.'

'I don't think so,' she said. 'A girl has to stay a virgin to be a world-class gymnast, everybody knows that.'

'Who's everybody?' he asked. 'Who told you that, Vikki?'

'My coach at school, Mr Jarvis. He was very definite about it. He said that once you let a boy put his hard-on up your kitty you were done for as a gymnast.'

'But you like holding mine,' he said, shaking with pleasure as her fingers slid over the bare head. 'Did Mr Jarvis teach you to play with them like that?'

'He explained that it's perfectly all right to diddle a man's *thing*,' she said. 'It helps to develop dexterity and concentration. He made us all do it to him all the time.'

'I bet he did,' Toby murmured, his eyes on her pretty face while her hand kept tirelessly sliding up and down and giving him thrills. 'What did he say about feeling your kitty?'

'It's all right to let a man tongue you,' she said. 'He told me it's very good for muscle-tone and he did it to me two or three times a day – he said I have real talent.'

'No doubt about that,' Toby sighed.

He could see she'd become very excited by playing with him. His fingers under the edge of her leotard stroked her kitty – the way she sat across his thighs had parted the lips for him. He pressed a finger inside and touched her moist little nubby.

'Did Mr Jarvis have a big one?' he asked, curious to hear more about her schoolgirl experiences.

'Not as big as yours,' she said, smiling at him. 'His was short and thick – yours is a lot longer than his.'

'And he never put this short thick hard-on inside a girl?'

'Only the ones he said had no chance of being world-class. He'd give them a last opportunity to show what they could do, and then ask if they wanted to go on trying. If they said no he had them on their back in the gym and put his *thing* in.'

'And that never happened to you.'

'I'm glad it didn't,' she said, sounding close to her big moment. 'Mr Jarvis did it to a friend of mine and she told me that having his hard-on inside you wasn't nearly as nice as being tongued by him.'

'Now you're at Lechlade I shall tongue you a lot,' Toby gasped, his fingertip slipping over her wet nubby. 'I'll make certain that your muscle-tone is kept at top pitch.'

Vikki's mouth opened in a silent squeal. Her long back arched and her head went back. Quick spasms shook her body. Toby glanced down as his belly-muscles clenched and saw the surge of his cream through her rapidly-pumping hand.

Which was all very well, and enjoyable at the time, but a lot like a Chinese meal – half an hour later you're hungry for another one.

Enid Uppingham naked on her hands and knees on the bed was a very different proposition – a solid meaty chunk of woman to get stuck into.

'Good thighs,' Toby murmured, putting his hand on her belly again and sliding it under the elastic of her knickers. Her belly was very warm and plump and pleasing. He reached further and touched her curls, soft and springy. A little further and he felt the full lips of her chuffie.

There was no word of protest yet from Enid – although she couldn't possibly believe that being felt like this had anything to do with a serious examination. Clearly it suited her to close her mind to the fact that she was being interfered with, just as if she were a sixteen-year-old girl with Toby in the gym.

His fingers lay along the hot cleft between the lips of Enid's chuffie but he didn't press inside yet. That would come later, when he'd got her to the point when she wanted so

106

desperately to be done that she'd forget she despised him for wanting to do her.

The fingers of his other hand rested in the cleft between the full-moon cheeks of her bum. The tip of his longest finger pressed on the little knot of muscle.

He could hear her sighing – she was reaching the point of no return. He'd have it up her very soon. This evening he intended to have it up Sharon. And one of these days soon he'd have it up Sharon's girlfriend Claudine.

'What are you going to do about Sharon?' Enid asked.

Her question took him by surprise. Surely she couldn't read his mind just because he'd got two fingers in her chuffie? It was very lucky he'd only been touching her thighs when he was thinking about playing with Vikki. If he'd had his fingers inside Enid then, she might have guessed that he'd been diddling one of the new girls.

No, no, that's ridiculous he said to himself, Enid can't read minds – she's asking about Sharon to take her mind off what she really wants me to do to her.

'What do you think I should do about Sharon?' he asked, his fingers sliding skilfully around Enid's nubby. Her thighs were well parted; she was making it easy for him to diddle her. But she was going to get more than a finger inside her.

'For the good of the college you must end this relationship with her,' Enid said. 'There's no telling what complications might arise if the two of you continue on this unwise course.'

'Yes,' Toby said, meaning nothing at all, 'and will you also advise Claudine to end her relationship with Sharon?'

'That is for me to decide,' Enid gasped – she was very close now to the big thrill.

'Of course,' Toby agreed, 'and I know that you'll bear in mind while you're deciding that Claudine and I both do the same thing to Sharon.'

'What do you mean?' Enid sounded shrill and shaky.

'We do it in different ways,' Toby said, 'Claudine and I. We do it to Sharon at different times. We each view the other as a hated rival. But we do the same thing. We undress Sharon and feel her titties. We lay her on her back and play with her kitty. We make her come – Claudine does it with

107

her tongue and I do it with my hard-on.'

Enid shrieked and shook. Toby didn't wait another second – he dragged her expensive knickers down her legs and tossed them away behind him. He jumped up on the bed, ripped the zipper of his tennis shorts down and flipped his throbbing twanger out.

Enid was still in the throes of coming when he brought the head to her open chuffie and pushed in.

'What are you doing . . .' she sighed, her belly shaking.

His arms were round her and under her and he clasped her big heavy titties while he thrust in a steady rhythm. He was thoroughly enjoying doing Enid, sliding his hard-on in and out of her big fleshy body, her bare bum against his belly. He was lying forward over her back while he rode her like a well-fed dray-horse.

'If I listen to you and give up Sharon,' he said, 'how shall I relieve my natural urges? If I became desperate, it's not beyond the bounds of possibility that I might be tempted to take advantage of some of the girls – have you thought about that, Enid?'

'Oh my god,' she moaned, her body shaking to his thrusts as they grew faster, 'not the girls . . . you wouldn't interfere with any of the girls . . .'

Had she but known, he'd already interfered with many of the girls – and he meant to interfere with many more.

'Men have strong natural urges,' he gasped, giving free rein to his own. 'They must find release.'

'Use *me*,' Enid wailed. 'Forget Sharon – you can use *me*!'

'Oh . . .' Toby moaned, 'oh, yes . . .'

Enid felt him jerk against her bum as he shot his cream into her. Five seconds later, shuddering and shrieking, she came herself, greatly to her amazement and pride.

Chapter 7

The college showers were in almost constant use, from early morning to late in the evening. This was only partly because the young ladies were encouraged to be exceptionally clean – another reason was that the showers were the scene of more girlish thrills a day than could ever be counted.

The boilers that Keith the caretaker looked after served several sets of showers. There were central showers in each of the four houses where the young ladies lived and slept. There was a larger shower block attached to the gymnasium, another one close to the tennis courts, and another for the swimming pool. This gave Keith plenty of scope to watch girls dressing and undressing.

All the shower rooms were built the same, with tiled and open-fronted stalls along both sides. There were curtains that could in theory be drawn across the front of each stall, if a girl was too shy to be seen naked. But by a long-standing tradition, these curtains were never used. Not even when two girls shared the same stall.

The sight was a familiar one, a pair of naked sixteen-year-olds under the cascading water, chatting while they soaped each other's titties and giggling as they rubbed a soapy palm between each other's legs. It was so familiar a sight that no one stood and stared when wet bodies were pressed together, titties against titties, nimble fingers at work down below . . . until gasps and long shudders signalled that the girls had reached the big thrill together. That is to say, no one watched these little scenes openly. Keith tried his best to get a look, but it wasn't easy. The architect who designed the showers had been fully aware of his responsibilities to the students and the proper protection of their modesty. There were no windows in any of the shower blocks. There were large skylights, but these were made of frosted glass.

Many a time Keith had lurked on the roof of the biggest block, by the gymnasium, but all he had ever seen was a pinkish moving blur where wet girlish bodies were in contact below. This was intensely frustrating – he was certain they were playing with each other down there, feeling kitties and titties – and he was shut out from the fun.

He had considered secretly replacing a pane of frosted glass with clear glass, dabbled over with a tint to resemble frosting. He could leave a clear circle that he could put an eye to and watch the frolics below. So far he hadn't dared do it, but he hadn't given up the idea.

The Lechlade custom of leaving the shower stalls open was another old tradition whose origins no one remembered. But if anyone had bothered to delve into the dusty old files up in the attics – the files that dated back to the dimly recalled era before the War – they'd have discovered a clue.

The person responsible for starting the college tradition of leaving shower curtains undrawn was Miss Stella Briston. She was a brunette in her thirties when she taught classics at Lechlade in the late 1920s and early 1930s. Besides Latin and Greek languages and literature, she taught classical history and, above all, she taught the appreciation of classical art.

As is well known, classical art consists mainly of life-size marble statues of naked gods and goddesses, without concealing fig-leaves to preserve the viewer's tranquillity of mind.

There were no men in Miss Briston's life, and never had been, but she could and did explain to her students the elegance of line when she showed them pictures of unclothed male statues. Gods, they were supposed to be, but the models had been living men. The girls were interested and whispered humorous comments to each other about the smallness of the dingle-dangles – even on statues of the mighty and muscular Hercules.

Miss Briston did not find men sexually alluring, but as a

110

connoisseur of art she understood the aesthetic qualities of the nude male body. In her own student days she had attended life drawing classes and sketched nude models – although the men usually sat on chairs and crossed their legs, to preserve their modesty.

Teaching her class, Miss Briston ignored the danglers and explained the artistic possibilities of the human body, male as well as female. She pointed out the curve of a shoulder, the line of a flank, the turn of a muscular thigh. If instead of marble the figure had been made of warm and living male flesh, her enthusiasm would have been much reduced.

When it came to statues of beautiful naked goddesses, such as Aphrodite or Artemis, Miss Briston's enthusiasm was unlimited. Sometimes she hung a large picture of one of them on the wall and told the girls to copy it. She hovered over each girl in turn, advising on her drawing, pointing out the soft curve of a tittie, the roundness of a bum cheek, the delicate line of a thigh.

Every summer vacation she organised a tour for a party of girls to the better-known Roman and Greek archaeological sites. A dozen or more students went with her each year, first by channel ferry to Calais and then by train to Rome, to see the Forum and the Colosseum and the Pantheon.

After a few days they took the train south to Naples to explore the ruins at Pompeii and the temples at Paestum. Then from Bari they sailed by the overnight ferry across the Adriatic Sea to Greece, to visit the site of Delphi and the ruins of old Corinth and other tourist-book sights, till they ended their journey at the Acropolis in Athens.

Like all good teachers, Miss Briston was very keen about the subjects she taught. She believed that the classical age had been a time of joy and beauty. It was her conviction that ancient Romans and Greeks had worn hardly any clothes at all in their sunny lands – and she was certain that at the slightest excuse they shed the little they did wear.

They went proudly naked and free on every possible occasion, she told her class, because they understood the glory of the nude human body. Sometimes an impudent girl giggled and asked her if the naked Greek men ever got

111

themselves into an awkward predicament when they met naked Greek women in the street.

To questions of that type Stella Briston said very firmly, 'Of course not, the ancients were pure in heart as well as in body.' The girls did not believe her, though they pretended to. Even back in the 1930s they had been kissed by boyfriends during vacations and had felt something hard and long press against them through layers of clothing.

In the days when Stella was organising her tours there were far, far fewer tourists than there are today. Travel was cheap and the people of Italy and Greece were poverty-stricken. Which meant that small bribes to the guides who haunted classical sites made it possible for her and her girls to have the old ruins with their cracked pillars and fallen marble walls to themselves for an hour or two.

To help them experience the grandeur of the past, Stella assigned Roman or Greek first names to the girls on the tour. Names such as Lucretia and Flavia, Cassandra and Atalanta. On ruined sites, after the guides had been paid to go away, she persuaded the young ladies to strip naked and dance hand in hand in a circle with her.

This was the true spirit of classicism, she said, this was how in the past the nine beautiful Muses had danced naked and singing on Mount Helicon. When the girls were out of breath, they sat on the fallen pedestals and arches – with clothes spread on the sun-roasted stones to protect their bare bums – while Stella recited the poems of Sappho and told them about other joys of classical times.

Needless to say, the tourist guides never went far away after they'd taken the bribe to do so. They were fascinated and excited by the sight of so many young and pretty English girls. They were curious why they had been paid to vanish. Accordingly, they concealed themselves among the fallen stones to watch – just as, many years later, Keith Mason would hide behind trees and under bushes at Lechlade to watch girls in the swimming pool and on the tennis courts.

The fortunate Italian or Greek tourist guide peeping from among the rocks on a sun-beaten hillside saw much more than Keith generally did. Most of these guides, no doubt,

112

could hardly believe their eyes when they saw a circle of naked girls dancing around their naked lady teacher. Because of local customs they'd never seen a totally naked female before in their lives, not even the married guides. To see so many naked girls' bodies all at one time would have been mind-boggling for them.

All those young titties bouncing about in the sun, all those curly-haired little chuffies on show ... *all of them virgins*, the concealed guide would say to himself with a moan, not knowing for sure but assuming they were.

By then he'd have his trousers wide open and his hand inside to clasp his leaping twanger. Long before the dance was over and the girls were sitting on the hot stones to listen to Miss Briston recite poems by old Romans and Greeks, the impassioned guide would have shot his little lot, gasping ferociously as he did so, before sinking back onto the ground with a blissful and foolish smile on his face.

Stella was devoted to young girls, and never more so than when they were naked. Throughout the month-long tour of the antique past the party stayed in small hotels. It was the most natural thing in the world for the whole group to shower at the same time, Stella included. Or 'Sabina', that being the Roman name she gave herself on these tours.

This was, she pointed out, the way the ancients bathed, not alone in small private bathrooms, but together in large communal baths. As the young ladies had seen for themselves in Rome at the huge ruined Baths of Caracalla. Men only were allowed on some days, women only on other days, there being no such arrangement as mixed bathing, she told them. Women were to be trusted, but men being what they were, mixed bathing would most surely lead to all sorts of unfortunate results.

When a dozen pretty girls press naked together under a warm shower, the results are invariably interesting. Titties rub against titties, and hands touch bellies and bums.

In the good-natured confusion, hands slide between thighs and lather soap-suds on kitties. It can be difficult to know whose hand is touching whose kitty in the general throng. 'Sabina' was always in the thick of the action and her hands were very expert indeed, and extremely willing to deal with wet and lather-covered chuffies.

These group bathing sessions lasted a long time. Long enough for every one of the young ladies to study Miss Briston's slim naked body and her small elegant titties. The sessions were friendly and relaxed enough for young ladies to put their arms around their teacher and to slide their hands over her belly and titties and between her thighs.

There was time for each of the group to be thoroughly felt by Stella, for their virginal kitties to be lathered and rinsed off, fingered and admired and kissed. There wasn't time for her to give every girl the big thrill every time, so some of them happily diddled each other. But she never failed to give everyone present a feel – and during the session she would reach the climactic moment herself five or six times.

When they were back at college for a new term the travellers asserted their superiority over girls who hadn't seen the classical landscapes by continuing the showering customs they had learned abroad. They left the curtains undrawn and they shared stalls. They played with each other under the hot water and didn't even bother to hide what they were doing.

If anyone dared draw attention to what went on or ask about it, Miss Briston's students said in a very superior manner that they were being 'noble, nude and classical'. After the initial shock wore off, the rest of the girls took up the same ways. In this way a tradition was established, one that has remained a major feature of student life at Lechlade.

There were those – teachers and students – who said with bated breath that Stella Briston must surely have diddled every girl in the college. Not just one year, they said, but year after year, as the eighteen-year-olds went on to university and sixteen-year-olds arrived to take their place.

Perhaps it was true and perhaps it wasn't. The only person who knew the truth was Stella herself. And she never said.

After a lapse of time, she was forgotten, and so was the reason shower curtains were never drawn. But anyone who searched the old records in the attics would have found a bundle of dusty drawings and water-colours proving that

Stella had real artistic talent – though her only subject was naked young girls. She sketched them and painted them among the ruins of Italy and Greece, their pretty bodies posed by cracked stone columns or ruined fountains.

The manner of Stella Briston's leaving Lechlade College was as unusual as her teaching methods. A girl named Hetty Bradshaw fell in love with her, after being diddled all across Europe on trains and in small hotels and among the ancient ruins.

Hetty was a dark-haired seventeen-year-old, in her second year at the college, when she fell for Stella Briston. Hetty discovered a new outlook on life in a small hotel in Calais, where Stella had her down on her back on a bed, pushed her legs wide apart – and tongued her to a screaming climax.

By the time the party reached Greece, Stella had recognised Hetty's special potential. She gave her a leading part in a enactment of an incident from classical mythology – or at least Stella claimed it was. It took the interesting form of a hand-to-hand fight between an Amazon warrior-woman raiding a temple and a virgin priestess defending the temple's gold treasures.

The location for this unusual school play was the temple of Venus at Miseno, a ruined site some miles west of Naples.

It was a forlorn and lonely site, reached by a rough track and far from any sign of human habitation. On this area of dry scrubland were to be seen a few broken columns and fallen stones and a bit of mosaic pavement with a dove on it. The temple had been half-excavated and then deserted.

Not enough tourists ever came here to make it worthwhile for anyone to offer guided tours, a fact Stella counted on to ensure privacy for the gambol she planned. She appointed Hetty to be the virgin priestess of the temple, and she chose Priscilla Lanesborough to be the wild Amazonian marauder.

The rest of the party seated themselves on fallen columns and bits of pediment to watch the myth recreated. Hetty and Prissy stripped naked and prepared to do battle on the stretch of faded mosaic pavement that represented the interior of the temple where the gold was kept – Hetty stood

115

guard there while Prissy came running at her, shouting a battle-cry.

Ahhhh the audience sighed as they watched the pair clash and their strong young naked bodies lock together in grappling combat under the hot sun. They heaved and sweated trying to trip and throw each other, titties squashed flat against titties, until Prissy got Hetty down on her back and sat on her face.

She reached down to squeeze her hand between Hetty's thighs and press two fingers into her naked chuffie – to demonstrate her victory over Hetty. Stella Briston had become so engrossed in this living theatre based on ancient events that she had let a hand drift between her own thighs and was fingering herself dreamily.

Hetty was not to be so easily beaten – she bucked her body upward and slid her head out from between Prissy's thighs. There was a scuffle and then Prissy was on her hands and knees, with Hetty sitting on her bare back as if on a mare, her heels kicking up into Prissy's belly to wind her.

Prissy squealed and collapsed onto her face, her bare bum up in the air and her titties flattened on the straw-dry grass under her. Hetty, still astride her, twisted sideways to put a foot on the nape of Prissy's neck to hold her down, while her hand reached back over Prissy's bum to hook fingers into her exposed kitty.

The mortal combat between guardian priestess and raiding Amazon lasted a satisfactorily long time. Now Hetty was on top, now Prissy threw her and pinned her on her back and lay on her belly, then Hetty's thighs were clenched about Prissy's head to wrench her over sideways . . . and so it continued, until both girls collapsed exhausted on their backs.

Stella divided the rest of her flock into Amazonian raiders and virgin priestesses and sent them in all together to carry on the battle. Thirteen naked young bodies launched themselves at the few feet of cracked mosaic pavement and writhed over the prostrate forms of their worn-out champions. Minutes later the shrill shrieks of young girls in climax could be heard halfway back to the outskirts of Naples.

That was the afternoon when a new and startling view of life opened up for Hetty Bradshaw. Her father was the founder and majority shareholder of a Bradford bicycle-pedal manufacturing company. He died about a year before Stella demonstrated to Hetty the true possibilities of girl-to-girl pleasures, as distinct from the casual schoolgirl fumblings she had known before.

She was Ephraim Bradshaw's only child and she inherited his fortune. By his will the directors of the Bradford Penny Bank were appointed her guardians until she reached the age of thirty.

After her shattering experiences with Stella, the prospect of going on to Oxford University seemed pointless to Hetty. She had all the income she needed, and her guardians took the old-fashioned view that higher education was wasted on young women. They accepted her suggestion that she should abandon her studies.

They assumed that her wealth and position would soon attract suitable young men as suitors. Under the terms of her father's will, the guardians had to approve of any person who proposed marriage to Hetty, which was only right and proper, since her husband would take control of her fortune. In the view of the Bradford Penny Bank directors, no young woman could be trusted to make the right choice unassisted.

None of this mattered as things turned out. As soon as Hetty secured her guardians' consent to her request to leave Lechlade College, Stella resigned her position there and the two of them went abroad together to find a place to live in the sun. They eventually settled on the Greek island of Lesbos, which was only to be expected.

In the 1990s, so long after these events, it was no longer entirely true to say that no one stood to stare at girls showering together, even when there were two or more soaping each other in a stall. It wasn't other girls who stared – they were too well-behaved for that. But there were some teachers who did.

Eleanor Redruth was one teacher who never missed an opportunity to watch naked girls. And Miss Monica Howlett, who taught modern languages, was another who liked to see what was going on.

When this happened, the girls sharing a stall continued to wash each other, but they were suddenly careful not to touch each other's titties or chuffies. They soaped each other's backs and they squatted on their haunches to wash each other's feet. They tried to pretend this was innocent co-operation. The watching teacher – Eleanor, say – would grin and pretend she believed the girls were virtuous and proper.

Eleanor Redruth had never heard of Stella Briston, but she was busily trying to equal Stella's rumoured achievement of diddling every girl in the college – all one hundred and sixty of them. It was in the showers that Eleanor herself fell in love with Rachel Fermor.

Rachel's friends had nicknamed her 'Monkey' because of the jet-black bush between her legs. It was as thick as fur and it grew halfway up to her belly-button. And it was the reason Eleanor had fallen for her.

The shower block by the gym was the recognised place for making new friends. Soon after the new term began Rachel met Caroline Wilton there. More accurately, Caroline met Rachel, since it was Caroline who first displayed an interest, even though she was a new girl and Rachel was in her second year.

Rachel was alone under the spray when Caroline approached her. The stalls on either side were not being used, though there were a dozen or more girls elsewhere in the showers, chattering away and giggling, sharing stalls two or three together.

Caroline didn't stand staring at Rachel, enchanted though she was by her thick black bush – new girls were told the first time they visited the showers that staring was insulting. So being a bold young lady, she slipped uninvited into the stall where Rachel stood with water streaming down her naked young body.

'Who are you?' Rachel asked. 'You're new here.'

'I'm Caroline Wilton. I know who you are.'

The two of them were very nearly the same height, but Rachel was more robust of body. She looked at Caroline's

118

titties. They were beautifully round though no bigger than apples. She looked down Caroline's slender body, at her long, flat belly and her slender thighs. Like everyone else who saw Caroline naked, Rachel was struck by the contrast between the girlish titties and the full-lipped and prominent chuffie.

'Which house are you in?' Rachel asked.

'Wexby. And you're in Sawby House.'

'How do you know so much about me when you've only been here for a week?'

'I saw a teacher looking at you under the shower the other day and it made me interested enough to ask about you.'

'Who was that?' Rachel asked with a grin. 'Miss Redruth?'

'It was obvious what she was thinking while she was looking at you,' said Caroline. 'Have you let her diddle you?'

'That's a cheeky question for a first-year girl,' Rachel said in surprise.

She turned her bare wet back to Caroline and carried on with her shower. Caroline looked down at the round cheeks of her bum and grinned – she knew her own were smaller and tighter.

'Come off it, Rachel,' she said, 'by the time anyone's been here for a week they know what's going on – unless they're simple. And I'm not.'

'She's very nice, Miss Redruth,' Rachel said. She turned to face Caroline again, her titties swinging with her sudden rotation. 'You'll find out for yourself before the end of term. She has all the prettiest girls and I'm sure she'll have you.'

Caroline reached out to put one hand on Rachel's hip while she glanced down at the famous black bush between her thighs. 'I can see why she wants *you*,' she said. 'I suppose everybody wants to stroke your kitty.'

'They all want to, but only the ones I choose get to touch me,' Rachel said softly. 'Miss Redruth likes to comb through my curls – she's got an antique ivory comb, and she makes me take my knickers off and lie on her bed while she combs my bush. It's a very thrilling sensation.'

'She won't be able to do that to me – I've hardly any hair at all – as you can see.'

119

The girls were standing face to face in the tiled shower stall, close together, Caroline's hand on Rachel's hip. The water was spraying down both their fronts, running over their titties to the pink bobbles, and down their bellies to their contrasting fleeces.

Rachel looked at the light-brown fluff on Caroline's well-developed mound. She stroked it with her fingertips.

'You've had a boy's *thing* up you,' she said.

'Oh yes,' Caroline agreed, 'but how can you tell?'

'It must be instinct, I suppose,' Rachel said with a grin. 'There's a lovely wicked look about your chuffie that says it's had a lot more done to it than being diddled by other girls. What does it feel like to have a hard-on inside you?'

'Haven't you ever tried?'

'I've let my boyfriend feel me,' Rachel said. 'I've even let him lie on top of me, to see what that's like. And it was exciting, lying on my back with my legs open and feeling his weight on me.'

'Did he have his flies open and his hard-on out?'

'Yes – I'd been stroking it and it was huge and hard – it was trapped between our bellies. I could feel it throbbing against me. I'd let him take my knickers off and it was pressing on my bare skin.'

'He'd got you right where he wanted you. Why didn't he push it in? You couldn't have stopped him.'

'He wanted to, he kept on saying, "Let me, let me do you". But I said no. You're right – he did try to push it into me and with his weight on top and my legs wide apart I couldn't have stopped him, though I kept telling him not to. I think he might have got it in, except he was so excited that he came over my bush first.'

'We're going to be friends, you and I,' Caroline said.

'Do you think I should have let him?'

'I think you should let *me*,' Caroline said. 'Lean against the wall.'

Rachel leaned her back against the tiled wall, clear of the cascade of hot water. Caroline slid in close and soaped her new friend's wet body. She covered Rachel's titties in white foam, then her belly and then at last her black-haired kitty.

Her hand moved slowly between Rachel's thighs and hid her curls in thick creamy lather. Caroline's fingertips found the soft lips under the curls and stroked them until Rachel's eyes were closed and she was breathing quickly. Caroline stood back from her, Rachel took a step forward and then the water was splashing down her front, washing the soap-suds away.

When Rachel's titties were rinsed clean, Caroline put her head down to lick their pink bobbles. She sucked each in turn and heard Rachel's gasps of pleasure. They put their arms round each other, belly to belly, titties to titties, cheek to cheek, and made their chuffies rub slowly together by thrusting with their hips.

'When Miss Redruth does you,' Caroline asked, 'does she just diddle you with her fingers or does she tongue you?'

'You'll find out when she has you,' Rachel sighed.

'If I let her.'

'You will if she wants to – everybody lets her.'

'Why?' Caroline asked. The fleshy lips of her kitty were rubbing on Rachel's thick wet curls. 'Who says I have to let her feel me, if I don't want to?'

'Why wouldn't you want to? She's absolutely super at it – she gives you fantastic thrills.'

'I didn't say I didn't want to. I said I didn't have to.'

'You'll want to, when she gets her hand inside your knickers,' Rachel said knowingly, while she rubbed her titties harder against Caroline's tiny ones.

'If I had the choice,' Caroline said pertly, 'I'd rather open my legs for the head of my house, Miss Locksley.'

'We'd all like to be diddled by her,' Rachel murmured, 'but she never seems to be interested. Not like Miss Redruth – she's interested all the time. She's been known to have as many as five of us on the same day.'

'How do you know that?'

'It was her birthday last term, in the middle of June. She went round for a week in advance telling everyone she was going to give herself a special treat to celebrate it. We were all trying to guess what it would be – but we didn't find out till the day itself.'

'She diddled five of you as a birthday treat?' Caroline asked with a broad grin.

'Five of us – I was one of the five and the others are friends of mine – we talked about it for days afterwards.'

'Did she have you all there at the same time?'

'No, only one at a time. She arranged it all beforehand. We each had a set time to go to her sitting-room. She had a big birthday cake with thick white icing and her name on it in pink – and a bottle of champagne in an ice-bucket.'

'It sounds super,' said Caroline, 'I hope she does the same next year and invites me. What did she do to you?'

'First she gave me a glass of bubbly and a slice of cake and then she asked me to sit on the table. There was a white tablecloth spread on it, and glasses and two or three big boxes of chocolates. I sat on the edge of the table and while I was eating my cake and sipping my champagne she put both hands up my skirt and pulled my knickers down my legs.'

'Champagne and cake and kitty for her birthday,' Caroline giggled.

'She pushed my skirt up my thighs to look at my bush and feel it, and she said it was beautiful – she says that every time she sees it.'

'That's because it *is* beautiful,' Caroline agreed, sliding her own fluff-covered kitty against the raven-black thatch.

'She stood between my legs, and put her arm round my waist while she felt me. And all of a sudden she pushed her finger inside me.'

'Had you finished eating your cake?' Caroline asked.

'I still had half a slice in my hand and half a glass of champagne in the other, while Eleanor was diddling me. I couldn't put my arms round her to hang on . . .'

'It sounds as if she's got a wicked sense of humour.'

'She played with me till I came sitting there on the table. It sounds silly, but it was marvellous. Then she told me to get down on my knees, because it was time for me to wish her a happy birthday properly.'

'She wanted you to kiss her kitty?'

'That's what she always wants. She was wearing a button-front dress with a belt. I got off the table and down on my knees while she was unbuckling the belt and unbuttoning her dress all down the front – she had absolutely nothing on at all under it.'

'Ooh . . . I like the sound of that,' Caroline murmured. 'Show me what you did to her.'

Rachel went down on her knees; her wet hands slid down Caroline's body and held her hips while she kissed her belly. She slipped a hand between Caroline's parted thighs and opened the lips of her down-covered chuffie to reveal the little nubby.

'This is how I did it to her,' she murmured.

'Ah,' Caroline breathed, lost in pleasurable sensations as the tip of Rachel's tongue slid over her pink nubby.

She moved her feet further apart on the tiling and pushed her belly forward against Rachel's tongue. She moaned as the tip flicked faster and quickly put her hands on Rachel's shoulders for support.

'I've come,' she gasped, her body shaking to the big thrill.

'That's too soon,' Rachel exclaimed in surprise and dismay. 'I've only just started on you.'

Caroline's recovery was equally quick – she rose to her feet grinning and pushed Rachel back against the wall.

'I've got this thing about you, Rachel,' she said. 'Another reason why we're going to be good friends.'

She pressed her mouth to Rachel's in a long kiss and slipped her hand between the older girl's legs. Rachel slid her feet apart on the slippery floor and Caroline's fingers parted black curls to press in between the smooth wet lips.

'For a new girl you take a lot of liberties,' Rachel said, trying to assert her superior status. 'You can't just march naked into my shower and do what you like to me. Second-year girls always have the pick of the new ones – I don't know whether I'd pick you or not, your titties are smaller than I like. Just you remember that anything you try to do to me, I'll do the same to you, twice over.'

It could be a threat or a promise, depending on how you looked at it.

'Maybe you will, maybe I'll make sure you can't,' Caroline said with a grin.

Rachel's wet titties were heaving against Caroline's little apples now that the younger girl's fingers were fluttering over her nubby. Her own fingernails dug into Caroline's taut bum, her belly was pressing close to Caroline's and bucking.

'Oh yes,' Rachel moaned, and then she was trembling in the throes of her thrill.

Two naked girls moved into the next shower stall, giggling, and turned the water on. Rachel leaned back against the wall, resting and getting her breath back.

'That was far too quick,' she complained.

'You've got a thing about me,' Caroline said with a shrug, 'but the second time is always better.'

'Who said anything about letting you diddle me a second time? For a new girl you're even cheekier than I thought.'

'Never mind all that,' Caroline said, 'there's something important I want to talk to you about.'

Rachel put her arm round Caroline's waist and pulled her close until their bellies were pressed wetly together. She slipped her hand between their thighs and clasped Caroline's prominent chuffie.

'What is it you're so concerned about?' she asked.

'The college caretaker.'

'Oh, Keith – has he been spying on you?'

'My second day here, would you believe! I was changing clothes when I noticed a face at the window. He was gone in a second and I don't know how long he'd been there. The girl I'm sharing with – Marjorie Newmill – told me later that it was the caretaker.'

'He walks round the college all day with his stiff *thing* showing in his trousers, trying to get a look at a pair of titties,' Rachel said.

'He saw more than my titties,' Caroline told her. 'I'd got my knickers in my hand when I realised I was being watched. Marjorie says he has his *thing* out in his hand when he looks through windows. She caught him up a ladder once behind the gym – he'd got it out, she said, and he was playing with it while he spied on the girls inside.'

'Keith's our resident sex maniac,' Rachel told her, 'but he doesn't get away with it all the time. A gang of us from Sawby House jumped on him behind the pavilion one afternoon last term. That's where we go in the summer to sunbathe topless. We knew Keith would be spying on us, so we laid a trap for him.'

'How many of you were there?'

'Four sitting on the grass with bare titties to catch his attention and keep him occupied, and three more of us creeping quietly round behind him.'

'I heard how you caught him,' Caroline said. 'You're famous in Wexby House, as well as your own house. And that's another reason why you and I are going to be friends.'

'He was lying in the long grass,' Rachel said. 'He was quite close to the girls with bare titties, but he'd got a pair of binoculars for an even closer look. He was much too busy to notice the three of us creeping up on him. We jumped on his back together and blindfolded him with a bathing towel so he wouldn't know who we were.'

'Didn't he struggle? I mean, men are stronger than we are.'

'He was too shocked. By the time he reacted we'd tied his wrists together behind his back and there wasn't much he could do. We rolled him over – you should have seen the bulge in his jeans, it looked the size of a french loaf.'

'He hadn't come while he was spying on you, then,' Caroline said. 'What did you do – yank his twanger out?'

'We had it out and took snaps of it with my instant camera. What a hard-on he'd got – eight inches long at least, and as thick as my wrist. Tessa Bowland got hold of it to keep it still for the photos, because it was jerking about all over the place. Miranda Yardley sat on his head to stop him rolling around on the grass – he was in a tremendous state.'

'Did you make him come while you watched?'

'Tessa diddled him till he shot his *stuff* in her hand. Even with a towel round his head he made so much noise we were sure he'd be heard clear across in the main building.'

'Have you still got the photos?' Caroline asked, pressing her belly closer to Rachel's.

'I've still got one, if you want to see it – I took a whole pack and gave the others away. Everybody wanted to see the picture and have a laugh at Keith helpless on his back with his *thing* standing up.

'What I want,' said Caroline, 'is to get my own back on Keith for spying on me while I was undressing. I want you to help me, because you've done it before and you know how to catch him.'

'I've been under the shower too long,' Rachel said, 'I'm starting to go wrinkly. Let's get dried and dressed and go to my room and I'll show you the photo. Then we can talk about what to do.'

'You know what we're going to do,' Caroline said with a grin, 'but first we're going to decide how to deal with Keith.'

Chapter 8

Toby's romance with Sharon Pomeroy did not develop in the way he hoped. From his point of view the reason he shared her with Claudine was that he imagined the arrangement might lead to Claudine opening her legs for him, as well as Sharon.

Halfway through term there was no sign it would ever happen – when he talked to Claudine she displayed no sign of interest in him at all.

Even Sharon's attitude toward him had changed – she was less and less enthusiastic about letting him undress her and slide his hard-on into her. A displeasing conclusion was staring him in the face – Claudine's sexual attentions to Sharon were more welcome than his own, and Claudine was slowly turning Sharon against him.

He decided to put this suspicion to the test by eavesdropping on the two of them when they were together, to hear what Claudine was telling Sharon about him. There were no lessons on Saturdays, but when he suggested to Sharon that they should have lunch in town and watch the local rugger team play a home game afterwards, she said she was too busy with half-term papers.

Sharon's quarters were on the ground floor of Wexby House, halfway along a corridor of similar doors. Toby found a spot where he had a view of Sharon's door – his hiding-place was a small store-room where the cleaners kept brushes and vacuum cleaners and buckets. He went in and lurked, an eye to the keyhole – and as he'd guessed might happen, Claudine turned up mid-morning.

Being off-duty, so to speak, Claudine was wearing tight black leather trousers and a black roll-top sweater. Toby's eyes bulged at the view of Claudine's rear as she stood knocking at Sharon's door – the black leather was stretched deliciously tight over the cheeks of her nicely shaped bum. His twanger instantly began stirring in his jockstrap.

He wanted to press himself against her bum with his flies unzipped and rub his hard-on against the thin leather – and then put his arms round her, slide his hands up inside her sweater and get hold of her titties . . . It was a mystery to him why Claudine was so indifferent to his male attractions.

He waited five minutes after she'd gone in before he moved across the passage to Sharon's door and put his ear to it. He could hear nothing at all, not a word. He dropped to one knee and peered through the keyhole – luckily for him there was no key in it. He could see most of the room, desk and chairs and sofa, but he couldn't see either Sharon or Claudine.

They had to be in the bedroom, he realised. Further investigation was out of the question. He was about to stand up and leave when a thought occurred to him – what better place for Claudine to say nasty offensive things about him to Sharon than the intimacy of the bedroom? It was an ideal chance to discover the truth about her.

Toby was no Keith Mason. Spying on girls and women undressing might be a hobby to Keith but to Toby it was impolite and unthinkable. If he were to go any further with his investigation into Claudine's dislike of him it would be with the best of motives – he would only listen to what was being said and he would certainly not try to see what the two women were doing.

Even that had its problems – suppose they found him listening to them, what on earth could he possibly say to justify the intrusion? He'd be shamed. At that moment he heard footsteps and girls' voices approaching round the corner of the corridor – he was about to be discovered lurking outside Sharon's door . . .

In a flash he was up on his feet and inside Sharon's sitting-room, the fortuitously unlocked door shut behind him. The room was empty and on the far side the door to the bedroom was almost closed, but not quite. He took his shoes off and walked slowly and silently across the room. At the bedroom door he sank down on his knees and put his ear to the inch-wide opening.

He could hear their voices, but he couldn't make out any words. But that was the whole point of taking the terrible risk of intruding into Sharon's room, to hear what lies and slander Claudine was telling her about him.

He pressed his cheek against the door and looked round it into the bedroom. The reason he couldn't hear what they were saying to each other was that they were close together and speaking very intimately. Sharon lay on her side on the bed, her pretty body naked. Claudine had taken off her sweater and leather trousers and was wearing only a pair of tiny black knickers. She was sitting on the side of the bed and leaning over to stroke Sharon's titties.

Toby knew about the caretaker's spare-time activities – everyone did, with the exception of the Principal. Toby reckoned himself a cut above a peeper like Keith. It took most of Toby's time and much of his energy to do or diddle all the females who threw themselves at him – he had no need to play Peeping Tom to see a pair of uncovered titties.

Nevertheless, he was so fascinated by the scene on the bed that he instantly forgot his scruples and watched eagerly as Sharon opened her long legs by putting one knee up. It was a beautiful erotic tableau: blonde Sharon, leaning on one elbow, her long hair hanging over her right shoulder, while Claudine stroked her fair-haired kitty.

You can stroke her and you can diddle her, Toby said to himself as he watched, *but you can't do what I did to her the day before yesterday, you haven't got a dick to do it with.*

The last time he'd had Sharon was in the gym late in the lunch break. He'd been teaching a class of adoring sixteen-year-olds martial arts as self-defence against rapists. The girls had gone to lunch, but Toby had stayed on to practice his back-kick to the crotch, not being entirely satisfied with the way he had demonstrated it to the girls.

Sharon came into the empty gym. They hadn't arranged to meet but he was pleased to see her.

'What are you doing, Toby?' she asked as he whirled on one leg and slammed his heel into a punching-bag.

'It's an anti-rape technique,' he said. 'When the would-be molester makes a grab at you, you swivel round and use your foot to mash his bean-bag flat.'

'It looks effective enough,' Sharon said with a shudder, 'though no one's ever tried to rape me, I'm delighted to say.'

'If you promise not to kick me I'll demonstrate molestation to you now,' Toby offered. 'No harm in being prepared.'

He was hot and sweating and in the mood. The sixteen-year-old girls he had been coaching wore thin tee-shirts and shorts, and the vigour of their kicking the punch-bag had set their titties joggling and bouncing. Long bare thighs were exposed as the girls whirled and kicked, all the way up to their smooth groins and tiny briefs.

'Here?' Sharon said, smiling. 'With all these windows?'

The walls of the gymnasium were almost entirely of plate-glass from floor to roof, but it stood at a distance from other college buildings and at this time of day everyone would be eating. Toby didn't hesitate – he picked Sharon up and threw her across his shoulder and ran with her to a vaulting-horse on the other side of the gym.

It was a large piece of equipment, four feet long, chest-high, padded on top. He laid Sharon on it and reached with both hands under her skirt to pull her knickers down.

'Not here, you idiot,' she said, half-laughing. 'Everyone can see us.'

Her tiny knickers were halfway down her thighs, revealing a neat blondish triangle of curls. Toby leaned over to kiss it.

'Nobody can see us,' he said, 'they're in the dining-room.'

He slid her knickers all the way down her legs and off, then pulled her legs apart. She trembled and begged him to stop when she felt his fingers parting the lips of her kitty.

'You're being molested,' he said, grinning down at her. 'It doesn't make any difference if you struggle or plead with me, I'm going to do you anyway.'

He was wearing a white track-suit, and at the crotch there was a long bulge visible in spite of his close-fitting jockstrap. He put both hands on the top of the vaulting-horse and

130

demonstrated his athletic ability by leaping up and landing with both feet between Sharon's legs.

He ripped his one-piece track-suit open from chest to groin and had it down round his knees in a split second. Then he was on top of Sharon with his stiff twanger in his hand, steering it between the lips of her chuffie. He pushed in, and she was slippery and ready.

'You've been overpowered and flung down on your back and now you're being ravished,' he whispered as he slid rapidly in and out.

'No, you mustn't . . .' she moaned, tremors running through her body. She pushed at his shoulders and tried to arch her back to throw him off.

'This is it!' he gasped as he felt his cream shoot into her chuffie. 'You've been well and truly done, Sharon . . .'

Two days after that he was thinking *You can't do her the way I do her, Claudine* while he watched the two women on Sharon's bed. Claudine had her hand between Sharon's legs. Sharon's head was on Claudine's thigh and she was smiling up at her.

Claudine stood up to take her knickers off and reveal her dark-brown curls. Toby stared at her lean flanks and long thighs as she stretched herself proudly, her bare feet planted wide apart and her arms high in the air, fists clenched, so that she was like a naked human X. She lay down on the bed with Sharon and they put their arms around each other while they kissed.

Toby wanted to be there on the bed with them, lying between them and feeling their naked bodies press close. He wanted the feel of their titties and bellies against him, their wet chuffies sliding on his bare skin. He could imagine their hands stroking him all over – his hard-on in Claudine's hand being joggled up and down, Sharon's hand reaching between his legs to hold his bean-bag.

There'd be another hand rubbing his belly and a hand stroking his bum. Two pairs of titties and two soft wet chuffies gliding over his face and his chest and his belly – thirty seconds of that and he'd come in long spasms and shoot his cream over both women . . . he'd see it splatter on their titties, see it trickle down their faces.

By now Toby's hard-on was straining so fiercely that he couldn't bear the tightness of his jockstrap. He was dressed to go to town, in blazer and slacks – he flicked his zip open and pushed his black posing-pouch down to liberate his throbbing shaft.

He was almost panting while he wondered if Claudine and Sharon played heads-and-tails together. Perhaps he would see one of them turn about on the bed so that they could lie for hours with their faces between each other's open thighs, flicking their tongues over each other's little pink nubby.

His mind was in a whirl. At this point there was no difference between him and Keith Mason. That thought steadied him and made him feel ashamed of what he was doing. He tore his gaze away from the scene on the bed and forced his bounding hard-on back into his underwear.

It was only for an underling like Keith Mason to spy on naked women and diddle himself, Toby admonished himself. A superior person like himself had no need for such antics, he could always find a friendly slit to slide his shaft up. In fact, there was someone right nearby who was always at his disposal – someone who'd gladly drop her knickers and open her legs for him – Keith's wife.

He could hear a soft moaning from the bed as he tiptoed away from Sharon's bedroom door and across her sitting-room. He'd heard Sharon moan like that before and knew she must be almost at the point of coming – he was tempted to go back to the bedroom door and watch while Claudine diddled her over the edge.

And stay after that to watch Sharon return the favour. He'd never seen Claudine in the spasms of coming, much as he wanted to give her the big thrill himself.

Today was the first time he'd ever seen Claudine naked. He liked her long, lean body and he thought her pointed titties very sexy and her patch of brunette curls elegant.

But staying to see Sharon play with Claudine would only be tormenting himself. There was no chance of getting his hard-on into either of them. He put his shoes on and went

132

swiftly along the corridor and out of Wexby House. There were plenty of girls about, but he didn't stop to speak to any of them – he was too anxious to rid himself of his throbbing stand. Five minutes later he was at the gatehouse. He'd trotted all the way and was glowing with wound-up energy when he went in.

Sally was coming down the stairs with a laundry bag in her hand. She was wearing a short skirt and a broad-striped shirt. She was so eager day and night to be rattled that she could read a man's mind at twenty paces and tell whether he was a goer.

One look at Toby standing inside the front door with his blazer open and a bulge in his trousers told her all she needed to know.

'Where's Keith?' Toby asked, advancing to the bottom of the stairs. 'He's out, I hope.'

For answer Sally dropped the laundry bag she was carrying and jumped at him from halfway up the staircase. Her thin arms wound about his neck, her long skinny legs clamped tight around his waist. Strong enough not to stagger, he put both hands under her taut bum to support her while she rubbed herself against his body.

'Is Keith out, then?' he whispered in her ear.

'It's all right,' she said. 'Do me fast – I've been dying for it since I got up this morning.'

Toby was in too much of a state to really take in what she'd said. He was desperate to get his hard-on into a warm wet chuffie and relieve his tension. He climbed up a step or two and laid Sally on her back on the brown-carpeted stairs.

'Do me hard,' she moaned, pulling her skirt up to her hips.

'I'm going to, Sally,' he moaned back at her as he lay over her and pulled her shirt up to her neck. She wore no bra, and he cupped her small titties in his hands while she felt down between their bodies and deftly freed his straining twanger.

In spite of the awkwardness of being on the staircase with his feet braced on a step to stop him sliding down, he had

Sally's knickers off in a flash. Her legs moved apart like a pair of scissors opening as she jammed his hard-on into her kitty.

'Oh yes, yes,' he sighed gratefully, ramming it all the way home.

He felt the moist grip of her soft chuffie holding him while he did her with hard little jabs. She was hanging on to his shoulders for dear life to prevent herself slipping down the stairs while she bucked her belly up at him.

'You're nearly coming,' she gasped.

'So are you,' he said, his voice strained as tremendous sensations surged through him and he fired his cream into her.

'Oh my god, I'm coming too,' Sally groaned. Her thin belly was smacking against him in her throes.

Five seconds later she was pushing him away from her and telling him that Keith was upstairs changing a tap-washer in the bathroom and might find them on the stairs any second now. Toby was alarmed and dismayed by this news – he yanked his wet shaft out of Sally and scrambled downstairs backwards, stuffing it into his trousers and dragging up his zip as he went.

Sally lay there on the staircase with her legs apart, the open chuffie he'd just creamed into fully on show. She was grinning at him. She sat up and pulled her shirt down over her titties, then slipped her knickers on and wriggled them up over her knees and up her thighs. She stood up and smoothed her skirt down, still apparently in no great hurry.

Finally she came down the stairs to stand facing him, her hands on her hips, a grin on her face.

'That got you going,' she said, 'I've never seen a man jump off the nest and tuck his gear away as fast as you did.'

'You played a trick on me,' Toby said, still trembling from the shock. 'Keith isn't up in the bathroom at all, is he?'

'Something else got you going before you rushed in with a stand like a poker,' Sally said, ignoring the question. 'You were only inside me for five seconds before you shot your bolt. What have you been up to, Mr Sports Coach? Have you been fingering one of the girls behind the pavilion – or maybe one of them was playing with your diddler?'

'Nothing of the sort,' Toby said, sounding very sincere.

'Then you must have been feeling that stuck-up teacher with the long hair and she wouldn't let you slip it up her,' Sally mocked him. 'That's what made you rush back here to stick it up me instead, am I right?'

'If you mean Sharon Pomeroy, I haven't been anywhere near her today.'

Toby was wondering how Sally came to know of his interest in Sharon. The other teachers all knew, and he guessed many of the girls knew, but it was unlikely that either teachers or girls were on gossiping terms with the caretaker's wife. She must have had it from Keith – but where could he have picked up the news? Toby resigned himself to the thought that no one had any secrets at Lechlade.

It was worth trying to keep some things confidential, though, hard as it was. Telling Sally he hadn't been near Sharon that day was untrue, of course; he'd been close enough to watch her being diddled and tongued by Claudine Stanhope. If he'd stayed a minute or two longer he'd have seen her come and would have shot his cream in his hand.

'I'm sure you were doing something you shouldn't, to get yourself into a state like you were in,' Sally persisted.

She moved closer and groped the front of his trousers.

'It wouldn't take much to make it stand up for another go,' she said, offering her expert opinion. 'You might last longer, second time round. What got you all hot and bothered, Toby?'

He was wracking his brain for an answer – it had to be believable, but he didn't want to give anything away about his private arrangements with girls or teachers.

'I was minding my own business,' he said, grinning, 'when I remembered that first time you came into my room with a morning cup of tea. Before I was properly awake you had your knickers off to straddle me. Thinking of it just now gave me such a huge stand that I broke into a run to get to you, and there you were coming down the stairs in a skirt showing your thighs nearly all the way up – and you were as ready for it as I was.'

135

'You know me,' Sally said as she rubbed her hand over his bulge, 'I'm always ready for it. But you remembered wrong about the first time we did it together.'

'No, I didn't – I was so surprised at the time that it's stayed clear in my mind, every detail.'

'You'd been here about a week,' Sally told him, 'and on the morning in question you didn't even wake up when I brought your cup of tea to you. You were lying with one hand underneath the pillow and you'd thrown the sheets off in the night. Your dickie had slipped out through the slit of your pyjama trousers, so I had a good eyeful.'

'Yes, I always wake up with a hard-on,' he said proudly.

'You've got a real hard-on now,' Sally said, squeezing it through his trousers, 'but that morning it was dangling down small and soft – I was very disappointed. I had a good look and thought it might be a big one when it stood up, so I ran my finger along it lightly – I didn't want to wake you. After a while it stirred and began to get longer and thicker.'

'I don't remember any of that,' Toby said foolishly.

'How could you? You were fast asleep at the time. When you'd got a big hard stand I circled my forefinger and thumb just below the head and gave you a very slow finger-wave. That put a silly smile on your face.'

'You must have given me a sexy dream by playing with me.'

'I was wondering if I could make you shoot in your sleep.'

'But I didn't, did I – or I'd have woken up when I came and found you diddling me.'

'You muttered and took your hand from under the pillow and I could see you were waking up. I stood away from the bed and said "Good morning", as if I'd just that minute come in the door.'

Toby grinned at her and slid his zip down to let her feel inside his trousers and get hold of his hard-on – it was at full stretch again now, and he wanted to slip it back into her. Not on the staircase this time, there were more comfortable places.

'Let's go into your sitting-room and I'll have you on the sofa,' he suggested, his hand squeezing her left tittie through

136

her loose shirt. 'This time I'll do you long and slow and keep you on the edge of coming till you scream for mercy. I'll make you beg and plead to come before I shoot off inside you – you'll come so hard that you'll pass out.'

'It sounds lovely,' she said, pulling her hand out of his flies, 'but I can't.'

Before he could ask her why not, he heard a step on the landing above and Keith came into view, carrying a big toolbox. Toby dropped his hand from Sally's tittie and took a step back from her. Without any sign of concern she turned to look up the stairs at Keith as he came down.

'Have you fixed that leaky tap?' she asked.

'All done,' he said, 'I've put in a new washer.'

Toby was red in the face, but he had the presence of mind to stand behind Sally and use her as cover while he pulled up his zip. He was stunned to discover that he really had been on top of Sally while her husband was only a few steps away. Suppose Keith had finished changing the tap sooner and come out of the bathroom – he'd have seen Sally being done on the stairs!

Halfway down the stairs lay the laundry bag that Sally had dropped when she hurled herself at Toby. Keith picked it up and brought it down. He gave it to Sally, who moved aside to let him past.

'I dropped it when I went to answer the door,' she said, 'but it was only somebody collecting for the handicapped.'

'Hello, Mr Dundale,' Keith said, looking at him curiously. 'I thought you were going into town today. You look a bit flushed – is everything all right?'

'Yes, fine, I'm just off now,' Toby said. Behind Keith's back Sally was grinning and making up-and-down motions at waist level with her clenched hand.

The awkward fact was, Toby acknowledged as he went out of the college gates and strolled toward the town a mile away, the quickie with Sally hadn't relieved his tension. Watching Claudine and Sharon playing with each other naked had excited him so much that it was going to take a lot more than a twenty-second rattle on the stairs to settle him down.

It was that confounded Keith's fault. Sally would have

spread herself on the sofa with her legs wide open for as long as Toby wanted her to. He'd told her what he wanted to do to her, while she had her hand in his flies making his twanger stand again. And she wanted him to do it – she always wanted him to do it.

Why was Keith lurking about the bathroom fiddling with taps, instead of being out round the college? He should have been spying on half-naked girls through windows, with his dick in his hand, not at home changing washers and stopping Sally being done till she passed out.

In addition to the raging frustration of a hard-on and no chuffie to slide it into, there was another emotion gnawing at Toby. It was anxiety – a sense of foreboding. The question was, had Keith seen anything when he came out of the bathroom? Toby remembered with a blush that he was feeling Sally's titties when Keith suddenly loomed up on the landing.

Her hand was deep inside his flies and she was holding his hard-on. They'd pulled away from each other instantly, but was that fast enough? If Keith saw or suspected that Sally was flipping Toby's twanger, he'd certainly guess the rest. Which meant trouble.

There was something else to worry about. When Sally reached her climax on the stairs, had she come noisily? She'd come hard and fast, he knew, and she'd smacked her belly violently against him ten or twelve times during her big thrill. But had she squealed or screamed, as she often did when they were alone in the house?

The bathroom where Keith was mending a tap was right at the top of the stairs, and he wouldn't have been likely to close the door while he was working. If Sally squealed when she came, Keith must have heard her. And he'd heard her make that sound enough times to know what was going on.

The natural reaction would have been for Keith to look round the door and down the stairs to see what was happening – he might have seen Toby on top of Sally ramming away for dear life. But he hadn't rushed down to drag Toby off her and punch him all the way down the stairs and right out of the house. So he must not have seen anything.

Or perhaps he had and he was playing it deviously. *Oh my*

138

god, Toby thought, *he might have seen me banging away at Sally … was there anything in his manner to suggest he knew I'd just done her when he came downstairs? If he goes to the Principal and makes a complaint about me, I'll surely be sacked – the Trustees will never condone a teacher having it off with the caretaker's wife.*

In spite of all that, Toby was an optimist by nature. By the time he'd walked into town and round the market-place, had a couple of pints in the Cock Inn and walked back to the college, he'd decided Keith knew nothing and suspected nothing. There was no need to worry.

The only thing that was still troubling Toby by six o'clock that day was his permanent stand. From the moment Sally had handled it at the foot of the stairs, it had refused to go slack. It stood up hard against his belly inside his jockstrap, demanding to be given help and alleviation.

When Toby changed into running-shorts for the evening jog, he looked at himself sideways on in the long mirror, to see how prominent it was. He very nearly decided to give himself a finger-wave before he ventured out of his room, but that seemed a defeatist thing to do when he was surrounded by so many pretty young girls.

Since his first week at Lechlade, Toby had encouraged jogging. It was entirely voluntary, so girls joined him at eight-thirty in the morning or at six in the evening for a two-mile trot only if they wanted to. Quite a few did, mainly because he was popular with the girls. On sunny mornings in summer he'd sometimes had as many as fifty girls running with him.

There were never many on a Saturday, however. On that day the girls were free from breakfast until dinner at seven. Many of them went into town to look around the shops or go to the flicks if there was a good movie on. It was rumoured that some girls knew boys their own age in the town and let themselves be groped in the dark at the back of the cinema.

It was even said of Patty Bambridge, a dark-haired girl with big round breasts who'd left Lechlade at the end of last term, that she had fallen for a boy in the town. Every Saturday afternoon, rain or shine, she went to meet him and would stand with her back against the wall in the cinema car park while he pushed his *thing* up her and did her properly.

On this particular Saturday there were fourteen girls waiting outside the gymnasium when Toby arrived at six o'clock.

'Hi,' he said cheerfully as he looked them over.

He was sorry that Patty had left Lechlade. All last term, morning and evening, the sight of her big bouncing young titties when she jogged had given Toby a most tremendous hard-on. Not that he needed much in the way of encouragement – trotting along with a crowd of girls in little shorts and thin tee-shirts never failed to give him an enormous stand. He wore a strong athletic support under his shorts to hold his stand tight to his belly, so that it wasn't obvious to the girls. Or so he hoped.

Marjorie Newmill had turned up to jog, he noticed, but not her friend Hilary. Marjorie was a plumpish brunette of seventeen, with a good-sized pair of titties and a permanent gleam in her eye that said she knew what kitties were for – and what hard-ons were for. She stared at Toby with a smile on her round face, then dropped her gaze to the bulge he'd hoped was hidden under his running shorts.

The group set off, jogging easily along the road to the gatehouse. As usual, Toby was alongside the straggle of girls, checking that they were moving without strain, elbows in to their sides, heads up, backs straight. Marjorie Newmill was back towards the tail end of the party – she didn't like games and took part in the jogging only to stop herself getting any plumper.

'Your lace isn't tied properly,' Toby told her as she jogged alongside, 'it will come undone and trip you.'

Marjorie pulled out of the line onto the grass beside the roadway and stopped. She went down on one knee to check the laces on her trainers – then looked up with a puzzled expression at Toby, having found nothing wrong.

'Keep going,' he called to the other girls, waving them on toward the gate and the road outside the grounds. 'We'll catch you up.'

The line of joggers swept on by. Toby held his hand out to Marjorie and pulled her to her feet.

'I'll re-tie your laces,' he said. 'Come behind that tree.'

There were tall chestnut trees all round the perimeter of the college grounds, just inside the six-foot boundary wall. Trees with trunks thick enough to hide behind from passers-by. Now it was Toby's turn to drop to one knee. He raised Marjorie's foot onto his other knee while he pretended that he was checking her laces. She had good legs, with well-shaped calves and strong young thighs.

Toby stopped fidgeting with her laces and massaged her calves briskly, telling her it was to loosen up the muscles. He said the same when his hands moved above her knees and massaged her thighs. His cheeks were pink and he had a distant expression by the time his hands worked their way up to the tops of her thighs.

'You've got your hands in my shorts,' Marjorie said.

'Yes, I have,' Toby said with a grin. 'I'm checking to make sure you haven't got groin-strain.'

'I don't think so,' she said, 'but you'd better find out.'

She found it thrilling to have Toby's hands in her shorts – and then inside the briefs she wore under them. He stood up and pressed her against the tree trunk – she stood with feet apart while he had a good feel inside her little briefs.

'Put your hand in my shorts,' he suggested, abandoning all pretences of professional detachment, while he slid his own hands under her tee-shirt to undo her sports bra and have a feel of her big breasts.

'I know what you want,' she said. 'You want me to get your *thing* out and stroke it. It's gone long and stiff inside that funny little pouch you wear to stop it flopping about. That doesn't hide it, you know – everyone had a giggle when they saw you like that.'

'No . . .' he breathed. 'It wasn't that obvious, was it?'

'Looks as if you've got a stick of rock in those tight shorts,' Marjorie said with a wide grin. 'Orline Ashby pinched my bum when she saw it and asked if I fancied having that up me.'

'What did you say?' Toby murmured, his hands playing

141

with her billowing titties. 'Yes, you would? Why don't you get it out and hold it?'

She opened his shorts and grasped his stiff twanger, 'I told her I'm not having a *thing* that size in me – I'd be split open all the way up to my belly. I refuse to let any horrid big *thing* get into me and stretch me open like an old purse with the zip gone.'

He laughed and pulled his shaft out of her grasp and slipped it up the leg of her tennis shorts, into the little briefs inside them, and stood very close to her, so it was held tight to her belly by her underwear.

'You think I've got a big one, Marjorie?'

'A super big one,' she said, 'it's nice to have it in my hand. And it feels hard and strong against my belly – but don't get any ideas about putting it inside me.'

Toby had his hands on her hips and was steadying her against the pressing and rubbing of his shaft on her warm chubby belly. He knew that she was excited, he could feel her body trembling against him – he'd played with her before and knew she usually came easily. Just as well, because he didn't want the joggers to get too far ahead.

What he really wanted was to thrust his throbbing hard-on up her kitty and shoot his cream in long spurts. But that was out – his experience of Lechlade girls was that they were very keen to be diddled and given the big thrill, but they closed their legs fast at any suggestion of a dick inside them.

Somehow he had to get the satisfaction his body had been shrieking for since Sally stroked his shaft to a mighty stand and then did nothing to ease his frantic plight – because her stupid pervert of a husband put in an unwelcome appearance at the wrong moment.

His grip on Marjorie tightened and he rubbed the head of his twanger against the soft skin of her belly. His knees trembled, he gave a long wailing moan and shot off furiously.

'Beast – you've come all over me!' Marjorie gasped.

Chapter 9

On Monday it began to rain soon after two o'clock, which meant that the tennis courts couldn't be used. The swimming-pool was also out of action – something had gone wrong with the filter device. As a result the water was too heavily chlorinated to be usable, until Keith mended whatever was wrong. Toby decided to take the afternoon off – any girls who wanted to use the gym could manage on their own for once.

He trotted through the drizzle towards the gatehouse to shower and change his clothes. His brief tennis shorts and shirt were soaked before he got there. The shirt was clammy and uncomfortable against his chest and belly, so he stripped it off and jogged on across the grass naked to the waist.

He saw the Principal walking along the road toward the main buildings. She was wearing a beige mac and had a big sensible umbrella up. He gave her a wave as they passed, but she didn't return it and he could guess what she was thinking – a bare-chested and bare-thighed man running in broad daylight through the grounds of a college for young ladies. Disgraceful, scandalous, shameful – those were the kindest words that would come to Enid's mind.

Only two days had passed since he'd had Enid on her hands and knees, shrieking and shuddering in climactic pleasure. He'd been on her bed behind her, his tennis shorts gaping open and his hard-on in his hand – she was still coming when he pushed it hard up into her chuffie. Even then, though she could hardly speak for the erotic tremors racking her body, she'd pretended not to understand what he was doing to her.

To Enid's way of thinking, men were simply a nuisance to

143

be seen off. They didn't exist as sexual objects. Secretly she wanted to be done hard and often, but she would never admit it. Even while it was happening to her, while a long thick hard-on was sliding in and out of her chuffie in a strong and steady rhythm, she refused to accept that she was being properly done and loving it.

This only served to make the act more enjoyable for Toby as he lay forward on her broad back, her big bare bum pressing against his belly, while he rode her to a long squelchy second climax. But he knew she'd never admit she'd been done – if he mentioned it to her, she'd go red in the face and deny anything of the sort had ever taken place. She hadn't even waved back to him just now.

He reached the gatehouse and dashed into the entrance hall out of the rain. He had his foot on the bottom stair, about to go up for a hot shower, when he saw that the door to the Masons' living room was open.

He glanced in, and there was Sally in a quilted dressing-gown, with a towel wrapped round her head. She was just out of the bath; she stood at an ironing-board and was smoothing an electric iron over a pair of small pale-blue knickers.

Her back was to Toby. He stood with a foot on the first stair and a hand on the banister, staring at her. He was fascinated by the sight of the hot, shiny steel iron gliding over the knickers on the board. It would make them very warm, he was thinking, and he'd like to be there to watch when Sally opened her dressing-gown and put them on.

She would feel the heat between her thighs and against her chuffie. It was sure to make her instantly excited, that dry heat radiating against her flesh from the thin just-ironed knickers. The long lips of her kitty would open up, ready for a hard-on, or a finger, to slide in . . .

Without knowing it, Toby was demonstrating the truth of the Principal's views on men in general – that their minds were occupied all the time with lewd thoughts about women's bodies. It was Enid's view that if a man saw a pair of knickers he instantly started to think about what went inside them. He would think about slipping his hand into a woman's knickers for a feel. And that thought would lead on automatically to a desperate desire to get his *thing* into the woman's chuffie, to slake his vile lust on her body. As far as Toby Dundale was concerned, Enid was absolutely right – a mere glimpse of thigh and knicker on the tennis court, when a girl's skirt swirled up in a forehand smash over the net, was all it took to give him a stand.

Jogging in the mornings and evenings with the volunteers was even more arousing. The sight of bare thighs in little shorts pumping up and down and firm young titties bouncing under close-clinging tee-shirts never failed to give Toby a tremendous hard-on. On more than one occasion he'd come in his shorts as he led the girls along the road toward town.

If he felt the familiar lurch of his twanger and a sudden racing surge up his shaft, he'd wave the girls on while he turned sharply aside into some nearby shrubbery or behind a tree. He would stand there gasping and trembling, his hand clasped tightly over the front of his running shorts while his cream spurted out into his tight jockstrap.

One exceptional jogging incident was the time he stopped Marjorie Newmill to check her laces and then backed her up against a tree and slipped his hard-on up the leg of her shorts and into the little briefs she wore inside them. It was a crazy thing to do, out in the open like that, but that day he'd been too desperate for it to care.

That's why it was over so fast. He'd held Marjorie tight by the hips and immobilised her against the tree trunk. He rubbed his twanger against the skin of her belly for just about ten seconds – that's all it took – before he came and she squealed.

Usually he stuffed a hanky down into his athletic support before he went jogging with the girls, to be on the safe side in case watching their bouncing young titties made him shoot off accidentally. He hoped this artificial reinforcement of his natural bulge wasn't obvious to the girls, just as he hoped they didn't understand the reason for his sudden halts when he knew he was about to shoot his lot into his shorts.

He was wrong on both counts – the young ladies knew why he'd had to stop and they giggled. When he rejoined

145

them, half a mile further on, they furtively eyed the front of his shorts for stains seeping through. And at the start of a jog, they never failed to comment on the size of his bulge – and to discuss in whispers whether he'd got a hanky or two hankies in there. Or even a pair of tights, some suggested.

Seeing Sally at her ironing-board, with a pair of knickers under the hot iron, brought Toby up hard inside his tennis shorts and changed his mind about taking a shower – he could do that later. Something else was far more important to him first. If Enid could have seen his reaction to Sally's ordinary domestic activity, she would have congratulated herself for her own insight into the lewd nature of men.

Toby dropped his wet shirt on the carpet and went into the living room with one thing on his mind. Sally glanced over her shoulder and smiled at him as he moved behind her and stood close enough to press his hard-on against her bum. He wrapped his arms round her and slid his hands into the top of the dressing gown to hold a small tittie in each palm.

'I've got to have you, Sally,' he said. 'You know that without being told. Where's Keith this afternoon?'

That made her grin sideways at him. 'You're all right this time,' she said. 'He's not upstairs.'

'Yes, but where is he?' Toby asked again. He'd been nearly caught doing Sally on the stairs and he wasn't going to take another risk like that.

'I'd love you to do me,' Sally said as she rubbed her bum against him. 'I'm really in the mood for it.'

'You're always in the mood for it,' Toby said while he was squeezing her titties and rubbing the tips of his forefingers over their stiff little bobbles. 'If he's not upstairs, where is he? If you don't tell me this minute I'll get you all hot and bothered and then go for a bath and leave you to diddle yourself.'

Sally laughed at his anxiety. She could feel the hardness of his shaft through her dressing-gown and she knew he'd never walk away from her in that condition.

'Why don't you do me?' she said. 'I promise I'll tell you

146

where he is when I feel your hard-on inside me. And not before.'

Toby sighed in vexation, knowing he was in no state to think of refusing her offer. He untied the belt of her dressing-gown and pulled it open so he could run his hands up and down her hot bare body, feeling her soft little titties and narrow belly and her blondish-haired kitty.

'Come on, then,' she said, bumping her bum against him in a regular rhythm. 'Give me a good hard rattle.'

'You'll get all you want in a minute,' he said, 'just let me have a good feel first – there's nothing in the world as nice as having a pair of bare titties in your hands.'

'You can do all that later,' she said urgently.

He put a hand on the nape of her neck and bent her forward over the ironing board, until her bare titties lay on the warm knickers. He put the iron down on the floor out of the way, so she could stretch her arms out sideways and grip the ends of the board.

'Hold on tight,' he said, 'it's going to be a bumpy ride.' She twisted her head halfway round, trying to grin at him. Her lean bum was thrust at him in invitation, her thighs well parted to offer him the perfect target. He turned the dressing-gown up her back, finding her chuffie still warm and soft from the bath when he touched it from behind, fingering the hairy lips and pulling them open.

'Put it in me,' she urged him, 'I want to be done properly – you can diddle me all you want to later.'

Toby unzipped his flies left-handed and released his leaping shaft. He steered it to her chuffie and pressed the bare head in between the soft, moist lips.

'Right in,' she said, 'all the way – let me feel it in me.'

He pushed forward, looking down to watch his twanger disappearing into her, inch by inch. All the way into her, as she'd said, until his belly was pressed against her bum and he could see only his curls tight against her cheeks.

He held her bare hips, gripping very tight, while he jabbed in and out strongly. He wanted to do her hard and brutally – and Sally wanted to be ravaged and done to death.

'You're wet and slippery,' he gasped as he rammed her

hard, 'I'm all the way into your belly.'

'Keith's gone to Gloucester,' she said. 'The local dealer hadn't got the part he needs for the swimming pool so he'd taken the school van and driven over to the wholesaler. He'll be gone for hours.'

'Good,' Toby moaned – he'd forgotten Keith in the excitement of sliding forcefully in and out of Sally's wet chuffie.

The ironing board was rocking underneath her while she bumped her bare bum against him to meet his strokes. Her eyes were staring and she was moaning – he saw that she'd started to come already.

'You're being done hard,' Toby panted, 'I'm going to make you come till you can't take any more and you faint.'

'Don't stop,' she squealed, 'don't stop – keep going – I'm coming and coming and coming – I can't stop.'

'Oh yes, oh yes . . . I'm going to do it now,' he gasped, ramming in and out of her wet chuffie furiously.

'Yes!' she shrieked, staring at nothing. 'Give it to me!'

Toby's cream shot powerfully up into her belly and her body bucked on the ironing-board, threatening to overturn it and drop them both to the floor. Long hard spasms shook her and she squealed loudly as the biggest thrill of all took her.

All this frantic activity was finally too much for the ironing board. The locking-catch pulled loose beneath the flat top and the spindly cross-legs collapsed like a concertina. The board crashed to the floor, with Sally face-down and bare-bummed across it, her legs splayed wide.

Toby went down with her, landing on top of her, almost winded by the thump of her lean bum against his belly as they hit the floor together. His twanger was driven right into her to the very limit as it spouted the last of his cream.

'Oh my god, I've never come like that,' Sally panted when she was able to speak again. 'You shot your stuff so far up me that I could taste it on the back of my tongue.'

Toby eased his slackening shaft out of her and struggled up onto his knees. He gave her a hand; they helped each other to stand up and broke into laughter.

'We didn't do the ironing board any good,' Sally said, looking down at the wreckage, 'but I must say it was worth it. You can do that to me any afternoon you like, Toby.'

He bent down to pick up the small pale-blue knickers that she'd been ironing – they'd lain forgotten on the board under her bare belly all the time he was having her.

'That's what started it all,' he told her, 'the sight of you ironing these.'

'Is that so?' she said, grinning curiously.

She was facing him, her dressing-gown open to show her titties and the blondish thatch between her lean thighs. She held his dangler in her hand and was rolling it gently to see if it would go stiff again.

'If all it takes is the sight of a pair of knickers to get you going like that,' she said, 'you can do my weekly ironing for me. Will it give you a stand to iron my knickers? I've got pink ones and white and black – all sorts – you'd have lots to iron every week.'

'It wasn't just seeing them,' he explained, 'it was the thought of you putting them on hot from the iron and feeling the warmth between your legs – that's what set me off.'

His dangler was starting to stir in her hand.

'If you did do the ironing for me,' she said, tugging at it to make it grow harder, 'I'd stand behind you and put my arms round your waist and play with you – you'd like that.'

Toby's twanger was pointing upwards again. He had his hand between Sally's legs and hooked two fingers into her wet chuffie.

'Let's go up to my bedroom,' he suggested, 'if you're sure that Keith won't be back for a while.'

Two minutes later they were lying naked on his bed, face to face, kissing and feeling each other.

'Before you get stuck into me again,' Sally said, her hand sliding up and down his stiff shaft, 'there's something I ought to tell you.'

'What's that?' he asked lazily, ready to slide it into her.

'I think Keith suspects about you and me,' she said calmly.

Toby jerked himself up into a sitting position. 'What?' he gasped. 'What are you saying?'

149

'He suspects that you're having me while he's working.'

'This is terrible,' Toby said, dismayed. 'What has he said?'

'He hasn't said anything at all, but I know him – I can tell he thinks I've let you do me.'

'How can you be sure?'

'It started right after you had me on the stairs, when he was mending the bathroom tap. I know we were dressed and decent and standing in the hall talking when he came downstairs – but all the same, I think he must have heard us when you were doing me – and if he peeped round the bathroom door he'd have actually seen you on top of me.'

Toby thought the way Sally was putting it was unnecessarily one-sided and unfair – *when you had me . . . you were doing me . . . seen you on top of me.* It was as if she'd taken no part in it, as if she had been an innocent little housewife doing her daily duties and he'd jumped on her out of the blue and rammed it up her. In fact, the way she was speaking, it was almost as if she hadn't been there at all. He didn't like the sound of that.

'But you say he hasn't said anything about it, and you still haven't told me what he's done to make you think he really did hear us or see us,' Toby said, still sitting up on the bed.

Sally wriggled round until she could rest her cheek on his thigh and keep his twanger standing long and hard by tickling it with one finger.

'It's the way he's been acting since then,' she replied. 'That night when we went to bed, he jumped straight on me. He didn't even grope me first, he just grabbed me and rolled me onto my back, and then he was on top and all the way up me in a flash.'

'Which is not his usual way, I gather,' Toby said, an eyebrow raised.

He'd never asked Sally about Keith's bedtime habits and didn't really want to hear about them now. It seemed to him impolite to ask a married woman what her husband did to her when her knickers were off. But Sally had no such inhibitions.

'He likes to play about for quite a long time first,' she said, 'so I thought it was very strange when he had me flat on my back short and sharp like that. Not that I was complaining about it, mind.'

'Something put him in the mood,' Toby said, 'that's all there was to it. Were you watching a late movie on TV before you went to bed? They have bedroom scenes all the time.'

'Not the one we saw that night,' she said. 'It was a horror film – all about teenagers being murdered and mutilated by a maniac. But I did think while Keith was ramming it into me that he could have seen something on his last round before lock-up that got him all fired up.'

'Highly possible,' Toby agreed. He knew about Keith's peeping habits, but he didn't think Sally knew, so he wasn't going to say too much.

'He might have seen a young girl standing at a window in her nightie,' Sally said, 'so even though it was unusual for him to do me fast and furious like that, it didn't bother me at the time. To tell you the truth, I thoroughly enjoyed it. But early the next morning he did it again. I was fast asleep and he woke me up by pulling my legs open and jumping on top of me.'

'You mean he hasn't done that before?'

'No, never. You see, Keith's a slow waker in the mornings. It's always been me playing with him, to wake him up stiff and ready, never the other way round. So I knew there must be something on his mind.'

'On his mind, or on something lower down?' Toby asked. He wasn't worried now that he'd heard Sally's reasoning. 'You said it yourself, he might have seen something on his rounds of the college that got him going,' he told her casually. 'The girls play with each other, you know, or so I've been told. Keith might have spotted two of them with a hand in each other's knickers.'

'That would have made him frisky at bedtime,' Sally agreed, 'but he'd have had to dream about it all night as well, to wake up with a stand.'

'That's possible,' Toby said, starting to feel anxious again about where all this was leading.

'And after he woke me up with his hard-on in me, he must have seen the same scene again that morning, because

151

he came in early for his lunch and had me on my back on the table before he sat down to eat.'

Toby was astonished to be told all this. And even more astonished that Keith was up to it. But other sensations were pulsing through him just then, making his twanger stand bold and strong. Sally had it in her hot hand and would very soon have it in her wet chuffie. He lay back and stretched out comfortably on the bed.

'Keith did you on the table?' he said with a chuckle. 'You must be feeding him very well, to build him up for all this. He sounds more like Hercules unchained than Keith – what do you give him for breakfast, oysters and Guinness?'

'Laugh if you like,' Sally said, stroking Toby's throbbing tool, 'but I know him better than you do. He knows you've been ramming *this* into me.' She squeezed it for emphasis.

'Then he also knows that you've been lying down and opening your legs for me – it takes two, Sally. But I don't believe a word of it. He'd have had it out with both of us if he really suspected anything.'

'Not necessarily,' she said. 'He can be very sly.'

'I can't see anything sly about jumping on you three times a day. It's more as if he's trying to prove something.'

'That's what I mean,' Sally said. 'He's trying to prove that what's between my legs is his and not yours.'

As if to show what she meant, she put her hand over her chuffie and rubbed it slowly. The movement drew Toby's eyes and he put his own hand over hers.

'Suppose he is trying to prove his ownership of your kitty,' he said. 'Who's he proving it to – himself?'

'And to me,' she suggested.

She slipped her hand out from under his and he was left clasping her warm chuffie. The lips were loose and open. She turned on her back and opened her legs wide in invitation.

'How long did it last, this non-stop rattle?' Toby asked.

'That's the wrong question,' she said. 'It would be more to the point to ask how long it's *going* to last.'

'What!' Toby exclaimed. 'Are you telling me that he hasn't slowed down to normal yet?'

'That's right. He still wants it three times a day.'

'Good god, does that mean he did you this morning?'

'Before you were even awake,' Sally agreed with a long smile. 'I was on my back with my knees up to my ears being pumped full of sticky stuff while you were still dreaming. And that's not all – just wait till you hear this: when he came back about eleven this morning and said he had to drive over to Gloucester for the bit he needs for the swimming-pool filter, he asked me to go with him so he could give me a seeing-to in the back of the van in a country lane.'

'I'm glad you didn't go with him,' said Toby, 'or I'd have missed the chance of having you across the ironing-board.'

'Yes, but you see what I'm getting at,' she said. 'Keith is behaving very strangely. The only explanation is that he knows about you and me.'

'There could be half a dozen explanations,' Toby told her, unwilling to believe he'd been found out by the caretaker. 'What are you going to do about it?'

He deliberately asked the question that way instead of 'what are *we* going to do' because of the way she'd made him anxious earlier on by putting it in terms of *when you had me, saw you on top of me* and the like.

'I'm going to lie back and enjoy it,' she said with a lazy grin. 'What else can I do? When Keith has made up *his* mind what to do, you can be sure we'll hear all about it.'

'What do you think he'd do – would he be violent?'

'I told you before, Keith is sly. You never know what's in his mind or what he'll do. After he did me on the table he started to say something about putting in for a wage increase. A really big one. But when I asked him what he meant, he shut up very fast.'

'What do you think he was getting at?'

'For a minute I wondered if he thought he could ask the college for money to keep him quiet about you. But that doesn't make sense because Miss Uppingham would be more likely to give him the sack than pay him more money. And get the Trustees to sack you too.'

Toby was thinking hard – which wasn't easy while Sally was holding his hard-on and stroking it. She wanted him to slip it into her – and he wanted to do it. But this Keith business, what could it be about? Only the Principal could give him a wage increase, and why should she? As for a really big increase, his chances were zero.

Enid Uppingham had the quaintly old-fashioned opinion that the honour of serving a top-class educational establishment like Lechlade Ladies' College was reward enough in itself – salaries were very unimportant. She thought it was vulgar, the idea of asking for more money. Keith had no chance at all of a big increase.

'Does it make any sense to you?' Sally asked, tugging at his length.

'None at all,' Toby told her.

But he wasn't telling the truth. What she had said suddenly did make sense to him in a stomach-churning way – the Peeping Tom caretaker had found some sort of hold over Enid Uppingham.

Toby was blushing furiously, his twanger jerking and jumping in Sally's hand. She slid down the bed and took it in her hot mouth and licked it. Toby's sudden flush was brought on not by what Sally was doing to him, but by guilt. He could think of an event involving himself which would give Keith all the hold over Enid he wanted – assuming he'd been there to witness it.

After Toby and Enid had discussed her health in her bedroom and he had carried out a so-called examination of her body, she agreed it would be sensible to follow a plan of exercise he would devise for her. Gentle exercise, nothing too energetic or stressful, Enid insisted. And he must be there all the time to advise and guide.

She was convinced it would detract from her dignity and authority if the girls saw her exercising, puffing and panting and sweating – so all the sessions were to take place when there was little or no chance of anyone seeing her.

Toby arranged a half-hour evening swimming session for her after the girls had left the pool. And a half-hour morning jog before he took the girls out. Two games of tennis a week, when the courts were deserted for the evening. Half an hour in the gym when it was empty – easy stretching and bending

154

exercises over a vaulting-horse.

Not the tall horse on which he'd ravaged Sharon Pomeroy – a lower one. Enid could lie over it on her plump belly and stretch out her arms and legs. The position gave superb views of her full-moon bum in her close-fitting shorts. So that she wouldn't become bored with a regular routine, Toby swapped the evening and morning sessions about at random.

Enid took to it with less complaining than he expected. But he knew that the only way of sustaining her interest over a longer time would be to introduce a sexual thrill. That was simple enough in the swimming pool. He wore the disgracefully revealing swimming trunks that were really no more than a tight-fitting posing pouch and brazenly revealed the shape and size of his *thing*. Enid wore a black one-piece bathing costume that clung very closely to her ample body.

The costume supported her heavy titties well and stopped them sagging. It did nothing to hide her bobbles, which showed through very clearly. It fitted closely round her thighs and between her legs in a way that made her chuffie appear very prominent.

Toby persuaded her to start with five lengths of the pool. She did this in a slow and stately breast-stroke. He swam alongside her, to monitor her progress, he said – in a graceful side-stroke. He reached out every few strokes to touch her and encourage her.

At first he touched her bare back above the costume. By the time she was on her third length of the empty pool, he was stroking her round bum as she kicked her legs open and closed.

To give her confidence and let her recover after her five lengths, he taught her to float on her back. He stood in the shallow end, between her parted thighs. His hands were under her bum to support her, as she lay on the water on her back – with her legs gripping round his waist. In that suggestive position, floating was very simple.

So was stroking the prominent mound of her chuffie. Enid seemed not to notice when his hands left her bum and surfaced over her belly before diving down between her thighs. Toby continued to stroke her until her sturdy legs clamped round him in tight spasms and she panted as the big thrill took her.

Could Keith Mason have been lurking near the pool, Toby wondered, and have seen Enid's swimming lesson? He didn't think so, because there were few places to hide nearby. Even if Keith had been there with his famous binoculars, Toby didn't think he'd have been able to see the discreet manipulation of Enid's chuffie inside her swimming costume.

But the jogging – that was another story. For her very first outing Enid had turned up in a brand-new white track-suit and trainers. Toby wasn't going to take her far the first time. They weren't going out through the gates and along the road away from town, the route he took with the girls. Enid's first jog was going to be once round the inside perimeter of the college grounds.

He trotted alongside her, fascinated by the way her big round titties bounced up and down in her track-suit. *They're like two lovely melons in a string bag*, he thought to himself. His twanger was stiff and upright in his tight jock-strap. He dropped back a pace or two behind her, saying by way of explanation that he wanted to check the co-ordination of her running movement.

In reality, what he wanted to check was the slow and rotatory up-and-down movement of the big round cheeks of her bum inside her track-suit. *Oh yes*, he thought, feeling the rub of his twanger against his belly, *big and round and soft – I want to squeeze my hard-on in between those cheeks of hers . . .*

Jogging always had this effect on him. His twice daily outings with the girls were occasions of both torment and delight. He trotted up beside Enid to tell her that her co-ordination was good and she smiled at him gratefully, though she was red-faced from effort already. They'd done about half the trip round the college grounds and were two or three hundred yards from the gatehouse and well away from the main buildings.

He watched the jump and sway of Enid's titties again and suppressed a moan as his twanger bounded inside his running shorts. He knew he'd have to take some decisive action soon or he'd shoot his wet little load in his underwear. Enid was starting to breathe harshly – she was hopelessly out of condition by Toby's standards. This gave him all the reason he needed to call for a pause in the run.

'We'll rest while you get your breath back,' he said. 'We mustn't exhaust you on your first time out.'

He directed her into a clump of beech trees that stood not far from the boundary wall. She sank gratefully to the grass, her back against a tree and her legs stretched out.

'No sign of cramp?' Toby asked, on his knees beside her. Without waiting for an answer from her, he untied the drawstring of her track-suit bottom and put both hands down inside to feel her thighs.

'Good, good,' he murmured, 'no cramp there.'

Enid stared at him with an amazed expression as his fingers moved up and down her thighs inside the track-suit bottom. In another moment he had a hand down the top of her knickers and was stroking her belly.

'No stitch?' he asked.

Enid was too dumbfounded to remember that the stitch usually made itself felt twelve inches higher and six inches to one side or the other. Toby's fingers found her chuffie and stroked the lips slowly.

'No discomfort here?' he asked her while his fingers slid inside and massaged her gently.

'You mustn't do this to me,' she gasped. 'You know what I think about men and their disgraceful ways – I refuse to let any man penetrate me.'

What she claimed was totally untrue, as they both knew. Toby's twanger had been inside her and he'd shot his sticky stuff into her chuffie – but Enid had an obsession about it and denied it even to herself.

'Your strength of mind does you credit,' Toby said, easing her track-suit bottom and her knickers down her legs. 'Now I want you to lie flat on the grass while I check your responses.'

His shorts were halfway down his thighs and his jockstrap with them – his hard-on stood free and throbbing. Enid lay on her back and parted her legs. He lay between them and guided his stiff length to her chuffie.

'You're not to try to take advantage of me,' she said. 'I forbid it.'

'Trust me,' he gasped.

He slid his hard-on into her. In spite of her protest seconds earlier, she lifted her loins up to receive it and he sank in all the way until his belly lay on hers.

'No,' she said. 'I must insist you stop what you are doing.'

'Lie still,' he said in a comforting tone of voice, 'this is a special technique to soothe muscles aching from exercise.'

He lay on her, letting her feel his weight on her belly, but not giving her the usual vigorous in-and-out pistoning. What she experienced was a succession of delicate throbs and tiny slithers, only a fraction of an inch at a time.

Without realising what she was doing, Enid soon responded to this subtle internal stimulation with little movements of her own that were not much more than tremors at first. By degrees her breathing became faster and more ragged, though she was striving to keep her emotions under control and slow down her reactions. But the sensations increased by themselves, as Toby's hard-on throbbed inside her wet chuffie.

'I really can't understand the point of this technique,' she sighed. 'My legs are still aching from jogging.'

'Not for much longer,' Toby murmured.

After another five minutes of lying on her back she told him that her legs had stopped aching and he could get off her.

'Not yet,' he told her soothingly. 'The benefit will extend to all your muscles if you are patient for a little while.'

He could feel her chuffie gripping him and massaging like a hand. Her pelvic muscles were certainly getting the benefit.

Another five minutes passed, and Enid was starting to gasp and jerk under him. 'I don't think I can hold out any longer,' she moaned, 'I think I'm going to have to give in.'

'Not yet,' Toby said in a shaky voice. 'Clench the muscles of your thighs and belly and hold on for five more minutes.'

He'd stopped moving altogether, but his massively stiff shaft jerked of its own accord inside her.

'Just a few more minutes,' he moaned. 'Not yet . . .'

'Can't help it,' Enid gasped, 'I'm coming!'

Deep tremors ran through her plump body and she sighed again and again as the big thrill took over. Toby felt the long slow contractions of her velvety chuffie round his hard-on and he too was over the edge.

'Oh, oh,' he sighed as he felt the surge of his cream. He tightened his muscles from thighs to shoulders and lay still on her hot and twitching body, while he shot into her in long slow spurts.

The trees that screened them were not far from the gatehouse. Suppose Keith Mason was out and about at that time of day and had seen Toby and the Principal jogging together. And seen them turn off into the trees to sit down. Wicked thoughts might have stirred in his brain – suppose he crept up on them unseen to watch them from some nearby hiding place?

He'd have seen everything – Toby taking the Principal's knickers off, stretching her out on her back on the grass, lying on top of her – the whole performance. If he'd been close enough, perhaps behind one of the trees, he might even have heard what they said to each other.

'Keith knows nothing, and I'm certain he suspects nothing,' Toby lied.

'That's all right, then,' Sally said, and she parted her legs a little wider.

Toby rolled on top of her, his twanger hard as iron and slippery-wet from Sally's mouth. His bare belly pressed down on hers and he pushed into her with one long, strong thrust – and outside, below the bedroom window, there was the crunch of tyres on gravel.

'Keith's back!' he cried in horror, jerking his shaft out of Sally and leaping off her naked body. 'You said he'd be gone for hours yet!'

'He must have driven like a madman to get there and back so soon,' she gasped as she slid off the bed. 'I've only got my dressing-gown here to put on – what am I going to do?'

Toby was scrambling into his trousers, cramming his hard-on in and not bothering with underwear.

'Nip into the bathroom,' he said. 'Sprinkle talc all over yourself and pretend you've just got out of the bath.'

She dashed naked out of his room as they heard the front door open and Keith's voice calling her name. Toby waited breathless as Keith came up the stairs, still calling 'Sally, where are you?' She answered him and he went into the bathroom. Toby finished dressing and moved along the hall silently. The bathroom door was closed but he could hear voices behind it.

He put his ear to the door – and what he heard was not words at all but Sally's voice shouting shrilly *oh oh oh oh . . .* and Keith's voice moaning *ah ah ah ah*. What was going on in there was obvious – Keith had jumped on Sally the moment he found her naked and was exercising his marital rights.

Toby wondered how he was doing her, in that confined space. Maybe he'd told her to bend over the wash-basin, while he rammed his hard-on into her from behind. Maybe he was sitting on the loo with the lid closed and Sally on his lap, impaled on his tool. Maybe he'd got her down on her hands and knees on the bath-mat and was poking it into her from the rear.

If there had been a keyhole in the door, Toby would have dropped to his knees to look through it. Spying was against all his principles – but less than five minutes ago he'd had his hard-on inside Sally, and had to whip it out without getting satisfaction. It was hot and hard inside his trousers. In the circumstances, he wanted to know how Keith was getting what he should have been having. But the bathroom door had a bolt and no lock.

Toby crept very quietly down the stairs and out of the house. He had a lot to think about – he was fairly sure that Keith had seen him on top of Enid, under the tree, and was going to put pressure on her for a big wage rise. He was also fairly sure Keith knew about him and Sally.

He must have seen the whole thing, Toby thought anxiously, he was at the top of the stairs and he saw me banging Sally halfway down – and if he saw me do Enid as well, he's really got the upper hand. But what can I do about it?

If the bathroom door had been equipped with a keyhole to look through, Toby would have seen something rather different from the scenes he'd imagined. Keith had not bent Sally double over the basin and he wasn't stabbing it into her with his jeans round his knees. He was on his back on the floor, with his flies ripped open, and Sally was sitting over him.

She was doing him – she'd spiked herself on him. Her chuffie was wet from Toby's attentions and she'd easily slid all the way down Keith's shaft to sit on his belly. He was reaching up to hold her small round titties, while she bounced on him with more raw energy than anyone would expect of her skinny body.

If Toby had stayed long enough with his ear pressed to the door, he'd have heard Sally's enthusiastic *oh oh oh oh* change into a panting gasp of *You're coming, Keith . . .* and he'd have heard Keith wail as he bucked underneath her and shot his load into her hot belly.

Chapter 10

With so many girls and teachers living in close proximity, as they did at Lechlade College, sharing their rooms and showers and other facilities, privacy hardly existed. Secrets were virtually impossible to keep. There were inquisitive eyes everywhere, and it was inevitable that activities not meant to be seen by others were observed and talked about.

Keith Mason was notorious for his spying on girls in the changing-rooms – but that was because he was a man and everyone knew what he had in mind: he wanted to fondle their titties and take their knickers down.

But many of the teachers regularly watched naked girls in the showers, and their thoughts were as lustful as Keith's. They too wanted to stroke young titties and slip a hand between girls' bare thighs. No one paid much attention to teachers watching the girls, and no one regarded what they did as notorious, simply because they were women.

Like Keith, Toby Dundale never missed a chance of eyeing girls' bodies in the swimming pool, the gymnasium, or anywhere around the college. Long smooth thighs and taut little bums fascinated him as much as they did Keith. But whereas Keith couldn't hope to do more than spy on girls and stroke his own hard-on, Toby was in a position to put his hot fantasies into action. It was a rare day when he didn't at least get his hand up a girl's running-shorts or inside a well-filled tee-shirt.

No one except the Principal regarded Toby's interest in girls as notorious, even though he was a man. It was part of his job as Sports Coach to keep watch on the physical well-being of all the girls in his care. It wasn't part of his job to feel their titties or stroke their kitties – that was a private perk and he was careful not to be caught doing such very unprofessional things. Or he tried to be careful; he wasn't always successful.

One particular advantage Toby had in his pursuit of sixteen- and seventeen-year-old girls was his qualification in physiotherapy – and a college tradition of massage for sporting aches and pains.

Toby wasn't actually allowed to massage the young ladies of the college – in fact, he was strictly forbidden by the Principal to do so, on threat of instant dismissal. When he was appointed Sports Coach, Enid was genuinely appalled by the thought of a man's hands on innocent young bodies. There was no telling what might happen, she said. Actually, Enid could visualise perfectly well what might happen, but she refused to put it into words, even in her mind.

Toby's predecessor at Lechlade was Miss Maureen Plessy, who had been called the Games Mistress. She too was a qualified physiotherapist and a very expert masseuse. She was also as completely fascinated by girls' bodies as Toby was – and every day of the week she had at least two girls flat on their back on the massage-table.

Maureen Plessy's skill and willingness to oblige made her very popular with the girls. They'd arrive at the treatment room complaining mildly about twisted knees or strained thighs. Maureen would nod and smile and ask them to strip naked and get on the table.

She had a marvellous touch. The girls loved it when her hands glided over their firm young titties, rolling them and cupping them until their pink bobbles stood up proudly. And when she massaged their flat little bellies in a slow and deliberate motion and ran her fingers through the thin curls where their slender thighs met.

The girl on the table when Maureen reached this stage would be in seventh heaven. Long sighs would greet her request to 'open your legs, please.' Then her skilled fingers probed between the parted thighs to stroke soft lips and press inside. 'Raise your knees now, dear,' the Games Mistress would say, and the girl on the table would bend her knees and pull her heels up to touch her bum.

164

By this point Maureen had the soft lips of the girl's kitty well opened and would slip a finger inside to diddle her little pink nubby. The girl would stare glassy-eyed at Maureen's face smiling down at her, and then moan and shake as she came.

There was great concern throughout the college when Maureen Plessy had to leave and a *man* was appointed in her place. Yet it emerged before the end of Toby's first term as the new Sports Coach that being forbidden to give massage was really an advantage in disguise. The treatment room was locked and the key was safe in the Principal's desk. But Toby had a key of his own, left behind by Maureen Plessy in her office.

The word spread round the college that the dishy-looking Sports Coach would massage girls he liked – in total secrecy – and he was even better at it than Miss Plessy had been. From then onward Toby had no lack of eager young ladies wanting him to treat their strained muscles – though it was obvious to him that the only muscles they were at any risk of straining were those around their over-exercised kitties.

A girl he was particularly fond of massaging was Hilary Landor, a tall fair-haired stunner. She was seventeen now and in her second year at the college, but in spite of all the times Toby had seen her, his twanger rose and stood hard in his underwear whenever he was near her.

In the swimming pool and on the tennis court and out jogging, Hilary wore the skimpiest possible kit she dared. This gave Toby plenty of scope to study her titties through her swimsuit or her leotard or the skin-tight tee-shirts she wore. His hard-on jumped and twitched in his jockstrap as he stared at her and panted to feel her titties and to lick them.

At the swimming pool his gaze was always drawn to the thin wet material covering the mound between Hilary's long thighs – even before he'd seen her naked on the massage table he was certain that the girlish curls down there must be as blonde as her hair. Just thinking about feeling her blonde-haired kitty would send his temperature soaring upward.

On the tennis court, when she flopped down exhausted

on a bench after a fierce game, her long legs sprawled out inelegantly, Toby could look up her very short skirt to her tiny white briefs. He imagined how it would be to tongue Hilary's kitty, to hold the lips open with trembling fingers and lick her until she shuddered and came.

He couldn't believe his fantastic luck when she turned out to be one of those who wanted regular massage. There she was one day on his table with her beautiful legs open — elegantly tall, slim-waisted Hilary Landor. Twice a week she'd lie naked on his table and smile at him while he played with her.

The day after Toby's anxieties started about Keith and what he knew happened to be one of Hilary's days in the treatment room — and there she was, languidly stretched out on her back, her naked body tanned from her holiday abroad. This was the holiday on the Algarve, where she had lured a Frenchman to diddle himself on a hotel balcony while she watched and grinned till he shot his sticky little lot — but Toby knew nothing of that.

Hilary liked Toby — there wasn't a girl in the college who didn't. She teased him while he was stroking her.

'I can see your *thing* standing up,' she said with a cheeky smile. 'As usual you've got a big bulge in your trousers. Does it ever go slack, or do you walk round like that all day?'

She was still on her back and he was stroking down from her pointed titties to her fair-haired kitty.

'It will never go down while you're here,' he said.

'That's because you want to put it in me and you can't,' she said. 'I won't let you.'

'You will one day,' he said with a long sigh as he stroked her kitty. 'You'll beg me one day to put it up you . . .'

'Dream on,' Hilary said. 'You're my sex-slave and I can make you do what I like.'

Toby found it very exciting to be teased by such a pretty naked girl. He liked to tease her too, when her legs were spread. He stroked her inside the wet lips of her kitty.

'I don't suppose you're a virgin now, Hilary, after the long holiday,' he said with a sly grin. 'I believed you last term, when you said you'd never let any boyfriend slip his hard-on into you. But after all those weeks of vacation, and lying half-naked on a beach abroad, it must have happened – you've been done, haven't you?'

'No, I haven't,' she said, opening her long legs wider as little throbs of pleasure shook her belly from his fingering. 'I'm still a virgin.'

'Maybe,' Toby said, watching the way her belly trembled.

'It's absolutely true,' she insisted. 'Surely you can tell from just looking at me that I've never had a man's *thing* inside me – if I had, I'd be stretched.'

'Maybe,' Toby said again, while his fingertip slid over her nubby and made her shake and gasp. 'But you're seventeen, Hilary, you're grown up now. Grown-up girls love the feel of a hard-on inside them.'

'Not me,' Hilary sighed, ripples of pleasure running through her. 'No boy is going to shoot his sticky *stuff* into me.'

'Maybe you don't want anything to do with *boys*,' Toby agreed, feeling his hot shaft throb in his trousers, 'but the day will come when you'll feel *my* cream shooting into your kitty.'

'Never, never, never, never,' Hilary moaned, and she came under his artful fingers. Toby moaned softly himself as he felt the way his twanger was jerking against his belly – he was practically on the verge of shooting his lot into his underwear.

Hilary was grinning at his predicament. She rolled onto her side and closed her legs.

'Get it out, slave,' she said.

Toby, red in the face, wrenched his zipper down and flipped his hard-on out of his see-through posing pouch.

'It's positively huge,' Hilary said. 'You must be crazy to think I'd ever let you force a thing that size into me – it would split me open all the way up to my titties.'

'It wouldn't,' he gasped. 'Kitties stretch easily – believe me, I know what I'm talking about.'

'You're not going to stretch me with it,' she assured him. 'In fact I'm surprised you can get it into Miss Pomeroy without damaging her.'

167

Toby groaned – nothing was secret at Lechlade. And the annoying part was that his friendship with the geography mistress was virtually over, thanks to Claudine Stanhope.

'Look – your *thing* is nodding its head,' Hilary told him with a grin. 'It agrees with me that it's far too big to get into my kitty. Stroke it, slave.'

'Oh, oh, oh . . .' Toby gasped. His twanger was straining up toward his chin and had thickened to an impressive size. He clasped his hand round it and beat up and down slowly.

Hilary wondered what he would say if she told him about the Frenchman on the balcony she'd teased into playing with his stiffie. But it might put Toby off, she thought, to discover he wasn't the only one she'd got into this state.

'Does Miss Pomeroy finger-wave you when you feel like it?' she asked in a cheerful tone. 'She's got nice hands and long fingers – I'm sure she's good at it.'

Toby's knees were wobbling under him as he flicked his hand up and down and stared at Hilary's bare, pointed titties.

'I'll show you a way of getting a very special thrill,' he said, and climbed up on the massage table with her.

'You're not going to put that gigantic *thing* in me,' she told him instantly.

'I won't do that,' he promised. 'Trust me.'

He balanced over her while he parted the soft lips of her kitty with his fingers and then, instead of pushing his hard-on into her, he laid it along the open cleft. He rubbed it slowly backwards and forwards, the head sliding over slippery pink flesh and over her exposed and firm little nubby.

'Isn't that nice?' he sighed, 'and I haven't even tried to put it in.'

'I want to see,' she gasped.

Toby raised his body on his elbows so that she could look down between them to where his shaft was sliding along her open chuffie.

'It's great,' she said, 'I like it – is there a name for this way?'

'I don't know,' he sighed. 'I call it "high-flying".'

'Slow and gentle,' she said. 'Make it last . . .'

Massaging her body had made Toby too excited to last

long. 'Going to do it now,' he gasped.

'Do what?' she sighed. 'What . . .? Tell me . . .'

He lifted himself quickly on his arms again and she stared wide-eyed down her own naked body at what he was doing to her. She squealed when she saw his cream shoot powerfully up over her bare belly.

'I didn't say you could do that!' she shrilled, but at that very moment her back arched off the table and she came with him.

Toby was very content with what he had achieved. He couldn't say that he'd actually *done* Hilary, the girl he most wanted, but he'd gone a long way toward it. After she'd put her clothes on and gone, he stayed alone in the treatment room, gloating a little.

He was sitting on the side of the massage table, dangling his legs and thinking about Hilary and how he could get her to go the rest of the way with him, when the door opened sharply and in strode Eleanor Redruth.

She stood glaring at him, her arms crossed over her titties. 'Out of consideration for the girl,' she began, 'I thought it best to wait until she'd gone before confronting you.'

Toby had forgotten that there were inquisitive eyes everywhere in the college and nothing stayed secret for long. Apparently Eleanor had seen him demonstrate his special technique to Hilary – or she had seen enough to guess the rest.

'What do you want, Eleanor?' he asked.

'I need hardly say that I am horrified by your blatant exploitation of a young girl for your satisfaction. Give me just one good reason why I shouldn't march straight into the Principal's office and tell her how you have debauched Hilary Landor – she'll be surprised to learn of the use to which you put the massage-room.'

Considering Eleanor's reputation as a chaser of girls, Toby regarded her reaction as the purest hypocrisy.

'You're being idiotic,' he said, grinning at her. 'I'll give you four good reasons why you'll do nothing of the sort.'

'What do you mean – *four*? What four reasons?'

'The four girls who took part in your midnight netball

match at the end of last term,' he told her.

'I don't know what you're talking about,' Eleanor said – but her face was crimson and she very obviously did know.

'Yes, you do, Eleanor,' Toby said, sounding very off-hand about it. 'On the last night of term you staged a naked netball match in the gym – my gymnasium. I was outside in the dark watching you – I saw you there with four girls leaping about naked.'

'Rumour,' Eleanor said uncomfortably. 'You're guessing – and you're certainly lying about being there.'

'Hilary was one of the four,' Toby said, grinning more than ever. 'The girl you accused *me* of debauching, whatever that means. I wonder how you describe what you were doing with her in the gym. Linda Knight was there too – the girl with the vivid ginger-haired kitty. And there were two girls from Sawby House playing against Linda and Hilary, Tessa Bowland and Rachel Fermor – the girl they call "Monkey".'

'I regard this as a brutal invasion of my privacy,' Eleanor said. She was even more red-faced now.

'Oh, I agree with you completely,' Toby said cheerfully, 'and it was a great thrill to spy on you secretly. I'd never seen four pretty girls playing netball naked before – all those lovely young titties bouncing about made my efforts well worth while.'

'You are an insensitive male swine,' Eleanor said coldly.

Toby thought she looked very attractive when she was furious. She was wearing a pastel blue jacket with a white silk blouse and a grey skirt. She'd uncrossed her arms and thrust her hands into the jacket pockets. Her titties pressed forward against her soft silk blouse – they weren't big, but they were well-shaped, Toby thought.

He stayed where he was, sitting on the massage table, his hands gripping the edge on either side of him, his legs swinging. When Eleanor stared angrily at his lap, he realised that he hadn't zipped up his flies after Hilary left. He glanced down and grinned at what was on show. His flies were gaping wide open, but his posing-pouch was back in place, covering his flopper.

However, the pouch was see-through, so Eleanor was

being treated to a view of something she had no time or use for. Perhaps that was why she was angry, he thought. She was an elegant woman, slim and long-legged, and he would very much like to get a hand up her skirt.

He'd been told by one girl – he didn't recall which one – that Miss Redruth never wore knickers. He'd like to find out for himself if that was true. And have a feel of the famous Redruth chuffie – but he guessed it was totally unlikely that he would ever be given the privilege. Being called an insensitive swine confirmed his doubt.

All the same, thinking about Eleanor's bare chuffie under her skirt had made his flopper start to grow longer and thicker – it would soon be a twanger, not a flopper. He reached down and pulled up his zip to protect Eleanor from a sight which might send her into a screaming rage.

'Rudeness is the wrong response,' he told her, unruffled. 'After the netball match was won by the Sawby House girls, you lay down on a mat with little Linda and put your face between her legs.'

'Who'd believe you?' Eleanor said, smiling thinly. 'The girls will deny it as strongly as I shall.'

'Deny what?' Toby said, raising an eyebrow in amusement. 'I wasn't thinking of running to the Principal to tell tales.'

She had the grace to blush at the implied rebuke.

'As a matter of fact,' Toby went on, 'when I saw you push your tongue into Linda's kitty, I decided that I wanted to do the same to her.'

'I see,' Eleanor said thoughtfully. She leaned against the massage table, more at ease now, her brain working fast.

'I was sorry I hadn't a long-lens camera with me,' Toby said. 'It was one of the most exciting things I've ever seen, Linda bucking her bare belly upward to your tonguing – you were gripping the cheeks of her bum to try to hold her still.'

Eleanor shrugged and then smiled suddenly.

'I apologise for my rudeness,' she said, 'but you had me rattled for a second. The position seems to be a stand-off, would you agree? I say nothing about you and you say nothing about me – right?'

'Oh, agreed,' Toby said, 'but there's more to it than that.'

'Such as?'

'Our interests are very similar, whether you admit it or not. We like pretty girls and we're in the right place to indulge our liking. So let's be friends and help each other.'

'I doubt if I need any help from you,' she said, but not in a hostile way – she was interested.

'Have dinner with me tonight,' he suggested. 'There's a lot to talk about – and this is not a good place for it. Someone will have seen you come into the treatment room – whatever anyone does around here, someone sees it. Tongues will wag – and not the way you like to wag *your* tongue.'

'Hah!' she snorted.

'I don't mind a bit if the rumour spreads that I've had you naked on the massage table and done you,' Toby told her. 'In fact, I'd be flattered. But it might not do your standing in the college much good.'

'Good god, you're right,' she said, making for the door.

'Dinner tonight at the bistro in town,' Toby said, 'a good meal, a bottle of wine and a long chat – what do you say?'

'I know you've got a reputation with the girls – from what I hear you only have to look at them and they take their knickers down,' she said, 'but if you think you can have your way with me for the price of a meal, you're sadly mistaken.'

'Never entered my head,' Toby told her untruthfully. 'Just dinner and chat. Trust me.'

The French-style restaurant in the town called itself Bistro Chic and served very acceptable food. Toby booked a table for seven-thirty and drove Eleanor there in his small sports car. According to him, the car was a classic, but most women thought it old and uncomfortable. They ate a very pleasant meal of consomme and duck *a l'orange*, followed by *pot au chocolat*, and they shared two bottles of claret.

The food served in the Lechlade dining-room was good but plain. An outing to the local French restaurant was a treat for teachers who were not put off by the high prices. By the time Toby and Eleanor reached the coffee and cognac, they were in a good mood and feeling quite friendly towards each other.

'Before we can be friends, we have to know we can trust each other,' Toby told her.

'What do you suggest?' Eleanor said curiously.

'You know about me and Hilary,' he said, 'I know about you and Linda. But that doesn't really count, because the information came to both of us by chance, so to speak. We both happened to see something we were not supposed to. There's no question of trust there. What I think we should consider is a gesture of good will on either side.'

'Like what?' Eleanor said with a trace of suspicion.

Toby smiled at her. If it had been anyone else with him, sipping fine brandy after dinner, he'd have had his hand on her thigh under the table. With Eleanor that would be asking for trouble – she'd react violently, he was sure of it. Maybe even smack his face and stride out. Which was a pity, because he had a big stand in his jockstrap and he wanted to find out if she was wearing knickers tonight.

'To show I trust you,' he said, 'I'll name another girl I've played with – one you don't know about. Then you tell me one you've had that I don't know about.'

She thought about it for a few moments, swishing the brandy round in her glass.

'Drink it,' Toby said, raising a finger at the waiter to bring them more.

'All right then, we'll have an act of good will,' Eleanor said. 'You go first, as you said. You tell me one of yours and I'll tell you one of mine.'

'Orline Ashby,' he said, 'halfway through last term. She was the first girl I played with in the treatment room.'

'How did you persuade her to let you?' Eleanor asked. She sounded interested.

'It was more a case of Orline persuading me,' he said. 'She claimed she'd pulled a muscle jogging. She knew that I wasn't allowed to treat her, but she kept on until I gave in.'

'Lucky you,' Eleanor said. 'I haven't diddled her myself yet but she looks a hot little number. I'll get round to her.'

'She sat on the edge of the massage table and she wasn't wearing a bra under her tee-shirt,' Toby went on, recalling the moment with pleasure. 'I could see the little bobbles of her titties pressed against the tee-shirt. She slipped her jogging trousers off – and she wasn't wearing knickers either.'

'And you realised you'd been set up,' Eleanor said.

Toby nodded and grinned.

'The way she was sitting on the table with her legs apart, and me on my knees to knead her calf muscle, her kitty was right in front of my face – her curls are almost blonde.'

'An obvious invitation to you,' Eleanor commented. 'How did you handle the situation – I suppose *handle* is the right word?'

'I fingered her till she came,' Toby said frankly. 'As you can imagine, I was in a high old state – I turned her over and laid her face-down on the table with her legs dangling down toward the floor.'

'You forced your *thing* into her?' Eleanor exclaimed. 'But that's terrible!'

'I did no such thing,' Toby corrected her. 'I stood between her legs, close up, while I gave her bare bum a good feel. I wanted to do her and I had my *thing*, as you call it, in my hand. I nearly slid it into her, I was rubbing it against the lips of her kitty – but at the last moment I stopped myself from pushing it in.'

Eleanor was smiling thinly to hear of his discomfort.

'Thank goodness I have no such problem,' she said. 'I can slip my tongue into a girl without hesitation. Did you get the gratification you were so desperate for?'

'Not as I really and truly wanted, but some satisfaction, yes,' he said happily. 'I gave myself what the girls call a finger-wave and spurted over her bare bottom.'

'I see we're being very forthright with each other,' said Eleanor. 'Not just the girls' names, but how and where.'

'How can we establish confidence in each other if we don't exchange full details?' he replied. 'Your turn now, Eleanor.'

'Vikki Herbert,' she said, 'one of the new girls. Wears her hair in a pony-tail. I'm sure you know her, because she's a first-rate athlete.'

Toby said he knew Vikki – but he certainly wasn't going to volunteer that he'd diddled her too.

'Actually, it was in your gymnasium,' Eleanor said. 'She was on her own, working on the big vaulting-horse – balanced on straight arms and swinging her body round, you know the exercise I mean.'

He nodded and listened in fascination.

'I saw her through the big window and fancied her – so I went in to try my luck,' Eleanor told him. 'She sat down on the vaulting-horse and rested while we chatted for a minute. She was wearing a tight-fitting leotard and her little chuffie was perfectly outlined by it. I simply couldn't resist – I reached out and stroked those long slim thighs of hers. And without a word she moved her legs apart to let me touch her.'

'What time of day was this?' Toby asked. 'The gym's a very public place with all those big windows around.'

'Sometime after six one evening. There was nobody about.'

'The next time I use that vaulting-horse I shall think of you giving Vikki a thrill while she was sitting on it.'

'Why not? Give yourself a thrill,' Eleanor said. 'I stood between her legs with an arm round her waist and she put her hands on my shoulders. While I was diddling her she said it was good for muscle tone, whatever that means.'

Toby had to grin. He well remembered Vikki saying that her former coach, Mr Jarvis, had told her that being tongued was good for her and proved it by doing it to her two or three times a day.

'After you'd improved her muscle tone, did she attend to yours?' he enquired.

'Naturally. I pulled her off the vaulting-horse and down on her knees in front of me. I dropped my skirt and she slipped my knickers down far enough to use her tongue on me.'

'I've seen you without your knickers,' Toby reminded her with a grin, 'when you played with Linda after the midnight netball match. You have a neatly trimmed little triangle of dark-brunette curls – I thought it was very fetching.'

Eleanor didn't quite blush, though obviously the idea that a *male* had seen her chuffie was something of a shock. But she rallied.

'If it comes to that,' she said, 'don't forget I saw your *thing* when you were taking advantage of Hilary Landor. That makes us even.'

'Taking advantage,' Toby said with a chuckle. 'Lovely phrase, that.'

'So there we are,' Eleanor said, 'I've made my gesture of confidence by telling you about letting Vikki Herbert tongue me in the gym. Does that make us friends?'

'You stood with your legs apart and your knickers round your knees while she licked your nubby – did she make you come?' Toby asked.

'Oh, yes,' Eleanor sighed. 'She certainly did.'

'We *are* friends,' he assured her. 'We can be completely honest with each other. I bet we've both had Marjorie Newmill.'

'I have,' Eleanor said, 'and it doesn't surprise me to hear you have. She's got itchy knickers, that one. Where did you diddle her – in the treatment room?'

'No, out jogging one evening last week.'

'In the open air? What about the other girls? You usually have at least a dozen going out for a run with you – how did you manage it?'

'Easy enough,' he told her. 'Her lace was undone, I stopped her to tie it and sent the rest of them running on down the lane. I took Marjorie behind a tree and felt her titties – she has a nice plump pair.'

'I know,' Eleanor said dreamily, 'I've played with them.'

'She had her back to the tree trunk,' Toby said. 'She opened my shorts and pulled my shaft out. I pushed it up the leg of her shorts and inside the little briefs she was wearing under the shorts.'

'You put it in her?' Eleanor asked, not approving at all.

'No, too dangerous,' he assured her. 'I stood up close, so it was held tight to her belly by her underwear. I held her hips and rubbed it against her belly – she has a lovely warm belly, as I'm sure you know.'

'Oh, yes,' Eleanor said with a smile of happy reminiscence, 'warm and chubby – I've kissed Marjorie's belly many a time.'

'She liked what I was doing,' Toby went on. 'She pushed

her belly at me while I was rubbing against it. It didn't take long – I came inside her briefs and it felt marvellous – a real knee-trembler.'

'You beast,' Eleanor said, but she was grinning at him in understanding.

'When did you have her?' he asked.

'To tell you the truth, Toby, I've had Marjorie so many times that I can't remember the first time.'

He was pleased that she was using his first name easily – he took it to be a sign of her increasing acceptance of him as a near-equal. As a mere male he'd never qualify for real equality at Lechlade, with either the teaching staff or the students, he understood that well enough. But at least he was making some progress with Eleanor Redruth.

'I can tell you the most recent time I played with her,' Eleanor went on. 'It was a few days ago – one afternoon last week, in fact. Maybe it was the same day you interfered with her. Imagine – maybe I tongued her at four o'clock and you rubbed off on her belly at six o'clock!'

'Oh, yes,' Toby said softly, his hard-on jerking inside his trousers. 'It's like sharing her. I tell you what, Eleanor, we can prove what good friends we are by arranging to do the same girl on the same day, in our different ways. What do you say – shall we do it tomorrow?'

Eleanor had a strange expression in her eyes.

'You're a hopeless lecher, Toby Dundale,' she said, 'and it's a curiously exciting idea. Let's try for tomorrow, by all means. Is there any particular girl you fancy, or will you leave the choice to me?'

'It had better be someone we've both had already,' he said, 'so that there's no problem of persuasion.'

They were still discussing which of the many possible girls to choose when they left the restaurant. A mile out of town, on the long and empty lane that led to the college, Toby pulled off the road, stopping on the grass verge under the overhanging trees.

'We have to decide before we get there,' he said. 'I can't invite you into the gatehouse for a chat and you can't ask me to your rooms for a cup of coffee. We'd be seen, and that would really set tongues wagging.'

The car top was up. With engine and lights off, they were in the dark, sitting close together because of the car's small size.

'Just as long as you understand we've parked here to talk,' Eleanor said. 'I don't want you to get peculiar ideas about getting your hand up my skirt.'

'Understood,' Toby said at once, though his twanger was hard against his belly – and slipping his hand up her skirt was exactly what he had in mind, to find out whether she was wearing knickers tonight.

'How about Rachel Fermor for tomorrow's lark?' she asked. 'You know I've played with her – you've guessed that much from the fact that she was in the naked netball game that I organised last term.'

'Sexy black-haired "Monkey" – is she a regular playmate of yours, or was that a casual one-off?' Toby enquired.

'I like her – I invite her to my rooms pretty often. I made a good start this term by diddling her on the first day we were back.'

'Congratulations,' Toby said, 'I wish I had.'

He wasn't going to tell Eleanor, but on the first day of term he'd been with Sally Mason all afternoon. The girls were too busy settling in with their new roommates and checking the new timetable to want to swim or play tennis. Keith was kept busy with luggage and making sure that all the services were working properly. Sally and Toby had hours to do whatever they liked.

The first time was in his bedroom, after lunch. Both of them naked and Toby flat on his back on the bed, with Sally on top of him. Her chuffie was so wet and slippery that he went all the way in on her first down-stroke. He reached for her thin shoulders and pulled her down until he could get his mouth to a tittie and suck it hard while she rammed at him hard and fast.

'Not so fast,' he gasped, 'I'm nearly coming . . .'

She grinned and said, 'I want you to' – and thumped away at him until he shot his cream into her. That was only the first time. Fifteen minutes later it was Sally flat on her back with her knees up and Toby rattling away at her like a train going downhill.

Thinking about doing Sally reminded Toby of the problem with Keith – did he suspect that the Sports Coach was slipping it up his wife most days? And had he spotted Toby on top of the Principal on the grass? And what was he planning to do? It was very worrying.

'I had her on my sofa,' Eleanor said. Toby was puzzled for a second – he found it hard to imagine Eleanor fingering Sally. Then he remembered that she was talking about Rachel Fermor.

'She was wearing a regulation white blouse with a mini-skirt,' Eleanor said. 'She has nice thighs, as I'm sure you've noticed. I soon had her blouse open and her bra undone, so I could give her bare titties a good long feel. She wanted me to diddle her right away, but I made her wait before I put my hand up her skirt and fingered her.'

'Oh,' Toby sighed, visualising the scene. In the close darkness of the car he was pressing his hand over his flies to hold his jumping hard-on still. He was afraid that if he didn't, he'd shoot his lot in his trousers.

'Later on I took her into my bedroom and stripped her naked,' Eleanor said dreamily. 'She lay on the bed with her legs apart while I gave her a good tonguing – and I became so excited that I completely lost control of myself.'

'I find it very difficult to imagine you frantic with lust, Eleanor,' Toby murmured.

'I know,' she said softly, 'I pride myself on staying in control. But it was absolutely marvellous being so desperate for once. I ripped my skirt off and flung myself on top of Rachel as if I had a *thing* and was going to do her with it.'

'Oh,' Toby moaned, certain he was going to come in a second.

'I wrapped my legs round her,' said Eleanor, reliving the moment in her thoughts. 'I rubbed my kitty against hers through my tights. I was so far gone I came straight away.'

'She has the same effect on me,' Toby sighed. 'I was fingering her once in the tennis pavilion – she was leaning against the wall. I had my hand down the front of her shorts and two fingers in her wet little chuffie. She put her arms round my neck and pressed her cheek against mine and she came – you won't believe it, but that set me off too and I came in my shorts.'

'That settles it,' Eleanor said with a low chuckle. 'We'll do "Monkey" tomorrow, both of us.'

'You rubbed your chuffie on hers through your tights,' Toby said, 'Does that mean you weren't wearing knickers?'

'I often go without,' she informed him.

'How about tonight?' he asked. 'Are you wearing any now?'

'Wouldn't you like to know!' she said with a chuckle.

'Yes, I would,' he said with a sigh, 'and it wouldn't hurt you to tell me – we're friends, aren't we?'

She half-turned toward him on the bucket seat and, as far as he could tell in the darkness, moved her knees apart inside her skirt.

'See for yourself,' she said.

Toby could hardly believe his luck. He slipped his hand under her skirt and up between her thighs. She was wearing stockings, not tights; he laid his hand on warm bare flesh above her stocking-top. When he felt further upward, his fingertips touched thin smooth material between her legs – she *was* wearing knickers for her outing with him.

'Ah, ah, yes,' he murmured, stroking her chuffie through the material. His shaft leaped dangerously against his hot belly and he knew he was going to come.

'Satisfied now?' Eleanor asked. She pressed her legs together to stop him getting his fingers under the edge of her knickers, and then took his wrist to pull his hand away.

'Oh, oh, oh,' he gasped. His hard-on was straining upright and it seemed to have grown to a magnificent size. This was it, the magical moment – it was going to happen now.

'What's the matter?' Eleanor asked, puzzled by his gasping.

He pressed her hand over the bulge in his trousers at the very moment that his shaft bounded and shot its creamy splurge up his belly.

'Good heavens!' she exclaimed. 'You're actually coming!'

She rubbed her hand quickly and lightly over his flies, over his distended shaft, while his cream spurted furiously.

Chapter 11

The summer was hanging on well into September. The Principal was in her private garden, enjoying the sunshine, when Keith went to confront her. Enid was taking Toby's keep-fit advice seriously, swimming and jogging twice a week. And she was sun-bathing at every opportunity.

Each of these half-hour sessions of exercise ended with Toby giving her aching legs and back a firm massage. She sat upright while he did her legs and chatted to him, watching his skilful hands manipulating her calves and easing her knees.

He had long strong fingers and blond hair on the backs of his hands. Enid would rather die than admit it, but she found his hands very exciting to look at. Especially when they were touching some part of her body, as when he loosened the knotted muscles of her calves.

And even more so when his fingers were digging into the muscles of her thighs, working their way upward. She wanted to feel those fingers probing her groins . . . wanted to feel the blond hairs on his hands brushing the lips of her chuffie.

To massage her back properly Toby had to take off her bra and bare her swollen titties. A little later in the proceedings, when her bobbles were as firm as red berries, he would find it necessary to slip his hand inside her knickers. Although it was her back he claimed to be treating, he needed to rub her belly too.

She adored having her belly stroked by him. Not for sexual reasons, of course, that had nothing to do with it. Complete body massage required her belly to be rubbed. And when his hands slowly slipped down beneath her deep-set belly-button towards her thick patch of curls, that was all part of the treatment.

181

Enid pretended that it was only treatment for 'stress relief' even when Toby's fingers pressed into her plump chuffie to tickle her nubby. When he pushed her thighs apart and lay on her belly to slip his twanger into her, she preserved an outward appearance of calm – almost to the very moment when she dissolved in waves of pulsing sensation.

In addition to this regular exercise, sunshine on the skin was good for her, Toby said. It created vitamin something-or-other in the system, and various beneficial substances. It eliminated the risk of deficiency problems, he said, and he urged her to expose her body to the sun as often as the weather allowed. So far this September that had been quite often.

Enid had persuaded herself that she felt tremendously fit as a result of regular exercise and sunshine – although she was slightly alarmed to find that her natural urges had grown stronger. She deplored these urges in women, because she was convinced that they caused weaker-willed women to submit their bodies to men. It was a sign of weakness for a woman to let a man put his stiff *thing* inside her.

As for the natural urges of men, Enid was so far out of sympathy with them that she considered them to be almost *un*natural. In her opinion, to force a hard shaft of flesh into a woman's tender body was beastly. And it was the root cause of most of the world's troubles.

Being a strong-minded and independent woman, she knew she was above surrendering her body to a *man*. Her own natural urges were a nuisance, no more than that. Toby assured her there was nothing to worry about, even if her urges were stronger than before, since regular stress relief would keep them under control.

For most of her life until now, Enid's way of dealing with her urges had been to spread her thighs in bed at night, lying on her back in the dark with her nightie up round her waist. She would hold the lips of her chuffie open and diddle herself with a sure touch. And before long she would be moaning and shaking as the big thrill hit her.

The relief that Toby was providing as part of her exercise routine had nothing to do with her own fingers and everything to do with his *thing*. Contrary to all her settled beliefs, she was letting him handle her body and take liberties with it. More than that, she was allowing him to slide his long hard shaft into her and bring on that tremendous thrill.

And when she reflected on the situation, she had to confess to herself that she greatly enjoyed these 'stress relief' sessions that followed her swimming and jogging. She convinced herself that lying on her back with her legs open was part of a well-balanced keep-fit programme.

When Keith tapped at Enid's sitting-room door and got no answer, he let himself in. The room was unoccupied, but the French doors to the garden stood open and he could see her sitting out on the lawn in a deck-chair. She was wearing sun-glasses and had a book in her hands.

Keith was in a bold mood. He knew he'd got a hold over the Principal and he meant to make the most of it – he wanted a big pay increase. He went out into the well-kept high-walled garden and walked round the deck-chair until he stood directly in front of Enid. He thought that this gave him an advantage, he on his feet and she almost lying on her back in the striped deck-chair.

For the past three days, since new girl Caroline Wilton had taken her revenge on him, Keith had been a walking time-bomb. She had persuaded half a dozen other girls, including black-haired Rachel Fermor, to help her get her own back on Keith for spying on her through her window when she was undressing.

They'd waited for him down in the boiler-room just after lunch. They'd taken the electric light bulbs out and it was easy to hide in the dark. Keith came down the steps thinking both bulbs had gone at the same time and needed to be replaced. When he reached the bottom step the door was banged shut above him and he heard a rush of feet, then unseen hands gripped him from all sides.

It was hot down there near the boilers and there was a scent that made Keith's flopper immediately stand up hard – warm young female bodies. He knew what was going on – like last term, a bunch of girls had grabbed him and they were going to tie him up and expose his dick. He didn't struggle when he was dragged to the wall and his arms forced out sideways.

The lashings had been put there earlier. His wrists were tied to pipes running along the wall, his legs were pulled open and his ankles tied to lower pipes. A scarf was wound round his head to blindfold him before a light bulb was replaced and switched on. Keith knew he was on display, crucified against the wall, unable to move or break free.

'Gag him,' a girl's voice said.

Keith didn't recognise the voice. He guessed there were five or six girls staring at him. Maybe seven. Could there be ten of them? Or perhaps a dozen seventeen-year-old girls holding him captive so they could make him do anything they wanted. He began moaning in mindless pleasure.

'This will keep him quiet,' another voice said, and something soft was stuffed into his mouth to silence his moans.

He knew what it was – one of the girls had taken her knickers off. His hard-on bounded inside his white boiler-suit. Thin smooth knickers, warm from her sweet young kitty – he gulped and shook in his bonds, feeling that having them in his mouth was like tonguing her . . . whoever she was.

He made muffled mewing noises – in his mind he was pushing his tongue into a pretty teenage girl, who was holding her skirt up round her waist for him. He was sure he'd come in his boxer shorts in a minute.

'Get his *thing* out,' a voice said.

Fingers plucked at his flies. His twanger was dragged out and left sticking up boldly, while the ambushers studied it.

'Look how it's jumping,' someone said.

'Let's see what it can do,' another suggested. A hand took hold of his hard-on and began to diddle him firmly.

'Your number's up, Keith,' a girl told him cheerfully. 'You're going to suffer for your depraved ways. No more spying to get a look at our kitties – the best you can hope for after this is sitting down here in the boiler-room to give yourself a finger-wave.'

It was Caroline who was taunting him – and every word

she spoke made him more excited, as she intended.

Keith was past sensible thought. It would be the most wonderful moment of his life if he could get his hard-on into the warm kitty of the girl handling his twanger, or the one talking to him. He struggled to get a hand free, to reach out and feel a kitty, any kitty, but the bonds were too strong to break.

'See how big it's got,' the girl diddling him said.

He ground his teeth on the wadded knickers in his mouth. *I'm going to come*, he thought, *any second now and they'll see me shooting my lot* . . .

He felt a surge inside his belly and up through his throbbing hard-on. He shot his cream, shuddering and straining in his bonds. He could hear the young ladies giggling as they saw what they'd done to him.

Caroline hadn't finished with him – she needed more than a forced diddle to satisfy her thirst for revenge. Keith was left tied to the wall with a little pool of his cream at his feet, his boiler-suit gaping wide open and his flopper dangling out on show.

Word of his plight was spread round the college, and all through the afternoon girls came down the steps into the boiler-room to look at him and laugh. They came in twos and threes and some did more than stare and laugh, they touched his flopper and tugged at it. When it stood up, some of them went further and diddled him again.

By five o'clock every girl in the college had been to look at Keith's *thing*. More than half of them had touched it. An experience like that changes a man – having his twanger felt by a hundred young girls in an afternoon. When Keith got over the exhaustion of it he couldn't blank the thought of sex out of his head, day or night.

In the walled garden, he stood over the Principal and saw that she was wearing a swimsuit. He'd never seen her in anything but formal day wear before, and the sight made his eyes open wide.

It was a black one-piece that fitted close to Enid's ample body. It made her heavy titties look even larger, and it let their big bobbles show. As a general rule Keith was excited most by young girls' little pointed titties, but he couldn't stop staring at Enid's impressive pair.

Like a certain waiter, long ago by a hotel swimming pool while Enid was attending a teaching conference in Bognor Regis, Keith felt his dangler grow long and hard. This worried him, because he'd changed out of his work overalls for the confrontation with the Principal and was wearing tight jeans and a green polo shirt. Any bulge in his jeans would be very visible.

For sun-bathing, Enid had slipped the straps of her swimsuit off her shoulders. The costume had slipped down without her noticing it, so far down that her plump titties were hardly covered at all.

Keith gaped silently and stared at her fleshy melons. *What a fantastic pair*, he was thinking, *she's got the biggest bouncers in the college*.

By the time he was able to drop his gaze and look lower, his twanger was standing up very stiffly in his faded jeans. Memories of being tied up in the boiler-room with his dick sticking out ran through his mind.

Enid's swimsuit fitted so closely between her solid thighs that her chuffie looked very prominent. Keith stared at the chubby mound and had difficulty in breathing properly. He guessed she had a mat of dark curls there, maybe as glossy black as the hair on her head.

She was half-lying on the deck-chair, her legs stretched out and her bare feet apart. She'd been alone and relaxing, not expecting that she'd be interrupted – least of all by a man whose mind was raging with lustful thoughts. And because Keith was in this high old state, it seemed to him as if Enid's body was on offer to him – as if lying there half-naked she was silently pleading *do me, do me*!

She glanced up from her book at Keith through her stylish sunglasses. His mouth was hanging open and he had a foolish look on his face – it was easy to guess what was going through his mind. With a slight frown she pressed her thighs together modestly, but she stayed in her almost-lying-down position on the deck-chair.

'Well, Keith,' she said, 'what do you want?'

Using his first name was not a sign of friendship. To Enid he was not an equal, he was a college servant, on the same level as the kitchen staff and cleaners. He addressed her as Miss Uppingham and she addressed him as Keith, to reinforce the distance between them.

What did he want indeed, standing there with his hard-on bulging under his close-fitting jeans! What he wanted was to flip Enid's large soft titties out of the top of her swimsuit and weigh them on his hands and bounce them up and down. And run his fingertips over their bobbles till they were hard as acorns. And then lick them.

The thought of sucking her big solid titties was distracting and he tried to push it out of his mind. But there they were under his nose, two fleshy temptations – and short of closing his eyes, how could he be expected to think about anything else but those spectacular titties?

'If you've got a minute, Miss Uppingham,' he stammered, 'I'd like to talk to you.'

Under her direct stare his boldness evaporated and he had to force himself to stand his ground and present his ultimatum.

'Must it be now?' she asked, putting him in his place. 'I was in my office all morning. And you will find me at my desk tomorrow morning, between nine and twelve, if you have anything of importance to raise.'

In his feverish state of mind, Keith wondered if her words meant more than they seemed to. She'd said *raise* – had she already guessed that he was here to ask her to raise his wages? He didn't think so – it was more likely that she'd spotted the raise in his jeans.

If that's what she meant, his stand, maybe she was giving him a hint that she wouldn't say no. He couldn't stop his thoughts running away with him. He visualised himself sliding his hand down the front of her swimsuit, down over her domed belly, down between her thighs, to get a handful of warm and hairy chuffie.

'I'm sorry to interrupt your afternoon off,' he mumbled, 'but it won't take a minute.'

'Very well,' she said, closing her book, 'I'm all yours.'

Keith gulped. There it was again – that way of saying things so they could be taken to mean something different.

If she was all his, in the way he really wanted, he'd make a start by lifting her massive titties out of her swimsuit and pressing his hard-on between them. He'd squeeze all that soft flesh round his shaft while he slid it up and down her chest. He'd shoot his lot and it would gush right up to her chin . . .

But she didn't really mean it that way. She wasn't his to do whatever he liked with – the indifferent look on her face made that clear to him.

'It's about one of the teachers,' Keith said, not very sure how he was going to explain his grievance.

'Which one?' Enid asked. 'I fail to see what you have to do with the academic staff.'

The question was what a certain member of the academic staff had to do with Keith – or more exactly, with his blonde wife Sally. Now he had his chance to speak, Keith didn't think he could say it straight out – it sounded so feeble to say, 'Your teacher's doing my wife rotten.'

'Mr Dundale,' he said, 'the Sports Coach.'

'Ah,' Enid said thoughtfully.

She wondered what was coming next and she couldn't help being slightly apprehensive. Toby had given her a very thorough physical relief session after her swim earlier that day. She wanted those sessions to continue, because they were so good for her health. There was a time when her main ambition was to get Toby Dundale sacked from the college staff, but not any more. Now she would do almost anything to make sure he stayed.

On the other hand, as an intelligent person, Enid suspected Toby was taking advantage of the girls. He wasn't allowed to massage them, it would be scandalous for a man to lay his lustful hands on near-naked girls on the table. But he put his hands on them when he was teaching them to dive in the swimming-pool. Enid had seen for herself how he held them by the waist to position them.

However good-looking he was, however amiable he was,

he was still a *man* – and all men were beasts, which meant that Toby was a beast and not to be trusted near young girls. Though Enid had never caught him at it, she didn't doubt for a minute that when he touched girls during swimming lessons his hand slid secretly down over their pretty bums.

On the tennis courts, she'd seen him stand very close behind a girl to demonstrate the back-hand smash. She was certain that he pressed himself close to the girl when he put his arms round her and held her arms to guide her swing. His *thing* would be against the girl's bum . . .

A man's hands on these charming young girls – the idea made Enid blush with a mixture of anger and envy and outrage. Some nights she dreamed about Toby naked under a hot shower with Hilary Landor or Rachel Fermor – feeling their wet titties while his long stiff male *thing* stuck out in front of him.

So far she hadn't dreamed of herself being tampered with by him under a shower. It was in her mind to suggest to Toby that after her next jog with him, he should strip and join her under the spray, to teach her his technique of body-washing – she felt sure he must have a special way of showering.

She was dragged out of her reverie about Toby standing naked in a shower with his *thing* sticking out by Keith's complaining.

'It's not right,' Keith said, and he sounded aggrieved, 'I shouldn't have to put up with it, not somebody in my position of responsibility. I mean, nobody else would wear it. But I'm a loyal employee, I am, and I don't want to cause trouble for the college, not if things can be sorted out right.'

Enid still had no clear idea what he was on about, but anything to do with Toby Dundale was suggestive. She thought she detected a sort of threat in Keith's words. It was sensible to confirm that he was a loyal and valued college servant.

'You have always given satisfaction,' she said cautiously.

The word *satisfaction* had only one meaning for Keith. *Satisfaction* was when you put your twanger up a warm wet chuffie and banged away until the big moment happened.

189

Like when he came back from Gloucester and found Sally just out of the bath, stark naked and dusting her titties with scented talc. He walked into the bathroom and she didn't even say hello to him – she just grinned and ripped his flies open. Out flopped his diddler, long and soft and pale-skinned. Sally grabbed it and pushed him down on the bathroom floor.

She was over him in a flash, her legs straddling him. Her fist jerked up and down till she'd given him a hard-on – then she had it up her in one push. He grabbed hold of her titties and she bounced up and down like a bronco buster, till he shot his lot into her belly.

Three minutes from start to finish – from walking into the bathroom to shooting his cream. A lovely fast rattle – that's what Keith meant by *satisfaction*. He doubted whether that's what Miss Uppingham meant by the word. She must be nearly forty – and she was still a Miss.!

He wondered if she'd ever known the feel of a hard-on up her. Most likely she touched up girls and got them to diddle her, as most of the teachers did. To be fair though, Keith had never caught Enid at it, or seen any evidence.

On second thoughts, was it possible that she did mean the same as he did when she said *satisfaction*? Was she dropping him a hint?

'Well, Keith,' she said, 'why are you upset about Mr Dundale?'

'It's about him and my wife Sally,' Keith muttered. He was very nearly drooling as he stood staring down at Enid's big round titties. 'It's not right, you know, him and her.'

Enid sat up quickly and put her knees together. Keith hadn't stated his grievance clearly, but there was no mistaking what he was getting at. Toby was *doing* his blonde whippet of a wife, that was the gist of the accusation. But Enid was not going to let Keith off the hook with vague statements that could be ambiguous.

'Oh,' she said, '"him and her"? I think you'd better explain what you mean more clearly.'

Keith summoned up his courage and spoke the fateful words.

'He's doing her senseless – and she's letting him.'

'I take that to mean you believe they have formed a sexual liaison,' Enid said thoughtfully.

Keith nodded, red-faced. Now he'd said it out loud, he didn't want to repeat it to her.

'How do you know?' Enid asked him. 'Have you seen them together in an improper act? Has Mrs Mason admitted misconduct with the Sports Coach? What is your evidence for this alarming assertion?'

'Don't have to see him doing it to her,' Keith said, and he sounded surly now. 'I can tell.'

Enid pushed her dark glasses up her forehead and stared closely at him. Her mind was very active and fully focused now on Keith's accusations.

'You're making a serious allegation,' she said, 'and all you can offer to substantiate it is the vague statement that *you can tell*. That's not good enough. If you haven't seen them do anything, then probably there's nothing to see. Have you been told anything by a third party?'

'The only third party is me,' he mumbled. 'I've not been told anything direct, as you might say. But everybody in the college knows the Sports Coach can't keep his hands off the women teachers and the girls.'

'"Everybody" knows no such thing,' Enid informed him. 'I for one do not know of any inappropriate conduct on his part.'

She wasn't speaking the truth. With her own eyes she'd seen Toby with Sharon Pomeroy, rearing over her naked body as she sat on the edge of her bed. And seen Sharon reaching for his big hard-on and guiding it up into her. She'd seen Sharon convulse and come – and Toby pull his wet *thing* out and spurt his cream up her bare belly as high as her titties.

Keith wasn't going to be put off.

'He lives in the gatehouse with us,' he said. 'It stands to reason he's having his way with Sally. She thinks he's Mr Wonderful, she'd drop her knickers for him any time he asked.'

'This really will not do,' Enid told him firmly. 'Wild accusations will only get you into trouble.'

191

Mention of the gatehouse had put an anxious thought into her mind. It was in the grove of trees not far from the gatehouse that Toby usually gave her 'stress relief' when they went jogging together. Only the evening before, she'd stood behind a tree-trunk with her baggy grey track-suit pants round her knees. Normally Toby had her on her back, but the grass was still damp from a passing light shower.

'Bend over and touch your toes,' he'd murmured, 'let's see how agile you are, Enid. Hold your ankles.'

'I'm a lot more agile now than before you took me in hand,' she said seriously. 'Are we going to play leap-frog?'

'Not exactly,' he said. 'This is a different game.'

He untied the draw-string of her track-suit pants and stood behind her to pull them down over her bum, then the white briefs she was wearing underneath. She bent her knees to grip her ankles – but even then she could only reach down just below her knees.

The posture pushed her bare fleshy bum at him.

'Time I took you in hand,' he said, grinning as he repeated her words.

Her black-haired kitty was exposed between her thighs to his roving fingers. He pulled his hard-on out of his running-shorts and pressed it upright in the crease between Enid's round and moon-like cheeks.

'This is a most demanding posture to hold for long,' she gasped from her bent-over position. 'It makes me more out of breath than I was from the actual jogging.'

'Really?' Toby murmured. 'Breathe slowly, very slowly.'

His busy fingers were sending thrills through her body. This was the part of the exercise routine she liked the most. When her kitty was wet and ready – which took only a few seconds – he used both hands to hold her by the hips and steady her against the press and rub of his shaft.

Enid was excited, he could feel her body shaking in his grip. For him it had become almost a sort of daily chore, giving her a good *doing*. It didn't compare with playing with any of the girls, say Hilary or Vikki, but it kept the Principal happy and it made sure he held on to his job.

'It's always better to relieve the tension as it builds up,' he said. 'Deal with it as we go along – not let it increase uncomfortably.'

'Oh, yes,' Enid agreed in a strained voice as she felt his long thick *thing* slide into her wet chuffie. 'Oh, yes – you're so right about that, Toby . . .'

His grip on her hips tightened and he rammed in and out strongly. Enid braced herself with stiff arms, hands on her knees – any breathlessness she was now experiencing had nothing to do with jogging. Her legs began to tremble; she locked her knees to stop herself falling to the grass.

'Now!' Toby exclaimed. 'Yes, yes, yes – go for it!'

Enid gave a long wailing moan as she came enthusiastically.

That session with Toby had seemed very satisfactory at the time, but now, with the College caretaker looming over her and uttering vague threats, there was a panicky question in her mind – *had Keith been anywhere near the clump of trees and seen her bending over bare-bummed while she was being treated by Toby for stress and tension?*

'Have you spoken to your wife about your suspicions?' she asked Keith. 'That would seem the first logical thing to do.'

When he didn't answer, she realised that he wasn't listening. He was staring down at her titties, and the lump in his jeans seemed impossibly big. *Good heavens, he looks as if he's going to fling himself on me and ravish my body,* Enid thought, *just look at the shocking size of that thing in his jeans – the man's a raving sex maniac.*

Enid had never used female wiles on a man in her life – she considered ruses of that kind as totally unworthy of an intelligent and educated woman. But perhaps there were exceptional circumstances that justified the use of a feminine stratagem. By instinct she knew just what to do.

From sitting upright, she settled back again in the deck-chair to a semi-lying position, with her bare legs stretched out straight and her knees apart. During this innocent manoeuvre, the top of her swimsuit somehow slipped down. Being unsupported by shoulder-straps, it slipped unchecked till her imposing titties were totally uncovered.

She seemed not to notice her condition. Nor did she hear Keith's long throaty moan, as he stared with eyes almost popping out of his head at her bare bouncers. And if she happened to observe the sudden jerk of his twanger in his tight jeans, she gave no sign, though there might have been the hint of a smile about the corners of her mouth.

'Look at the position sensibly,' she said. 'You believe that your wife is deceiving you. You have not a scrap of evidence, but you insist that you *know*. Prove it to me by telling me when was the last time.'

Keith was too busy staring at her titties and wishing he could get his hands on them to pay attention to her words. He completely misunderstood the question.

'This morning early,' he sighed.

Enid found that difficult to believe. At ten past eight that morning, after her four-pool-length swim, Toby had given her full physical relief for tension on the wet tile surround of the deserted swimming pool. Naked and on her back, her legs wide open and her plump bare belly like a well-stuffed cushion for him to lie on.

Men were lustful beasts, capable of any infamy, Enid knew that – but she found it virtually impossible to accept that Toby had serviced two different women before breakfast.

'Absurd,' she said sharply. 'I cannot believe Mr Dundale and your wife committed an improper act together early today.'

'Not him,' Keith gasped. 'It was me gave her a right seeing-to before we got up this morning.'

Enid's hands lay on her bare thighs, palms down, fingers curled, not far below her chuffie. Keith was staring at them in fascination – they were moving a little, as if to draw attention to the plump mound between her legs under the tight-stretched swimsuit.

'I see,' Enid said softly. 'She took her nightie off and lay on her back, I suppose. You lay on top of her and penetrated her, did you?'

'Right up her,' he panted. 'She was all wet and warm . . .'

'Then you made the usual reciprocating movements, no

194

doubt – all the way to an emission – am I correct?'

'Till I shot my lot,' he moaned.

'I'm sure you found it satisfactory, Keith,' Enid said, and it seemed to him that her thighs drifted apart an inch or two more. 'I have no experience of the marriage bed. How frequent is the act between you and Sally? Once a week?'

'Did her last night before we fell asleep,' he said. 'She never pulls her nightie down afterward. It's still up round her waist when I wake up and give her a feel.'

Enid wasn't quite touching herself, but the effect on Keith was the same. If her fingers moved another inch upward, she'd be stroking her own chuffie, he thought, his hard-on twitching inside his underwear.

'The reason I ask this personal question,' Enid said, 'is to find if there is any cause for her to feel neglected and look to another man for consolation. It would appear that she is being adequately gratified.'

'Early in the morning and last thing at night,' Keith said proudly, 'and sometimes in the middle of the day when I'm home for my lunch.'

'Heavens, what a very virile person you are!' she exclaimed.

He took that as a compliment, which was not the way Enid meant it. In her book he was a brute who subjected his wife to molestation morning, noon and night. Three times a day was excessive by any standard – she herself never required stress relief from Toby more than twice in any one day.

The jerky movement under Keith's jeans was very noticeable and Enid guessed that he was at the end of his tether. She was right – he fell to his knees on the grass between her feet, clawing at his flies to get them open in time. Out sprang his twanger, huge and hard and hot, as he fell forward onto her plump belly.

He was too far gone to realise that her thighs were gripping him to hold him in place. His flushed face was between her bare massive titties and he had his hands on them to press them to his cheeks.

His raging *thing* was squeezed between his own bare belly and Enid's chubby mound – that unseen chuffie under her tightly stretched swimsuit. There was only a thin layer of cloth between him and her warm plump lips. 'Oh, oh, oh,' Keith wailed, as his body jerked two or three times and he felt his cream shooting onto her black swimsuit.

With his face pressed between her titties he couldn't see the look on her face as she too came very abruptly. The stimulus that pushed her to climax was emotional and intellectual. Keith had lost his self-control, and this let her pretend to herself that she was being ravaged.

Flung down on her back by a coarse and brutal man, her knickers torn from her shaking body, the weight of his body crushing her as he rammed a great thick hard-on into her . . . slamming it in and out, impaling her and bursting her wide open . . .

Her hot fantasy took her over the edge into gasping orgasm. She recovered quickly and pushed at Keith's shoulders to get him off her body.

'You are trying to violate me,' she cried out. 'Stop it at once – this very instant. Get off me!'

Keith had shot his bolt; with returning sense came the realisation of the outrage he had committed. He scrambled away from Enid and fell over backward, his sticky twanger standing up out of his flies.

His first thought was to tuck it out of sight and pull his zipper up.

'Leave it,' Enid ordered sharply. 'Get on your knees and clasp your hands behind your back.'

He did as he was told. He scrambled onto his knees on the grass, sat back on his heels and put his hands behind him. He stared down in red-faced shame and dismay, unable to meet Enid's eyes. He could see that her legs were close together now – if he'd looked higher he'd have seen that she'd pulled her swimsuit up to cover her titties and put the straps over her shoulders.

There was a long, dark wet stain on the front of her swimsuit. It was all over the mound between her thighs and it went halfway up her belly. Keith looked at it and cringed. He didn't know what had come over him, but he knew there was a heavy price to be paid for what he'd done.

'Do you know the penalty for attempted rape?' Enid

demanded, looking up from the same wet patch. 'Look at me when I'm speaking to you.'

Keith raised his eyes reluctantly to meet her accusing gaze.

'Instant dismissal,' she said, 'and then the police and the courts become involved, and you are in prison for five years. Think about that.'

'I couldn't help myself,' he mumbled. 'I don't understand what came over me – it was like a red mist in my brain – nothing like that's ever happened to me before.'

'I should certainly hope it hasn't,' Enid said coldly as she stared at his flopper hanging forlornly out of his open flies. It was small and soft now and had a hang-dog air about it, as if ashamed of itself.

'I find it impossible to understand why you allowed yourself to lose control,' she said. 'You told me that you have relations with your wife frequently. You are not deprived – why did you try to ravage me?'

'I don't know,' he muttered. 'I'm very sorry. You said yourself that I'm very virile.'

'Not so virile at the moment, are you?' she said in a chilly tone as she stared at his dangler. 'It seems to have lost the brutal strength it displayed a few minutes ago. Look at my costume – you've stained it – it's ruined.'

'It'll wash out,' he said hopefully.

'Are you suggesting I lower myself to wash a garment you have soiled? I wouldn't even give it to a charity shop – it will go straight into the dustbin.'

Keith's face turned pink. Anything he said upset her – it was better to keep his mouth shut. He was in a nasty position and the only good sign was that she hadn't jumped up and run screaming into the building to phone the police.

'I am trying to understand you,' she said. 'You've always been a loyal and willing college employee. It would be a pity to see your life ruined for a moment of madness.'

'That's what it was,' he said eagerly, 'a moment of madness. It'll never happen again, I promise.'

'Ah, but can I believe your promise?' Enid said, one fingertip touching the wet stain on her belly. 'I have responsibilities toward the young women of the college.'

197

'I'd never harm a hair of their heads,' Keith vowed.

'Can you be trusted?' she said. 'Suppose you had one of these moments of madness when a girl was nearby – what then? I am a grown woman and I was able to resist and stop you completing your indecent attempt. Could a seventeen-year-old girl stop you?'

'You can trust me – I swear it on the Bible.'

'I cannot rid myself of this vision of you flinging a young girl flat on her back and ripping her knickers from her helpless body with your strong, coarse hands . . .' Enid said.

In his mind Keith was back in the boiler-room, bound hand and foot, his flies ripped open and his twanger out. A ring of seventeen-year-old girls were staring at it; one of them was holding it and diddling him.

'. . . lying on the poor girl with your full weight and crushing her,' Enid went on, 'forcing that huge thick *thing* into her . . .'

'I give you my solemn oath,' Keith gurgled – his dick had raised its head and grown stiff and long again.

'Deny it if you dare,' Enid continued relentlessly, 'it is the natural conduct of all men – you not excepted – to drive your *thing* into girls and ram it in and out . . . admit it!'

Down on his knees on the grass, with his flies unzipped and his hard-on standing out free, Keith was pleading with Enid in his mind. *Pin me down on the lawn . . . Strip your swimsuit off and sit on my belly . . . Grind me into the grass with that fat round bum . . . Show me your black-haired chuffie . . . Let me lick your titties till I come over you . . .*

He shuffled closer to Enid on his knees. She was leaning back in her deck-chair, her face turned up to the sky, while she set forth all her fears of the dreadful fate of young women at the hands of brutish men like Keith. He listened, his hand clasped round his stiff shaft, jerking up and down.

'You cannot appreciate the tenderness of the female parts,' Enid told him. 'Penetration by that monstrous *thing* must be excruciating . . .'

'Ah,' Keith moaned softly, 'my monstrous *thing* . . .'

His hand beat fast, his hard-on strained up toward his chin and it had grown to a menacing size. His mouth fell open and his eyes went out of focus as he moaned and shuddered. Enid was watching him slyly from under her eyelids.

'My god – you're doing it again!' she cried out in sham anger. 'I was absolutely right – you are a deranged sex-mad monster. We can't have you here at Lechlade a day longer, you are a living menace to every girl and woman in the college.'

'Please,' Keith gasped, confused and scared, stowing his shaft hastily in his jeans. 'Don't sack me, Miss Uppingham – it won't happen again.'

There was a pause while Enid stared at him icily.

'Give me one good reason,' she said eventually.

'It's this worry about the Sports Coach and Sally,' he said, 'it's been preying on my mind and I don't know what I'm doing half the time. I get these sudden flashes in my head where I see Sally on her back and him on top whamming it in. Is it any wonder I lose control?'

'A poor excuse,' she said scornfully, fully aware that he was making it up.

'Give me another chance, you won't be sorry,' he begged.

'I'm a fool to listen to you,' she told him, 'but in view of your blameless record in the past, I'll give you the benefit of the doubt.'

'Thank you, thank you,' he babbled, 'I won't let you down.'

It was obvious to him that she hadn't the slightest suspicion of his part-time activities, spying on undressed girls, or she would have given him the sack there and then. It was cheering to think he could carry on looking at bare titties and kitties through windows.

'As for your suspicions about your wife and Mr Dundale,' Enid said, 'you may put your mind at rest. I shall speak to him myself and demand his assurance that nothing irregular has taken place between him and her. I shall secure his promise that nothing ever will in future. Will that satisfy you, Keith?'

'Yes,' he said at once, 'if you make him promise – he'd never dare break his word to you.'

'Very well, let's hear no more about this. You may go now.'

He left in a shuffling walk across the grass, due to the pressure of his twitching hard-on in his tight jeans. Enid stared after him with a cruel smile and then went inside. Though she despised men and their obscene and paltry lusts, seeing Keith handle his stiff *thing* had aroused her. She needed the Sports Coach to deal with her stress.

The scene was vivid in her mind – Toby spreading her naked on her own bed with her legs wide open, sliding his *thing* into her and riding her until she dissolved moaning in a long wet sticky thrill. But it was only mid-afternoon and she couldn't expect him to turn up for the evening jog for hours yet.

She stripped off the swimsuit with the stain between the legs. Men were beasts, she told herself, their lustful emissions were messy and inconvenient.

On the bed, flat on her back, she slipped her hand between her plump thighs to feel her black-haired chuffie. She opened the soft lips and pressed a finger inside to bring on the thrill she was gasping for.

'Oh, that's nice,' she murmured as her fingertip slid over her nubby, 'I can feel it starting . . . I'm coming already . . .'

Chapter 12

On the last night of the previous term a lucky chance had made Toby a secret observer of Eleanor Redruth's naked netball game in the gym. It was extra lucky because it gave him the edge he needed this term to get closer to her. At first she was highly suspicious of him – she was as little impressed by men and their *things* as the Principal. Eventually she saw that his interest was the same as hers – a hot desire for girls' smooth young bodies.

Their wary exchanges developed into something like friendship after they diddled Rachel Fermor on the same day. Eleanor insisted on going first, and Toby agreed – he didn't think it mattered much. Eleanor invited Rachel to her rooms after lunch and soon had her lolling back on the settee with her mini-skirt up around her waist.

Eleanor was expert at playing with young ladies' kitties – she'd had a lot of practice and could make any girl come in ten or twelve seconds if she wanted. In her classroom, when she was feeling unexpectedly lusty, she sometimes kept one girl behind when the class dismissed.

The others knew what was going on when Miss Redruth kept one of them back. The ones with wristwatches timed the event and grinned – it never took more than two minutes before their friend rejoined them, her cheeks pink and her eyes gleaming.

On the settee with 'Monkey', however, Eleanor took her time. She smoothed her fingers through the girl's jet-black fleece, tickled her nubby, whispered in her ear and licked her titties. She kept her on the settee with her legs apart for half an hour, and in that time she made her come three times.

Let's see if dear Toby can get a flicker out of her after that, Eleanor thought with a secret grin. *I bet he won't even get as far as putting his hand down her knickers. He thinks the girls hero-worship him and can't wait to get their hands on his hard-on, but he'll learn in time that nothing beats girl-to-girl playtime.*

In spite of all her experience, Eleanor underestimated the attraction that tall, blond, athletic Toby had for teenage girls. Later that day, in the long grass behind the pavilion, Rachel lay down quite willingly to let him put his hand up her white tennis skirt and finger her.

She was slow to become aroused, as well she might be after her half-hour on Eleanor's settee. His touch on her kitty was nice enough but it wasn't going to give her another big thrill. After a while she pushed him onto his back and unzipped his shorts. His twanger sprang out into her hand and she gave him a quick finger-wave.

Toby had been so fascinated by Eleanor's secret midnight netball match last term that he wanted to be involved in planning a repeat game this term. Eleanor was doubtful, but she finally came round to his way of thinking. Secretly she thought it would be interesting to see how differently the girls might behave with a naked man present.

They discussed the arrangements for a week before settling what they would do. A suggestion of his that she accepted was not to wait for the last night of term. If their midnight caper was the huge success they expected, there'd be time to do it again before the end of term, he pointed out.

They chose the girls after much eager discussion and fixed the night. After Lights Out at ten-thirty they would be able to move about the college without much fear of being seen. Soon after eleven, Toby put his ear to the door of Keith and Sally's bedroom before slipping silently out of the gatehouse. He didn't want them to hear him going out – that might lead to awkward questions later.

As he expected, he could hear panting and moaning behind the bedroom door. He stood on the dark landing, wondering if Sally was on her back with her legs open and Keith thumping away on top on her – or if it was Keith flat on his back, with Sally straddling him and bouncing up and down. A quick look through the keyhole should settle it.

Toby's flopper was starting to rise – the sexy moans and the squeaking of bed-springs were having an effect on him. He told himself that he didn't really want to know whether Keith was doing Sally or Sally was doing Keith. It was wrong to spy on people in bed together. But now his twanger was standing hard and it made the decision for him. Without a sound he dropped to one knee and put his eye to the keyhole.

After his pangs of conscience about spying, he saw nothing because it was dark in the bedroom. He heard Sally gasping 'Make me come again' but that didn't settle it one way or the other. She'd said the same to Toby, many a time, whichever of them was on top.

Toby was wearing a black track-suit. Once he was out of the house he trotted unseen in the dark across the college grounds, toward the main buildings. Eleanor's rooms were on the ground floor of Wexby House, where Toby found the corridor deserted, the main lights off, and only a small blue emergency light burning. He tapped on her door with one knuckle.

Eleanor was in blue jeans and a white shirt and looked younger than her years – she could almost be a student rather than a teacher. Toby eased into the room past her and, as soon as the door was closed, put his hands on her waist and moved her gently back against the wall.

He wanted to kiss her but he guessed she'd object. She stared at him curiously and said nothing.

'Our big night tonight,' Toby said, excitement in his voice.

'Yes,' Eleanor agreed, smiling, her hand brushing over his flies lightly. 'Are you in the right state of mind for it?'

'I'm ready and enthusiastic,' he said, liking the way she stroked his shaft through his track-suit. It leaped strongly to her touch.

'Heavens above!' she said. 'Judging by the feel of *that* you're not just ready, you're well on the way to coming. You'll be finished before the games even begin.'

'No, I won't,' he said firmly. 'I shall discipline myself and not let anything happen till I'm prepared for it.'

Bold words, but his hard-on was standing up very big

and stiff under his jockstrap. He hoped he could live up to his stated intent.

'We'll see about that,' Eleanor said, pressing her hand close over his bulge to feel it jerking against his belly. 'I don't think you'll last out.'

'There's a very simple way of slowing me down,' he said, grinning to show her he was making a joke – though actually he was serious. 'Stand there against the wall with your legs apart for two minutes.'

'Not a chance,' she said instantly, her fingers clenched tight round his twanger through the track-suit. 'Just because you've got an inconvenient stand, that doesn't mean I have to let you stick it in me.'

'No obligation,' he said, his boyish grin growing wider, 'it would be an act of pure mercy if you did.'

'I'm not a merciful person – I'm a wildcat. Haven't you heard that I ravish half a dozen young girls before breakfast?' she said with a chuckle.

'You can ravish me any time of day, Eleanor, before breakfast, after lunch, during dinner – I won't struggle.'

The grip of her fingers was so very tight as to be sexily painful. She had only to flip up and down a dozen times and he'd shoot his lot in his underwear. Just as he had on that first night he took her out to dinner, when they were sitting in his car. He didn't want that to happen now, not tonight, when he'd be diddling naked girls in an hour's time. He took her wrist to pull her hand away.

'You're worried you'll lose it too soon,' she said with a laugh. 'It must be terribly awkward for you men, to have a *thing* that goes soft and useless after a quick come. Not like me – I've never said no to a good feel in my life.'

'That's the nicest thing I've heard all day,' Toby said, tugging at the zipper of her jeans.

She moved her feet apart on the floor and pressed her back to the wall while he undid her jeans and stroked her bare belly. He was pleased that she would let him go that far – it was a sign that she was starting to trust him. It surprised him to find that she was wearing white cotton briefs under her skin-tight jeans – the sort of knickers a schoolgirl might wear. He slipped his hand down inside the elastic to clasp her warm chuffie.

'I said a feel, you know, nothing else,' she reminded him, their faces close together.

'You said a *good* feel,' he reminded her. 'I'm brilliant at it – you can ask any girl you like.'

Inside her open jeans he slid her knickers down over her hips to the top of her thighs. More than her belly was bare now – he could see her neatly trimmed patch of dark curly hair. And long well-developed lips – they seemed to be pouting slightly. This was a big moment – the first glimpse he'd ever had of Eleanor's chuffie.

'*Very* pretty,' he said in a whisper, 'a beauty. Now you've let me see it I shan't be able to leave it alone. I'll diddle you silly.'

She grinned at him again. 'You should be so lucky,' she said. 'There's no man born who can keep up with me – I'll still be going strong long after you run out of steam and fall asleep.'

He hooked his middle finger between the lips and drew it up slowly to open them. Inside she was slippery and warm.

'You've been playing with yourself,' he said, his cheek against hers and his finger pressing in to find her nubby.

Her feet moved a little further apart on the floor as his palm clasped her well-trimmed kitty and his longest finger tickled inside. She had her hands on his waist and held him loosely, not pulling him close and not pushing him away.

'Why do you expect me to tell you my secrets?' she said.

'There's no secret about it,' Toby said. 'You're wet and slippery – I think you came not long ago.'

'I had a nap in the armchair after dinner, so I'd be fresh and strong for tonight,' Eleanor told him. 'I woke up all hot and bothered and had to diddle myself – in fact I've done it twice.'

The tip of Toby's finger played over her wet little nubby and he could feel her belly trembling from the sensations.

'Third time best,' he murmured.

'You're better at it than I'd have thought,' she said. 'It's all that practice on young girls, I suppose. And just in case 'you're wondering, I like it slow and easy – no slam-bam ten-second finger-waves for me.'

She wasn't telling the truth, but Toby nodded and said they'd better sit down so he could give her the full thirty minute treatment. She laughed and led him to the settee in her sitting room, slipped off her jeans and white briefs and lay back with her legs stretched out.

'This morning, during the break, I had Hilary Landor on this settee,' she told him. 'She sat in this same position I'm in now, knickers off and legs sprawling out. But I only played with her a little bit.'

'Didn't want to wear yourself out before tonight?'

'I can go on forever,' she countered, 'I just didn't want to wear Hilary out. Who have you played with today, Toby?'

'Linda Knight – I didn't want to wear myself out, but when I see her little ginger-haired kitty, I have to play with it.'

He slid the palm of his hand over Eleanor's trimmed dark curls. 'Lovely colour,' he said appreciatively. 'Maddeningly sexy.'

He unbuttoned Eleanor's shirt and found she wasn't wearing a bra. He'd have to ask her about that, why was she going to their Sports Night wearing knickers and no bra? Her titties were pointed and small. He licked their pink bobbles.

'You can think yourself very lucky,' she said. 'You're the first man to touch me since I was sixteen.'

He stroked slow and easy, round her prominent nubby. 'Is that how you like it?' he asked.

'That's good,' she sighed, her eyes half-closed, 'that's the way to diddle me . . . Well, it's one way – there are others . . .'

He knew what she meant. To prove his good will he knelt on the carpet between her thighs and bent over till his face was an inch above her bare pale belly. His tongue-tip could just reach her exposed nubby, but he made her wait.

'You don't fancy a hard-on up you,' he said, 'it's a tongue you like.'

'Stop talking and do me, do me,' she sighed, wriggling her bare bum on the settee.

He held her thighs in his hands and lashed her nubby with the tip of his tongue. When she started to make whimpering sounds he paused, to let her cool for a little while, then licked again. She was wet and warm and he desperately wanted to slide his straining shaft into her – but that would be the end of their friendship.

'I'm coming, Toby,' she gasped after five or six minutes of having her nubby tongued,' I'm coming *hard* . . .'

Her loins bucked up and she moaned loud and long. 'Oh god, oh god, I can't stop . . .' she was panting.

For the games that night they'd selected six girls. They'd both played with all of them at various times – and with others too – but these were the ones they found most exciting. There was fair-haired Hilary Landor, Rachel Fermor, Orline Ashby and new girl Caroline Wilton. They were both keen to include Vikki Herbert, the girl with great promise as a gymnast – apart from the promise of her smooth and slender body and her long lean thighs. The final choice to make up the six was Tessa Bowland.

At midnight Eleanor and Toby met the six in the gym. The college was dark and silent. The gym was located well away from the main buildings, so it was highly unlikely that if anyone woke up they'd see that the lights were on.

The girls were undressing without being asked and there were glimpses of young titties and bums as jeans and tee-shirts were stripped off.

Toby still had a hard-on from feeling Eleanor, and his twanger bounded in his underwear when the girls smiled at him. As for Eleanor, she sighed, held Toby's hand tight for a moment and murmured that the sight of all these beautiful bodies made her moist between the legs again. Toby daringly slipped his arm around her waist and murmured in her ear

'Suppose I unzip your flies and put my hand in your little white knickers?' he suggested.

'Not now I've got all these lovely naked young girls to tongue me,' she said, pulling away from his encircling arm.

Cheerful greetings were exchanged and the girls lined up.

'They're so gorgeous,' Toby sighed.

As indeed they were. Naked Rachel with her round titties and incomparable patch of thick black curls between her thighs. Long-haired brunette Tessa, with pointed titties and not much body hair. Tall fair-haired Hilary, who called Toby her sex-slave when she was on the massage table.

He'd responded by teaching her 'high-flying' – rubbing his hard-on along the open cleft of her kitty, the head sliding over the tip of her little pink nubby, until he shot his cream over her belly. He winked at her now as she stood naked in the line of girls and she smiled back.

Next to Hilary was Orline, who had an arm round her. Then new girl Caroline, exciting even though her titties were only the size of little apples and her belly was narrow and flat – her kitty was full-lipped and prominent, with just a light-brown fluff over it and a look that hinted at her lustful nature.

Right at the end of the line stood Vikki, her hair in a pony-tail. Toby stared admiringly at her long lean thighs and tight round bum.

Meanwhile Eleanor was undressing and the girls were looking on with interest. At thirty Eleanor was in good trim. Her titties were firm, her belly was flat, her kitty lips pouted through neatly trimmed brown hair.

When Eleanor was naked, her eyes and those of the girls all turned toward Toby. He grinned and took off his track-suit, enjoying the thought of so many desirable females staring at his body. It was a good strong body – he was long-legged and long of thigh, broad-chested, lean of bum. His body hair was blond – the little curls on his chest and legs made girls sigh.

He stripped down to his final small garment. Eleanor had insisted in advance that he should wear a jockstrap and keep it on – otherwise, she said, there would be a long heavy male *thing* flopping about every time he moved, and that would distract the girls. Or so she claimed, though he thought she was probably more worried that the girls might prefer it to what she was offering.

He didn't argue with her; he knew the strength of his

appeal to young girls. He stood with his feet apart and his hands on his hips, letting them have a good look at his athletic body. And at something else: he was wearing a posing-pouch that was transparent. It concealed nothing – his twanger stood proudly upright inside the thin nylon.

The girls nudged each other's bare waists and giggled. Eleanor very nearly blushed and seemed hardly able to drag her eyes away from the pouchful of hard male flesh.

'That's not what I meant,' she said.

'You didn't want me to flop about,' he said with a smile. 'Well, in this I won't. No need to worry about the girls – they've all seen my toy before. And played with it.'

Eleanor gave in and started the first event of this special secret Sports Night. It was a naked tug of war – three to a side. Hilary and Rachel were made team leaders and each picked the two girls they wanted on their side. They were all well-grown but slender, thanks to the emphasis on sports in the college curriculum.

For the event Toby had procured a soft rope. He wanted no rope-burns on tender naked bodies. The rope was laid out along the gym's polished wooden floor, fifteen metres of it, with white rags tied at the marker points. The teams lined up, Rachel and Hilary facing each other.

'No shouting, please,' said Eleanor. 'We mustn't risk being heard over in the main buildings. When I give the word, lean back into the pull and use your weight. Mr Dundale will referee. Now, pick up the rope.'

It was an exciting tussle. Toby stared entranced at beautiful young naked bodies straining backward as the girls heaved with all their weight and strength. Thighs rippled, titties were thrown into prominence as shoulders and heads leaned back.

Bum cheeks were clenched tight with effort, gasps escaped open mouths, drops of sweat were trickling down between swaying titties and over girlish bellies. Toby's hard-on was jerking madly in his pouch, and for a moment he thought of abandoning the refereeing and dropping to his knees to lick the sweat off Vikki's taut belly.

And Rachel – she was so exciting to look at while she stretched her body and limbs with all her might that Toby was dreaming feverishly of pulling her legs from under her so she would fall on her back – he'd jump on top of her as she lay on the floor and ram his hard-on into that soft young raven-haired chuffie between her thighs . . .

Back and forth the struggle went, the two sides well-matched and neither gaining much of an advantage. Eleanor was on the other side of the rope, equally enchanted by what she saw – as aroused as he was and equally ready to bury her face between the nearest pair of straining thighs.

It ended when Tessa leaned so far back that she lost her balance and fell on her bare bum. Without her weight on the rope, the opposing side reeled back, taking the marker over the line, before they fell down too.

Toby gazed transfixed at long legs waving in the air, kitties exposed, dark, blonde and brown, and he hardly had the presence of mind to raise his hand to signify a win. Eleanor was red-faced as she called out in a shaky voice, 'Rachel's team wins!'

They all needed a rest after that, Toby and Eleanor as much as the two teams. He adjusted his little pouch as best he could – the throbbing of his twanger was totally visible through it. Eleanor sat on a bench with the resting girls, her arm round Vikki's waist and her mouth close to the girl's ear – perhaps consoling her for losing the tug of war.

Before long, Eleanor was offering another sort of consolation. She was stroking Vikki's pointed titties slowly, making their tiny pink bobbles stand firm. Vikki closed her eyes blissfully and leaned her head on Eleanor's shoulder.

Soon she moved her thighs apart, Toby noted, to let Eleanor touch her kitty – but Eleanor had other ideas. She whispered something in her ear and Vikki slid off the bench and turned to face her. Now Eleanor's legs opened wide, and Vikki was bent over, her head between Eleanor's thighs.

Toby's *thing* was bounding in his transparent posing pouch – this was what he had been hoping to see, this *girlie-action*. The nearest he'd ever got to seeing it before was when he'd spied on his former girlfriend Sharon lying on her bed with her new girlfriend Claudine Stanhope.

That day he'd been down on his knees outside Sharon's

bedroom, spying round the edge of the door. Sharon was lying naked on the bed while Claudine, who had stripped down to a pair of tiny black knickers, sat on the edge feeling Sharon's titties.

But shame had overcome him on that occasion and he'd turned away and left before the two beautiful young women got down to the serious business of kissing each other's kitties and diddling each other. Here in the gym at midnight he had no such feeling of shame when he stared at Eleanor being tongued by sixteen-year-old Vikki. He was here by invitation, he was expected to watch.

Eleanor's hands were on Vikki's bare shoulders, holding and stroking them while little tremors were visibly flickering through her body from the action of the girl's tongue on her nubby.

'That's got you going,' Hilary said, pressing herself against Toby. 'We're having a bet, Rachel and me, on how long before you shoot off in your pouch. Any minute now, by the way it's jumping about – you'd better sit down before your knees give way.'

Toby put his arm round her and felt the taut cheeks of her bum. She led him to an empty bench by the wall and he sat down – she on one side of him and Rachel on the other.

'He's been trying to *do* me with his great big *thing* all term,' Hilary told her friend, 'and all last term. I haven't let him – I'm a virgin.'

While she was talking she pushed Toby's pouch down to free his hard-on. It pointed up at the ceiling, jerking furiously.

'He's always after my kitty with it too,' black-haired Rachel said, 'but he's not going to get it in.'

She clasped her hand round Toby's shaft and stroked up and down while Hilary watched.

'Look at the size of it,' Rachel said. 'Who'd want a monster like that up her? It would be terrifying.'

'That's right,' Hilary agreed. 'Anyway, we're too good for him – he's only a sex-slave. He's got above himself because I let him shoot his *stuff* on my belly as a special treat once, when he'd been very good with his massage. But that's the closest his *thing* is ever going to get to my kitty.'

Rachel was diddling Toby with a strong slow stroke, her hand moving up and down firmly. Hilary had her hand flat on his belly and was rubbing it. Toby had his arms round both girls, hugging their smooth warm bodies to him as his excitement raced toward a peak.

On the other side of the gym, Eleanor's legs were spread wide apart, the lips of her chuffie were pulled open and Vikki had her tongue inside to lick her exposed nubby. Toby saw Eleanor's legs start to shake and her hands fly to her own titties to squeeze them, and then she wailed loudly as the big thrill hit her.

It hit Toby at almost the same moment. Rachel's hand raced up and down and Hilary's fingers dug into the flesh of his belly – he shook as his cream jolted out in long flips that soared two metres across the floor.

'That will calm him down,' Rachel said with a grin.

'Not for very long,' Hilary said, 'he's nearly as non-stop as a girl.'

Toby sagged down on the wooden bench, trembling in the aftermath. His twanger was starting to droop, but when his breathing calmed down, he still felt exhilarated – the girls had given him a real seeing-to.

Five minutes later Eleanor decided that it was time to get on with the games. Another suggestion of Toby's she had accepted was to substitute basketball for netball this time. 'All that jumping and stretching up,' he told her, 'we'll have stunning views of titties and bellies . . .'

The two teams stood ready, Eleanor threw the ball in and Hilary caught it one-handed and ran bouncing it. The action was as fantastic as Toby had expected – naked bodies leaping and dashing and leaping, reaching for the ball, plump titties flipping up and down, long thighs scissoring open and closed, the cheeks of round little bums squeezed together.

Two minutes into the game Toby's twanger was standing up as hard as ever in his posing pouch. Eleanor had forgotten she was supposed to be refereeing and stood on the side-line open-mouthed. Toby moved around the court, seeing the delicious game from all sides, guessing that there would never be an other night like this in his life.

When he found himself next to Eleanor, she was so far gone in lustful emotion that she clutched at him. She hugged him to her hot and naked body, her fingers digging into the cheeks of his bum. He held her close, rubbing his stiff twanger in its thin pouch against her belly.

For a long time they clung to each other, both of them on the edge of the big jolt, but holding back.

The score was twenty-three to nineteen in favour of Rachel's team when Eleanor pushed Toby away from her, drew in a deep shuddering breath and stopped play. He wondered if she'd actually come while they were hanging on to each other – he thought she might have done, her body had been shaking like a leaf and her grip on him had been frantic.

Not that she'd ever admit it to a man. And whether she'd come or not, she knew exactly what she wanted to do now. She took new girl Caroline by the arm and got her to lie along the bench, legs apart and knees bent, her bare feet on the floor. In a moment she was kneeling at the end of the bench, leaning forward between Caroline's spread legs.

The other girls stood in a half-ring round the bench to watch Eleanor tongue Caroline. Toby joined them at once, not wanting to miss anything – he found a place between Tessa and Orline and put an arm round each of them and held them close to him. Tessa looked sideways at his bulging pouch and then grinned into his face.

Eleanor's lean bum was quivering as she raised herself above Caroline with her hands on the girl's bare shoulders. She ran her hands down Caroline's slim body and bowed her head to poke the tip of her tongue into the shallow little dent of the teenager's belly-button.

'She's a sex fiend, our Miss Eleanor Redruth,' Toby said, 'I admire the way she takes total advantage of all of you girls.'

'Oh, yes,' Tessa murmured, 'in her class we all sit with moist kitties and wish she'd sit by us and slide her hand down our knickers.'

'She's a beast,' Orline sighed on Toby's other side, 'and we all love her.'

Eleanor put her mouth to the pink bobbles of Caroline's tiny titties. Caroline closed her eyes and sighed. Eleanor sighed too and stroked the girl's full-lipped kitty.

'Do her,' Orline urged her teacher in a moan.

Eleanor rested her upper body on the bench between Caroline's girlish thighs and put her tongue to her kitty. She licked the light-brown fluff on it for a second, then pushed her tongue inside. Caroline was as hot for it as Eleanor was; she jerked her belly up to meet the probing tongue and press it harder against her nubby.

'I want to come,' she gasped, 'do me, do me . . .'

'Look,' Orline said, 'Caroline's coming – look at her . . .'

Orline's hot hand was pressed tight over Toby's bulge and he was so excited that he knew it wouldn't be long before he shot his lot into his little pouch.

Eleanor moved off Caroline, a smile on her face now she'd taken the girl all the way, and sat cross-legged on the floor. Toby stared down glassy-eyed at Caroline's naked young body stretched out on the bench, astounded by the sexiness of her tiny pointed titties and the childish fluff on her kitty. There was nothing childish about the long full lips that were pouting wetly open from Eleanor's tonguing.

He freed himself from Orline's hand and released his straining twanger from the pouch. In one lithe motion he sprang to the end of the bench and lowered himself down on Caroline, his belly on her hot and sweating belly. She was grinning at him as he steered his hard-on towards her slippery chuffie. He put the head between the loose wet lips and pushed – he was inside and up her at once.

Above him he heard the murmur of surprise as the girls watched – this was the first time any of them had seen a man penetrate a girl and it was a sight never to be forgotten. Sitting beside the bench on the gym floor, Eleanor was staring at him with a very strange look on her face.

'That feels wonderful,' Toby sighed to Caroline, 'I slid straight in – you're no virgin, are you?'

'I've had lots and lots of boyfriends,' she murmured back.

'Oh, have you?' he said. 'You like it, do you?'

'As much as you,' she said, 'and you were just as desperate

as any boyfriend I've ever had to get inside me . . . but you're probably better at it . . . I love being *done* . . .'

Toby was sliding his hard-on in and out, already on the short strokes, only a few heart-beats from shooting his creamy load into her.

'You've a lovely long hard dick,' Caroline gasped, her belly bucking under him, 'the first I've had in me since I've been here – make me come with it . . .'

Toby wailed and came in fast jerks. Eleanor was up on her knees beside him, one hand clawing at his heaving bum. She was scoring her nails down the cheeks, while her other hand was between her own thighs, diddling frantically. Toby was so lost in the sensations of fountaining his cream into the girl under him that he didn't know he was being love-marked by Eleanor.

And the new term at Lechlade College was just a few weeks old.

More Erotic Fiction from Headline Delta

Lust and Lady Saxon

LESLEY ASQUITH

Pretty Diana Saxon is devoted to her student husband, Harry, and she'd do anything to make their impoverished life in Oxford a little easier. Her sumptuously curved figure and shameless nature make her an ideal nude model for the local camera club – where she soon learns there's more than one way to make a bit on the side . . .

Elegant Lady Saxon is the most sought-after diplomat's wife in Rome and Bangkok. Success has followed Harry since his student days – not least because of the very special support lent by his wife. And now the glamorous Diana is a prized guest at the wealthiest tables – and in the most bedrooms afterwards . . .

From poverty to nobility, sex siren Diana Saxon never fails to make the most of her abundant talent for sensual pleasure!

FICTION / EROTICA 0 7472 4762 5

— *Sweet* — *Vibrations*

Jeff Charles

The business of lust

London in the sixties – city of fun and fashion and mind-blowing sex! Where the boys are horny, the girls are pretty and the vibrations they make together are honey-sweet . . .

At the Rose and Griffin theatrical agency it's business as usual – the business of lust. Hard-working agent Adrian Klein is renowned for his eye for new talent – particularly when the talent is blonde and gorgeous. Teddy Dixon, the agency's managing director, has discovered more promising performers than anyone – some afternoons his casting couch is red-hot! And their female colleague Carola Watforde is not to be outdone – when it comes to spotting a willing sex-pot it takes one to know one, they say!

FICTION / EROTICA 0 7472 4634 3

A Message from the Publisher

Headline Delta is a unique list of erotic fiction, covering many different styles and periods and appealing to a broad readership. As such, we would be most interested to hear from you.

Did you enjoy this book? Did it turn you on – or off? Did you like the story, the characters, the setting? What did you think of the cover presentation? How did this novel compare with others you have read? In short, what's your opinion? If you care to offer it, please write to:

> The Editor
> Headline Delta
> 338 Euston Road
> London NW1 3BH

Or maybe you think you could write a better erotic novel yourself. We are always looking for new authors. If you'd like to try your hand at writing a book for possible inclusion in the Delta list, here are our basic guidelines: we are looking for novels of approximately 75,000 words whose purpose is to inspire the sexual imagination of the reader. The erotic content should not describe illegal sexual activity (pedophilia, for example). The novel should contain sympathetic and interesting characters, pace, atmosphere and an intriguing storyline.

If you would like to have a go, please submit to the Editor a sample of at least 10,000 words, clearly typed in double-lined spacing on one side of the paper only, together with a short outline of the plot. Should you wish your material returned to you, please include a stamped addressed envelope. If we like it sufficiently, we will offer you a contract for publication.